THE IRON HE

This is the story of the American revolutionary Ernest Everhard. Written by Avis Everhard, his upper-class wife, the manuscript was to remain undiscovered for seven centuries, long after the final triumph of socialist democracy. With remarkable foresight Jack London describes the struggles of the working masses against the oligarchy and how, eventually, they were ruthlessly suppressed, particularly in the Chicago Commune. All too familiar now is the creation of "favoured" unions, the bomb that explodes in the House of Representatives, Black Hundreds wrecking the socialist presses, and military-style organisations hunting down revolutionaries— but not so familiar twenty years before the rise of fascism. Its publication in 1907 caused a sensation, yet sixty-eight years later its message is just as clear: allow the Revolution to be defeated and the ruling class, in their own words, will "walk upon your faces".

JACK LONDON

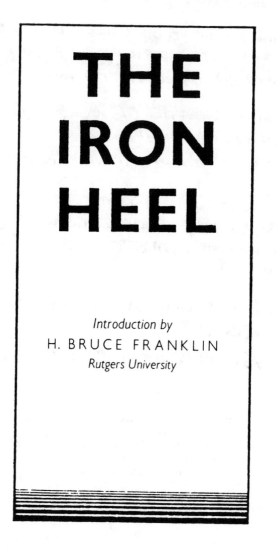

THE IRON HEEL

Introduction by
H. BRUCE FRANKLIN
Rutgers University

Lawrence Hill Books

FASCISM: EXALTS NATION AND RACE
ABOVE THE INDIVIDUAL - CENTRALIZED
AUTOCRATIC GOVERNMENT HEADED BY A
DICTATORIAL LEADER

SOCIALISM: ADVOCATING COLLECTIVE OR
GOVERNMENTAL OWNERSHIP OF THE MEANS
OF PRODUCTION AND DISTRIBUTION OF GOODS

CAPITALISM: PRIVATE OR CORPORATE
OWNERSHIP OF CAPITAL GOODS -
PRIVATE DECISION NOT STATE CONTROL

NAZISM: NATIONAL SOCIALIST GERMAN
WORKERS' PARTY - TOTALITARIAN PRINCIPLE
OF GOVERNMENT, STATE CONTROL OF ALL
INDUSTRY

OLIGARCHY: GOVERNMENT CONTROL BY A
SMALL GROUP

PLUTOCRACY: GOVERNMENT BY THE WEALTHY

First published in 1907

Published in The United States of America
by Lawrence Hill Books
an imprint of Chicago Review Press, Incorporated
814 North Franklin Street
Chicago, Illinois 60610

Reprinted by permission of the estate of Irving Shepherd

9

ISBN 1-55652-071-9 (paper),
previously ISBN 0-88208-118-7

Library of Congress Catalog Card Number 80-81804

Printed in the United States of America

Introduction

The Iron Heel appeared in 1908. By 1947, Philip Foner was calling it "probably the most amazingly prophetic work of the twentieth century." To us, looking backward from the closing decades of the century, this claim does not seem extravagant. For with every passing year, *The Iron Heel* now sems more timely, more vital.

When Jack London wrote this novel in 1906, the Russian revolution of 1905 was being crushed by the Czar's army, secret police, and terrorist gangs. Few people anticipated that out of this terrible defeat would emerge the triumphant Russian revolution of 1917. From our vantage point in time, we can see that these were the formative events of our century. For we live in the epoch of global revolution and counter-revolution, an age of fierce protracted combat to determine the future of the human race. This is the apocalyptic battle imagined in *The Iron Heel*, which foresees the struggle between the impoverished masses who do most of the world's work and the privileged minorities who live off the profits raging without resolution for three hundred years.

Some of London's prophecies came true very quickly. In July, 1908, just five months after the publication of *The Iron Heel*, a national secret police agency—then known as the Bureau of Investigation—was first established in the United States. Less than twelve years later, London's prevision of a violent suppression of the workers' political organizations was carried out. On one night alone—January 2, 1920—the Department of Justice struck simultaneously in seventy cities, in raids organized by Attorney General Palmer's youthful deputy J. Edgar Hoover. Workers were dragged from their homes and beaten, printing presses were destroyed, and ten thousand activists were imprisoned. Four years later, Hoover was made head of the organization soon to be renamed the Federal Bureau of Investigation.

Meanwhile Fascism—the form of capitalist political power envisioned in *The Iron Heel* and first brought into being by Benito Mussolini—was beginning its conquest of Europe. In 1922, the Fascists marched on Rome and toppled the government; within two years they were ruling Italy. In 1929, *The Iron Heel* was published in Italy. The translator, in a carefully guarded introduction foresees "the battle that will burst forth, who knows when, between the plutocracy and the people." Within months, the Fascist government had banned all cheap editions of *The Iron Heel* and London's other revolutionary works, labeling them as part of a plot to overthrow the regime. Expensive editions were allowed to remain in print, however, for the government saw no threat in this book as long as it stayed in "the hands of the cultured classes" (as reported on the front page of the *New York Times*, October 10, 1929). Three years later, speaking in Milan, the very city where *The Iron Heel* had been published, Benito Mussolini gave this assurance: "Today, with a fully tranquil conscience, I say to you, that the twentieth century will be a century of fascism. . . ."

London paints "the Iron Heel" of the oligarchy as though his models were the later twentieth-century fascist states of Italy, Spain, Portugal, Rumania, Bulgaria, Hungary, and Germany, with their ubiquitous secret police, unchecked militarism, and state-organized terror. And he points to the most essential fact about fascism: it is the form that the capitalist state assumes when the oligarchy feels that its economic and political power is seriously threatened by working-class revolution.

There are of course those today who think that Fascism and Nazism were defeated and expunged by the Second World War. These are the same people whom Aimé Césaire accuses (in *Discourse on Colonialism*) of being the "accomplices" of Nazism, because they have always "absolved it, shut their eyes to it, legitimized it" whenever it has "been applied only to non-European peoples." Thus it has been possible to define as part of "the Free World" the regimes of General Pinochet of Chile, the Shah of Iran, Chiang Kai-shek, President Duvalier of Haiti, General Zia of Pakistan, Generals Thieu and Ky of Vietnam, President Marcos of the Philippines, General Somoza of Nicaragua, King Faisal of Egypt, General Batista of Cuba, King Hassan of Morocco, the royal family of Saudi Arabia, General Stroessner of Paraguay, and, to name a few others, the present governments of Argentina, Brazil, Zaire, Indonesia, South Korea, and South Africa (where leaders of the governing party have repeatedly explained that their "Christian Nationalism" is merely the same form of government known as Facism in Italy and National Socialism in Germany).

But it is in America itself, the scene of London's Iron Heel, where his prophesies may now be most relevant. In 1961, Joseph Heller's *Catch-22* saw the ostensibly defeated fascist powers actually victorious in the American military-industrial complex that emerged from World War Two, with "mobs of policemen...in control everywhere," and with the features of Mussolini merging into those of the American men in power. The events of the 1960s and the 1970s have brought *The Iron Heel* back home.

London foresees: the creation of attractive suburbs for relatively privileged strata of the working class while the central cities are turned into what he calls "ghettoes" for the masses of unemployed and menial laborers, shoved into the darkest depths of human misery; the deliberate economic subversion of public education in order to spread illiteracy and ignorance; adequate food, health care, and housing priced above the reach of more and more people; the ubiquitous secret police infiltrating all organizations opposing the government; the establishment of a permanent mercenary army; the government conspiring in real and phony bomb plots, in the suppression of books and the destruction of printing presses, in witch hunts aimed at dissident labor leaders, professors, and authors, in destroying the reputations of some of its opponents, imprisoning many others, and murdering the few it finds too formidable; spontaneous mass rebellions of the downtrodden people of the central cities; urban guerrillas battling the government's army of mercenaries and police in the canyons of the cities. By the late 1960s, the Federal Bureau of Investigation, originating a few months after *The Iron Heel*, was merging into the novel's vision of the plutocracy's secret police: its agents and informers were planning and participating in the bombings and murders of civil rights workers, in the looting and burning of anti-war offices, and in the open assassination of prominent dissident leaders. It is fitting that the raid in which federal and state police officials riddled the sleeping bodies of Mark Clark and Fred Hampton occurred in Chicago, the city where London imagines the apocalyptic rebellion of "the People of the Abyss," who are slaughtered by the mercenaries and secret police of the plutocracy.

London understood better than any of his American intellectual contemporaries the utter ruthlessness and ferocity that the capitalist class would display if it felt its survival at stake. In fact, it was for these predictions that *The Iron Heel* was most reviled, even in the socialist press. But this was not the most remarkable of London's insights.

His most insightful prediction concerns the *strategy* of the capitalist class, a strategy that would prove to be the means of its preservation and power for decades to come. He predicts that the ruling class would use its superprofits to buy off a section of the working class, coopting it, turning it into an "aristocracy of labour" that would serve as the main agent of control over the rest of the working class. This concept was not entirely new to Marxist theory or American labor history. Yet in 1937 Leon Trotsky went so far as to claim that when *The Iron Heel* first appeared, "not one of the revolutionary Marxists...imagined so fully the ominous perspective of the alliance between finance capital and labor aristocracy."

How did London come to such a stunning vision of the future? The answer, I believe, lies in his own contradictory experience within different social classes. Jack London grew up in agonizing poverty and labor; his first class identity was forged in the slum and the factory. Turning away from the grinding routine of factory work, he became at the age of fifteen one of the most audacious oyster pirates on San Francisco Bay. As his life of wild adventures, brawling, and drinking merged with an avid self-education, he began to conceive of himself as an all-conquering superman straight out of Nietzsche. What converted him to socialism was his experience in a New York penitentiary, where, as a convict laborer, he found his heroic, superman view of himself crushed beneath the iron heel of the state. In "How I Became a Socialist" (1903), he explains that "no economic argument, no lucid demonstration of the logic and inevitableness of Socialism affects me as profoundly and convincingly as I was affected on the day when I first saw the walls of the Social Pit rise around me and felt myself slipping down, down, into the shambles at the bottom."

It is obvious that Ernest Everhard, whose name expresses his heroic role as the powerful socialist leader in *The Iron Heel*, is a projection of the man Jack London most wished to be. Everhard is physically a replica of London, who places in his mouth fiery socialist speeches which he himself had given. But the novel has been seriously misread by those who see Everhard as the *only* projection of London. The people of the abyss are also projections of the author, who had come perilously close to the bottom of capitalist society —in the penitentiary, in prolonged bouts of desperate drunkeness, in double shifts of cannery toil at ten cents an hour. And in 1906, as one of America's most popular and highest-paid authors, Jack London could also understand, from the inside, how it felt to be part of that bought-off aristocracy of labor. Even beyond lies one of the most revealing ironies of the novel: London sets the revolutionaries' secret underground hideaway on a ranch owned by one of the wealthiest and most vicious capitalists, a ranch that was in actuality owned by Jack London himself. London's uncanny prophetic vision came from the ability to explore and project the realities deep inside himself, a being created—and torn—by the contradictions between the extremes of life in capitalist society.

But in *The Iron Heel*, Jack London also transcends himself. Although Ernest Everhard is ostensibly the hero, the center of our interest gradually shifts to the actual protagonist, his wife Avis, who narrates the main story and who develops into the most skillful and intrepid revolutionary leader. The novel is of course a warning to London's American socialist comrades that their strategy of relying entirely on the ballot box to defeat the capitalists is a treacherous illusion. But the Everhard style of roaring supermasculine confrontation with the capitalists proves to be equally dangerous. As the Iron Heel consolidates its power, the revolutionaries are forced to rely on the intricate underground apparatus developed by the aptly name Avis ("bird") Everhard, nee Cunningham.

London's white supremacist ideas are surprisingly almost as absent as his male supremacist notions: the Japanese proletariat are seen as revolutionary socialists; the Mexican comrades turn out to be "far stronger than the Iron Heel dreamed"; the mulatto maid in the dressing-room of the train racing toward the cataclysm in Chicago turns out to be a revolutionary secret agent. But of course London, like his contemporary socialist comrades, was still a long way from understanding that the non-white peoples of the world were destined, in the second half of the twentieth century, to *lead* the revolutionary forces.

The Iron Heel presents with terrifying clarity the savagery of the struggle in which we are engaged. As we read brilliant scenes like the swirling urban warfare in Chicago we understand them far more deeply than do the scholars from the socialist world of the twenty-seventh century, who supply the bland Foreword and rather insipid footnotes. London suggests to us that we fellow creatures of capitalist society, in the epoch when capitalism is being torn asunder by its internal contradictions, must struggle as fiercely as his fictional revolutionaries to prevent the boast of the Iron Heel— to grind us down and walk upon our faces—from coming true.

H. Bruce Franklin
Newark, New Jersey
April 21, 1980

Foreword

IT CANNOT be said that the Everhard Manuscript is an important historical document. To the historian it bristles with errors —not errors of fact, but errors of interpretation. Looking back across the seven centuries that have lapsed since Avis Everhard completed her manuscript, events, and the bearings of events, that were confused and veiled to her, are clear to us. She lacked perspective. She was too close to the events she writes about. Nay, she was merged in the events she has described.

Nevertheless, as a personal document, the Everhard Manuscript is of inestimable value. But here again enter error of perspective, and vitiation due to the bias of love. Yet we smile, indeed, and forgive Avis Everhard for the heroic lines upon which she modelled her husband. We know to-day that he was not so colossal, and that he loomed among the events of his times less largely than the Manuscript would lead us to believe.

We know that Ernest Everhard was an exceptionally strong man, but not so exceptional as his wife thought him to be. He was, after all, but one of a large number of heroes who, throughout the world, devoted their lives to the Revolution; though it must be conceded that he did unusual work, especially in his elaboration and interpretation of working-class philosophy. "Proletarian science" and "proletarian philosophy" were his phrases for it, and therein he shows the provincialism of his mind—a defect, however, that was due to the times and that none in that day could escape.

But to return to the Manuscript. Especially valuable is it in communicating to us the *feel* of those terrible times. Nowhere do we find more vividly portrayed the psychology of the persons that lived in that turbulent period embraced between the years 1912 and 1932—their mistakes and ignorance, their doubts and fears and misapprehensions, their ethical delusions, their violent passions, their inconceivable sordidness and selfishness. These are the things that are so hard for us of this enlightened age to understand. History tells us that these things were, and biology and psychology tell us why they were; but history and biology and psychology do not make these things alive. We accept them as facts, but we are left without sympathetic comprehension of them.

This sympathy comes to us, however, as we peruse the Everhard Manuscript. We enter into the minds of the actors in that long-ago world-drama, and for the time being their mental processes are our mental processes. Not alone do we understand Avis Everhard's love for her hero-husband, but we feel, as he felt, in those first days, the vague and terrible loom of the Oligarchy. The Iron Heel (well named) we feel descending upon and crushing mankind.

And in passing we note that that historic phrase, the Iron Heel, originated in Ernest Everhard's mind. This, we may say, is the one moot question that this new-found document clears up. Previous to this, the earliest-known use of the phrase occurred in the pamphlet, "Ye Slaves", written by George Milford and published in December, 1912. This George Milford was an obscure agitator about whom nothing is known, save the one additional bit of information gained from the Manuscript, which mentions that he was shot in the Chicago Commune. Evidently he had heard Ernest Everhard make use of the phrase in some public speech, most probably when he was running for Congress in the fall of 1912. From the Manuscript we learn that Everhard used the phrase at a private dinner in the spring of 1912. This is, without discussion, the earliest-known occasion on which the Oligarchy was so designated.

The rise of the Oligarchy will always remain a cause of secret wonder to the historian and the philosopher. Other great historical events have their place in social evolution. They were inevitable. Their coming could have been predicted with the same certitude that astronomers to-day predict the outcome of the movements of stars. Without these other great historical events, social evolution could not have proceeded. Primitive communism, chattel slavery, serf slavery, and wage slavery were necessary stepping-stones in the evolution of society. But it were ridiculous to assert that the Iron Heel was a necessary stepping-stone. Rather, to-day, is it adjudged a step aside, or a step backward, to the social tyrannies that made the early world a hell, but that were as necessary as the Iron Heel was unnecessary.

Black as Feudalism was, yet the coming of it was inevitable. What else than Feudalism could have followed upon the breakdown of that great centralized governmental machine known as the Roman Empire ? Not so, however, with the Iron Heel. In the orderly procedure of social evolution there was no place for it. It was not necessary, and it was not inevitable. It must always remain the great curiosity of history—a whim, a fantasy, an apparition, a thing unexpected and undreamed; and it should serve as a warning to those rash political theorists of to-day who speak with certitude of social processes.

Capitalism was adjudged by the sociologists of the time to be the culmination of bourgeois rule, the ripened fruit of the bourgeois revolution. And we of to-day can but applaud that judgment. Following upon Capitalism, it was held, even by such intellectual and antagonistic giants as Herbert Spencer, that Socialism would come. Out of the decay of self-seeking capitalism, it was held, would arise that flower of the ages, the Brotherhood of Man. Instead of which, appalling alike to us who look back and to those that lived at the time, capitalism, rotten-ripe, sent forth that monstrous offshoot, the Oligarchy.

Too late did the socialist movement of the early twentieth century divine the coming of the Oligarchy. Even as it was divined, the Oligarchy was there—a fact established in blood, a stupendous and awful reality. Nor even then, as the Everhard Manuscript well shows, was any permanence attributed to the Iron Heel. Its overthrow was a matter of a few short years, was the judgment of the revolutionists. It is true, they realized that the Peasant Revolt was unplanned, and that the First Revolt was premature; but they little realized that the Second Revolt, planned and mature, was doomed to equal futility and more terrible punishment.

It is apparent that Avis Everhard completed the Manuscript during the last days of preparation for the Second Revolt; hence the fact that there is no mention of the disastrous outcome of the Second Revolt. It is quite clear that 'she intended the Manuscript for immediate publication, as soon as the Iron Heel was overthrown, so that her husband, so recently dead, should receive full credit for all that he had ventured and accomplished. Then came the frightful crushing of the Second Revolt, and it is probably that in the moment of danger, ere she fled or was captured by the Mercenaries, she hid the Manuscript in the hollow oak at Wake Robin Lodge.

Of Avis Everhard there is no further record. Undoubtedly she was executed by the Mercenaries; and, as is well known, no record of such executions was kept by the Iron Heel. But little did she realize, even then, as she hid the Manuscript and prepared to flee, how terrible had been the breakdown of the Second Revolt. Little did she realize that the tortuous and distorted evolution of the next three centuries would compel a Third Revolt and a Fourth Revolt, and many Revolts, all drowned in seas of blood, ere the world-movement of labor should come into its own. And little did she dream that for seven long centuries the tribute of her love to Ernest Everhard would repose undisturbed in the heart of the ancient oak at Wake Robin Lodge.

ANTHONY MEREDITH.

ARDIS,
   November 27, 419 B.O.M.

CHAPTER I

My Eagle

T H E S O F T summer wind stirs the redwoods, and Wild-Water ripples sweet cadences over its mossy stones. There are butterflies in the sunshine, and from everywhere arises the drowsy hum of bees. It is so quiet and peaceful, and I sit here, and ponder, and am restless. It is the quiet that makes me restless. It seems unreal. All the world is quiet, but it is the quiet before the storm. I strain my ears, and all my senses, for some betrayal of that impending storm. Oh, that it may not be premature! That it may not be premature![1]

Small wonder that I am restless. I think, and think, and I cannot cease from thinking. I have been in the thick of life so long that I am oppressed by the peace and quiet, and I cannot forbear from dwelling upon that mad maelstrom of death and destruction so soon to burst forth. In my ears are the cries of the stricken; and I can see, as I have seen in the past,[2] all the marring and mangling of the sweet, beautiful flesh, and the souls torn with violence from proud bodies and hurled to God. Thus do we poor humans attain our ends, striving through carnage and destruction to bring lasting peace and happiness upon the earth.

And then I am lonely. When I do not think of what is to come, I think of what has been and is no more—my Eagle, beating with tireless wings the void, soaring towards what was ever his sun, the flaming ideal of human freedom. I cannot sit idly by and wait the great event that is his making, though he is not here to see. He devoted all the years of his

---

[1] The Second Revolt was largely the work of Ernest Everhard, though he co-operated, of course, with the European leaders. The capture and secret execution of Everhard was the great event of the spring of A.D. 1932. Yet so thoroughly had he prepared for the revolt, that his fellow-conspirators were able, with little confusion or delay, to carry out his plans. It was after Everhard's execution that his wife went to Wake Robin Lodge, a small bungalow in the Sonoma Hills of California.

[2] Without doubt she here refers to the Chicago Commune.

manhood to it, and for it he gave his life. It is his handiwork. He made it.[3]

And so it is, in this anxious time of waiting, that I shall write of my husband. There is much light that I alone of all persons living can throw upon his character, and so noble a character cannot be blazoned forth too brightly. His was a great soul, and, when my love grows unselfish, my chiefest regret is that he is not here to witness tomorrow's dawn. We cannot fail. He has built too stoutly and too surely for that. Woe to the Iron Heel! Soon shall it be thrust back from off prostrate humanity. When the word goes forth, the labour hosts of all the world shall rise. There has been nothing like it in the history of the world. The solidarity of labour is assured, and for the first time will there be an international revolution wide as the world is wide.[4]

You see, I am full of what is impending. I have lived it day and night utterly and for so long that it is ever present in my mind. For that matter, I cannot think of my husband without thinking of it. He was the soul of it, and how can I possibly separate the two in thought?

As I have said, there is much light that I alone can throw upon his character. It is well known that he toiled hard for liberty and suffered sore. How hard he toiled and how greatly he suffered, I well know; for I have been with him during these twenty anxious years, and I know his patience, his untiring effort, his infinite devotion to the Cause for which, only two months gone, he laid down his life.

I shall try to write simply and to tell here how Ernest Everhard entered my life—how I first met him, how he grew until I became a part of him, and the tremendous changes

---

[3] With all respect to Avis Everhard, it must be pointed out that Everhard was but one of many able leaders who planned the Second Revolt. And we, today, looking back across the centuries, can safely say that even had he lived, the Second Revolt would not have been less calamitous in its outcome than it was.

[4] The Second Revolt was truly international. It was a colossal plan—too colossal to be wrought by the genius of one man alone. Labour, in all the oligarchies of the world, was prepared to rise at the signal. Germany, Italy, France, and all Australasia were labour countries—socialist states. They were ready to lend aid to the revolution. Gallantly they did; and it was for this reason, when the Second Revolt was crushed, that they, too, were crushed by the united oligarchies of the world, their socialist governments being replaced by oligarchical governments.

he wrought in my life. In this way you may look at him through my eyes and learn him as I learned him—in all save the things too secret and sweet for me to tell.

It was in February 1912 that I first met him, when, as a guest of my father's[5] at dinner, he came to our house in Berkeley. I cannot say that my very first impression of him was favourable. He was one of many at dinner, and in the drawing-room, where we gathered and waited for all to arrive, he made a rather incongruous appearance. It was ' preacher's night ', as my father privately called it, and Ernest was certainly out of place in the midst of the churchmen.

In the first place his clothes did not fit him. He wore a ready-made suit of dark cloth, that was ill adjusted to his body. In fact, no ready-made suit of clothes ever could fit his body. And on this night, as always, the cloth bulged with his muscles, while the coat between the shoulders, what of the heavy shoulder-development, was a maze of wrinkles. His neck was the neck of a prize-fighter,[6] thick and strong. So this was the social philosopher and ex-horseshoer my father had discovered, was my thought. And he certainly looked it, with those bulging muscles and that bull-throat. Immediately I classified him—a sort of prodigy, I thought, a Blind Tom[7] of the working class.

And then, when he shook hands with me! His handshake was firm and strong, but he looked at me boldly with his black eyes—too boldly, I thought. You see, I was a creature of environment, and at that time had strong class instincts.

[5] John Cunningham, Avis Everhard's father, was a professor at the State University at Berkeley, California. His chosen field was physics, and in addition he did much original research and was greatly distinguished as a scientist. His chief contribution to science was his studies of the electron, and his monumental work on the " Identification of Matter and Energy," wherein he established, beyond cavil and for all time, that the ultimate unit of matter and the ultimate unit of force were identical.

This idea had been earlier advanced, but not demonstrated, by Sir Oliver Lodge and other students in the new field of radioactivity.

[6] In that day it was the custom of men to compete for purses of money. They fought with their hands. When one was beaten into insensibility or killed, the survivor took the money.

[7] This obscure reference applies to a blind negro musician who took the world by storm in the latter half of the nineteenth century of the Christian Era.

Such boldness on the part of a man of my own class would have been almost unforgivable. I know that I could not avoid dropping my eyes, and I was quite relieved when I passed him on and turned to greet Bishop Morehouse—a favourite of mine, a sweet and serious man of middle age, Christ-like in appearance and goodness, and a scholar as well.

But this boldness that I took to be presumption was a vital clue to the nature of Ernest Everhard. He was simple, direct, afraid of nothing, and he refused to waste time on conventional mannerisms. 'You pleased me,' he explained long afterwards; 'and why should I not fill my eyes with that which pleases me?' I have said that he was afraid of nothing. He was a natural aristocrat—and this in spite of the fact that he was in the camp of the non-aristocrats. He was a superman, a blond beast such as Nietzsche[8] has described, and in addition he was aflame with democracy.

In the interest of meeting the other guests, and what of my unfavourable impression, I forgot all about the working-class philosopher, though once or twice at dinner I noticed him—especially the twinkle in his eye as he listened to the talk first of one minister and then of another. He has humour, I thought, and I almost forgave him his clothes. But the time went by, and the dinner went by, and he never opened his mouth to speak, while the ministers talked interminably about the working class and its relation to the Church, and what the Church had done and was doing for it. I noticed that my father was annoyed because Ernest did not talk. Once father took advantage of a lull and asked him to say something; but Ernest shrugged his shoulders and with an 'I have nothing to say' went on eating salted almonds.

But father was not to be denied. After a while he said:

'We have with us a member of the working class. I am sure that he can present things from a new point of view that will be interesting and refreshing. I refer to Mr Everhard.'

The others betrayed a well-mannered interest, and urged Ernest for a statement of his views. Their attitude towards him was so broadly tolerant and kindly that it was really

[8] Friedrich Nietzsche, the mad philosopher of the nineteenth century of the Christian Era, who caught wild glimpses of truth, but who, before he was done, reasoned himself around the great circle of human thought and off into madness.

patronising. And I saw that Ernest noted it and was amused. He looked slowly about him, and I saw the glint of laughter in his eyes.

'I am not versed in the courtesies of ecclesiastical controversy,' he began, and then hesitated with modesty and indecision.

'Go on,' they urged, and Dr Hammerfield said: 'We do not mind the truth that is in any man. If it is sincere,' he amended.

'Then you separate sincerity from truth?' Ernest laughed quickly.

Dr Hammerfield gasped, and managed to answer, 'The best of us may be mistaken, young man, the best of us.'

Ernest's manner changed on the instant. He became another man.

'All right, then,' he answered; 'and let me begin by saying that you are all mistaken. You know nothing, and worse than nothing, about the working class. Your sociology is as vicious and worthless as is your method of thinking.'

It was not so much what he said as how he said it. I roused at the first sound of his voice. It was as bold as his eyes. It was a clarion-call that thrilled me. And the whole table was aroused, shaken alive from monotony and drowsiness.

'What is so dreadfully vicious and worthless in our method of thinking, young man?' Dr Hammerfield demanded, and already there was something unpleasant in his voice and manner of utterance.

'You are metaphysicians. You can prove anything by metaphysics; and having done so, every metaphysician can prove every other metaphysician wrong—to his own satisfaction. You are anarchists in the realm of thought. And you are mad cosmos-makers. Each of you dwells in a cosmos of his own making, created out of his own fancies and desires. You do not know the real world in which you live, and your thinking has no place in the real world except in so far as it is phenomena of mental aberration.

'Do you know what I was reminded of as I sat at table and listened to you talk and talk? You reminded me for all the world of the scholastics of the Middle Ages who gravely and learnedly debated the absorbing question of how many angels could dance on the point of a needle. Why, my dear sirs, you are as remote from the intellectual life of the twentieth century as an Indian medicine man making incantation in the primeval forest ten thousand years ago.'

As Ernest talked he seemed in a fine passion; his face glowed, his eyes snapped and flashed, and his chin and jaw were eloquent with aggressiveness. But it was only a way he had. It always aroused people. His smashing, sledge-hammer manner of attack invariably made them forget themselves. And they were forgetting themselves now. Bishop Morehouse was leaning forward and listening intently. Exasperation and anger were flushing the face of Dr Hammerfield. And others were exasperated, too, and some were smiling in an amused and superior way. As for myself, I found it most enjoyable. I glanced at father, and I was afraid he was going to giggle at the effect of this human bombshell he had been guilty of launching amongst us.

' Your terms are rather vague,' Dr Hammerfield interrupted. ' Just precisely what do you mean when you call us metaphysicians?'

' I call you metaphysicians because you reason metaphysically,' Ernest went on. ' Your method of reasoning is the opposite to that of science. There is no validity to your conclusions. You can prove everything and nothing, and no two of you can agree upon anything. Each of you goes into his own consciousness to explain himself and the universe. As well may you lift yourselves by your own bootstraps as to explain consciousness by consciousness.'

' I do not understand,' Bishop Morehouse said. ' It seems to me that all things of the mind are metaphysical. That most exact and convincing of all sciences, mathematics, is sheerly metaphysical. Each and every thought-process of the scientific reasoner is metaphysical. Surely you will agree with me?'

' As you say, you do not understand,' Ernest replied. ' The metaphysician reasons deductively out of his own subjectivity. The scientist reasons inductively from the facts of experience. The metaphysician reasons from theory to facts, the scientist reasons from facts to theory. The metaphysician explains the universe by himself, the scientist explains himself by the universe.'

' Thank God we are not scientists,' Dr Hammerfield murmured complacently.

' What are you, then?' Ernest demanded.

' Philosophers.'

' There you go,' Ernest laughed. ' You have left the real

and solid earth and are up in the air with a word for a flying machine. Pray come down to earth and tell me precisely what you do mean by philosophy.'

'Philosophy is—' (Dr Hammerfield paused and cleared his throat)—'something that cannot be defined comprehensively except to such minds and temperaments as are philosophical. The narrow scientist with his nose in a test-tube cannot understand philosophy.'

Ernest ignored the thrust. It was always his way to turn the point back upon an opponent, and he did it now, with a beaming brotherliness of face and utterance.

'Then you will undoubtedly understand the definition I shall now make of philosophy. But before I make it, I shall challenge you to point out error in it or to remain a silent metaphysician. Philosophy is merely the widest science of all. Its reasoning method is the same as that of any particular science and of all particular sciences. And by that same method of reasoning, the inductive method, philosophy fuses all particular sciences into one great science. As Spencer says, the data of any particular science is partially unified knowledge. Philosophy unifies the knowledge that is contributed by all the sciences. Philosophy is the science of science, the master science, if you please. How do you like my definition?'

'Very creditable, very creditable,' Dr Hammerfield muttered lamely.

But Ernest was merciless.

'Remember,' he warned, ' my definition is fatal to metaphysics. If you do not now point out a flaw in my definition, you are disqualified later on from advancing metaphysical arguments. You must go through life seeking that flaw and remaining metaphysically silent until you have found it.'

Ernest waited. The silence was painful. Dr Hammerfield was pained. He was also puzzled. Ernest's sledge-hammer attack disconcerted him. He was not used to the simple and direct method of controversy. He looked appealingly around the table, but no one answered for him. I caught father grinning into his napkin.

'There is another way of disqualifying the metaphysicians,' Ernest said, when he had rendered Dr Hammerfield's discomfiture complete. ' Judge them by their works. What have they done for mankind beyond the spinning of airy fancies and the mistaking of their own shadows for gods? They

have added to the gaiety of mankind, I grant; but what tan-
gible good have they wrought for mankind? They philoso-
phised, if you will pardon my misuse of the word, about the
heart as the seat of the emotions, while the scientists were
formulating the circulation of the blood. They declaimed
about famine and pestilence as being scourges of God, while
the scientists were building granaries and draining cities.
They builded gods in their own shapes and out of their own
desires, while the scientists were building roads and bridges.
They were describing the earth as the centre of the universe,
while the scientists were discovering America and probing
space for the stars and the laws of the stars. In short, the
metaphysicians have done nothing, absolutely nothing, for
mankind. Step by step, before the advance of science, they
have been driven back. As fast as the ascertained facts of
science have overthrown their subjective explanations of
things, they have made new subjective explanations of
things, including explanations of the latest ascertained facts.
And this, I doubt not, they will go on doing to the end of
time. Gentlemen, a metaphysician is a medicine man. The
difference between you and the Eskimo who makes a fur-clad,
blubber-eating god is merely a difference of several thousand
years of ascertained facts. That is all.'

'Yet the thought of Aristotle ruled Europe for twelve
centuries,' Dr Ballingford announced pompously. 'And
Aristotle was a metaphysician.'

Dr Ballingford glanced around the table, and was awarded
by nods and smiles of approval.

'Your illustration is most unfortunate,' Ernest replied.
'You refer to a very dark period in human history. In fact
we call that period the Dark Ages. A period wherein science
was raped by the metaphysicians, wherein physics became a
search for the Philosopher's Stone, wherein chemistry became
alchemy, and astronomy became astrology. Sorry the domination of Aristotle's thought!'

Dr Ballingford looked pained, then he brightened up and
said:

'Granted this horrible picture you have drawn, yet you
must confess that metaphysics was inherently potent in so
far as it drew humanity out of this dark period and on into
the illumination of the succeeding centuries.'

'Metaphysics had nothing to do with it,' Ernest retorted.

'What?' Dr Hammerfield cried. 'It was not the thinking

and the speculation that led to the voyages of discovery?'

'Ah, my dear sir,' Ernest smiled, 'I thought you were disqualified. You have not yet picked out the flaw in my definition of philosophy. You are now on an unsubstantial basis. But it is the way of the metaphysicians, and I forgive you. No, I repeat, metaphysics had nothing to do with it. Bread and butter, silks and jewels, dollars and cents, and, incidentally, the closing up of the overland trade-routes to India, were the things that caused the voyages of discovery. With the fall of Constantinople in 1453, the Turks blocked the way of the caravans to India. The traders of Europe had to find another route. Here was the original cause for the voyages of discovery. Columbus sailed to find a new route to the Indies. It is so stated in all the history books. Incidentally, new facts were learned about the nature, size, and form of the earth, and the Ptolemaic system went glimmering.'

Dr Hammerfield snorted.

'You do not agree with me?' Ernest queried. 'Then wherein am I wrong?'

'I can only affirm my position,' Dr Hammerfield retorted tartly. 'It is too long a story to enter into now.'

'No story is too long for the scientist,' Ernest said sweetly. 'That is why the scientist gets to places. That is why he got to America.'

I shall not describe the whole evening, though it is a joy to me to recall every moment, every detail, of those first hours of my coming to know Ernest Everhard.

Battle royal raged, and the ministers grew red-faced and excited, especially at the moments when Ernest called them romantic philosophers, shadow-projectors, and similar things. And always he checked them back to facts. 'The fact, man, the irrefragable fact!' he would proclaim triumphantly, when he had brought one of them a cropper. He bristled with facts. He tripped them up with facts, ambuscaded them with facts, bombarded them with broadsides of facts.

'You seem to worship at the shrine of fact,' Dr Hammerfield taunted him.

'There is no God but Fact, and Mr Everhard is its prophet,' Dr Ballingford paraphrased.

Ernest smilingly acquiesced.

'I'm like the man from Texas,' he said. And, on being solicited, he explained. 'You see, the man from Missouri always says, " You've got to show me." But the man from

Texas says, "You've got to put it in my hand." From which it is apparent that he is no metaphysician.'

Another time when Ernest had just said that the metaphysical philosophers could never stand the test of truth, Dr Hammerfield suddenly demanded:

'What is the test of truth, young man? Will you kindly explain what has so long puzzled wiser heads than yours?'

'Certainly,' Ernest answered. His cocksureness irritated them. 'The wise heads have puzzled so sorely over truth because they went up into the air after it. Had they remained on the solid earth, they would have found it easily enough— ay, they would have found that they themselves were precisely testing truth with every practical act and thought of their lives.'

'The test, the test,' Dr Hammerfield repeated impatiently. 'Never mind the preamble. Give us that which we have sought so long—the test of truth. Give it us, and we will be as gods.'

There was an impolite and sneering scepticism in his words and manner that secretly pleased most of them at the table, though it seemed to bother Bishop Morehouse.

'Dr Jordan[9] has stated it very clearly,' Ernest said. 'His test of truth is: "Will it work? Will you trust your life to it?"'

'Pish!' Dr Hammerfield sneered. 'You have not taken Bishop Berkeley[10] into account. He has never been answered.'

'The noblest metaphysician of them all,' Ernest laughed. 'But your example is unfortunate. As Berkeley himself attested, his metaphysics didn't work.'

Dr Hammerfield was angry, righteously angry. It was as though he had caught Ernest in a theft or a lie.

'Young man,' he trumpeted, 'that statement is on a par with all you have uttered tonight. It is a base and unwarranted assumption.'

'I am quite crushed,' Ernest murmured meekly. 'Only

[9] A noted educator of the late nineteenth and early twentieth centuries of the Christian Era. He was president of the Stanford University, a private benefaction of the times.

[10] An idealistic monist who long puzzled the philosophers of that time with his denial of the existence of matter, but whose clever argument was finally demolished when the new empiric facts of science were philosophically generalised.

I don't know what hit me. You'll have to put it in my hand, Doctor.'

'I will, I will,' Dr Hammerfield spluttered. 'How do you know? You do not know that Bishop Berkeley attested that his metaphysics did not work. You have no proof. Young man, they have always worked.'

'I take it as proof that Berkeley's metaphysics did not work, because—' Ernest paused calmly for a moment. 'Because Berkeley made an invariable practice of going through doors instead of walls. Because he trusted his life to solid bread and butter and roast beef. Because he shaved himself with a razor that worked when it removed the hair from his face.'

'But those are actual things!' Dr Hammerfield cried. 'Metaphysics is of the mind.'

'And they work—in the mind?' Ernest queried softly.

The other nodded.

'And even a multitude of angels can dance on the point of a needle—in the mind,' Ernest went on reflectively. 'And a blubber-eating, fur-clad god can exist and work—in the mind; and there are no proofs to the contrary—in the mind. I suppose, Doctor, you live in the mind?'

'My mind to me a kingdom is,' was the answer.

'That's another way of saying that you live up in the air. But you come back to earth at mealtime, I am sure, or when an earthquake happens along. Or, tell me, Doctor, do you have no apprehension in an earthquake that that incorporeal body of yours will be hit by an immaterial brick?'

Instantly, and quite unconsciously, Dr Hammerfield's hand shot up to his head, where a scar disappeared under the hair. It happened that Ernest had blundered on an apposite illustration. Dr Hammerfield had been nearly killed in the Great Earthquake[11] by a falling chimney. Everybody broke out into roars of laughter.

'Well?' Ernest asked, when the merriment had subsided. 'Proofs to the contrary?'

And in the silence he asked again, 'Well?' Then he added, 'Still well, but not so well, that argument of yours.'

But Dr Hammerfield was temporarily crushed, and the battle raged on in new directions. On point after point,

[11] The Great Earthquake of A.D. 1906 that destroyed San Francisco.

Ernest challenged the ministers. When they affirmed that they knew the working class, he told them fundamental truths about the working class that they did not know, and challenged them for disproofs. He gave them facts, always facts, checked their excursions into the air, and brought them back to the solid earth and its facts.

How the scene comes back to me! I can hear him now, with that war-note in his voice, flaying them with his facts, each fact a lash that stung and stung again. And he was merciless. He took no quarter[12] and gave none. I can never forget the flaying he gave them in the end.

'You have repeatedly confessed tonight, by direct avowal or ignorant statement, that you do not know the working class. But you are not to be blamed for this. How can you know anything about the working class? You do not live in the same locality with the working class. You herd with the capitalist class in another locality. And why not? It is the capitalist class that pays you, that feeds you, that puts the very clothes on your backs that you are wearing here tonight. And in return you preach to your employers the brands of metaphysics that are especially acceptable to them; and the especially acceptable brands are acceptable because they do not menace the established order of society.'

Here there was a stir of dissent around the table.

'Oh, I am not challenging your sincerity,' Ernest continued. 'You are sincere. You preach what you believe. There lies your strength and your value—to the capitalist class. But should you change your belief to something that menaces the established order, your preaching would be unacceptable to your employers, and you would be discharged. Every little while some one or other of you is so discharged.[13] Am I not right?'

This time there was no dissent. They sat dumbly acquiescent, with the exception of Dr Hammerfield, who said:

'It is when their thinking is wrong that they are asked to resign.'

---

[12] This figure arises from the customs of the times. When, among men fighting to the death in their wild-animal way, a beaten man threw down his weapons, it was at the option of the victor to slay him or spare him.
[13] During this period there were many ministers cast out of the Church for preaching unacceptable doctrine. Especially were they cast out when their preaching became tainted with socialism.

'Which is another way of saying when their thinking is unacceptable,' Ernest answered, and then went on. 'So I say to you, go ahead and preach and earn your pay, but for goodness' sake leave the working class alone. You belong in the enemy's camp. You have nothing in common with the working class. Your hands are soft with the work others have performed for you. Your stomachs are round with the plenitude of eating.' (Here Dr Ballingford winced, and every eye glanced at his prodigious girth. It was said he had not seen his own feet in years.) 'And your minds are filled with doctrines that are buttresses of the established order. You are as much mercenaries (sincere mercenaries, I grant) as were the men of the Swiss Guard.[14] Be true to your salt and your hire; guard, with your preaching, the interests of your employers; but do not come down to the working class and serve as false leaders. You cannot honestly be in the two camps at once. The working class has done without you. Believe me, the working class will continue to do without you. And, furthermore, the working class can do better without you than with you.'

[14] The hired foreign palace guards of Louis XVI, a king of France who was beheaded by his people.

CHAPTER 2

Challenges

AFTER THE guests had gone, father threw himself into a chair and gave vent to roars of Gargantuan laughter. Not since the death of my mother had I known him to laugh so heartily.

'I'll wager Dr Hammerfield was never up against anything like it in his life,' he laughed. '"The courtesies of ecclesiastical controversy!" Did you notice how he began like a lamb—Everhard, I mean, and how quickly he became a roaring lion? He has a splendidly disciplined mind. He would have made a good scientist if his energies had been directed that way.'

I need scarcely say that I was deeply interested in Ernest Everhard. It was not alone what he had said and how he had said it, but it was the man himself. I had never met a man like him. I suppose that was why, in spite of my twenty-four years, I had not married. I liked him; I had to confess it to myself. And my liking for him was founded on things beyond intellect and argument. Regardless of his bulging muscles and prize-fighter's throat, he impressed me as an ingenuous boy. I felt that under the guise of an intellectual swashbuckler was a delicate and sensitive spirit. I sensed this, in ways I knew not, save that they were my woman's intuitions.

There was something in that clarion-call of his that went to my heart. It still rang in my ears, and I felt that I should like to hear it again—and to see again that glint of laughter in his eyes that belied the impassioned seriousness of his face. And there were further reaches of vague and indeterminate feelings that stirred in me. I almost loved him then, though I am confident, had I never seen him again, that the vague feelings would have passed away and that I should easily have forgotten him.

But I was not destined never to see him again. My father's new-born interest in sociology and the dinner parties he gave would not permit. Father was not a sociologist. His marriage with my mother had been very happy, and in the researches of his own science, physics, he had been very happy. But

when mother died, his own work could not fill the emptiness. At first, in a mild way, he had dabbled in philosophy;
then, becoming interested, he had drifted on into economics
and sociology. He had a strong sense of justice, and he soon
became fired with a passion to redress wrong. It was with
gratitude that I hailed these signs of a new interest in life,
though I little dreamed what the outcome would be. With
the enthusiasm of a boy he plunged excitedly into these new
pursuits, regardless of whither they led him.

He had been used always to the laboratory, and so it was
that he turned the dining-room into a sociological laboratory.
Here came to dinner all sorts and conditions of men—scientists, politicians, bankers, merchants, professors, labour
leaders, socialists, and anarchists. He stirred them to discussion, and analysed their thoughts on life and society.

He had met Ernest shortly prior to the ' preacher's night '.
And after the guests were gone, I learned how he had met
him, passing down a street at night and stopping to listen
to a man on a soap-box who was addressing a crowd of working men. The man on the box was Ernest. Not that he was a
mere soap-box orator. He stood high in the councils of the
socialist party, was one of the leaders, and was the acknowledged leader in the philosophy of socialism. But he had a
certain clear way of stating the abstruse in simple language,
was a born expositor and teacher, and was not above the
soap-box as a means of interpreting economics to the working men.

My father stopped to listen, became interested, effected
a meeting, and, after quite an acquaintance, invited him to
the ministers' dinner. It was after the dinner that father told
me what little he knew about him. He had been born in the
working class, though he was a descendant of the old line of
Everhards that for over two hundred years had lived in
America.[1] At ten years of age he had gone to work in the
mills, and later he served his apprenticeship and became a
horseshoer. He was self-educated, had taught himself German
and French, and at that time was earning a meagre living by
translating scientific and philosophical works for a struggling
socialist publishing house in Chicago. Also, his earnings were
added to by the royalties from the small sales of his own
economic and philosophical works.

[1] The distinction between being native born and foreign born
was sharp and invidious in those days.

This much I learned of him before I went to bed, and I lay long awake, listening in memory to the sound of his voice. I grew frightened at my thoughts. He was so unlike the men of my own class, so alien and so strong. His masterfulness delighted me and terrified me, for my fancies wantonly roved until I found myself considering him as a lover, as a husband. I had always heard that the strength of men was an irresistible attraction to women; but he was too strong. 'No, no!' I cried out. 'It is impossible, absurd!' And on the morrow I awoke to find in myself a longing to see him again. I wanted to see him mastering men in discussion, the warnote in his voice; to see him in all his certitude and strength shattering their complacency, shaking them out of their ruts of thinking. What if he did swashbuckle? To use his own phrase, 'it worked', it produced effects. And, besides, his swashbuckling was a fine thing to see. It stirred one like the onset of battle.

Several days passed, during which I read Ernest's books, borrowed from my father. His written word was as his spoken word, clear and convincing. It was its absolute simplicity that convinced even while one continued to doubt. He had the gift of lucidity. He was the perfect expositor. Yet, in spite of his style, there was much that I did not like. He laid too great stress on what he called the class struggle, the antagonism between labour and capital, the conflict of interest.

Father reported with glee Dr Hammerfield's judgement of Ernest, which was to the effect that he was 'an insolent young puppy, made bumptious by a little and very inadequate learning.' Also, Dr Hammerfield declined to meet Ernest again.

But Bishop Morehouse turned out to have become interested in Ernest, and was anxious for another meeting. 'A strong young man,' he said, 'and very much alive, very much alive. But he is too sure, too sure.'

Ernest came one afternoon with father. The Bishop had already arrived, and we were having tea on the veranda. Ernest's continued presence in Berkeley, by the way, was accounted for by the fact that he was taking special courses in biology at the university, and also that he was hard at work on a new book entitled *Philosophy and Revolution*.[2]

---

[2] This book continued to be secretly printed throughout the three centuries of the Iron Heel. There are several copies of various editions in the National Library of Ardis.

The veranda seemed suddenly to have become small when Ernest arrived. Not that he was so very large—he stood only five feet nine inches—but that he seemed to radiate an atmosphere of largeness. As he stopped to meet me, he betrayed a certain slight awkwardness that was strangely at variance with his bold-looking eyes and his firm, sure hand that clasped for a moment in greeting. And in that moment his eyes were just as steady and sure. There seemed a question in them this time, and as before he looked at me over long.

'I have been reading your *Working-class Philosophy*,' I said, and his eyes lighted in a pleased way.

'Of course,' he answered, 'you took into consideration the audience to which it was addressed.'

'I did, and it is because I did that I have a quarrel with you,' I challenged.

'I, too, have a quarrel with you, Mr Everhard,' Bishop Morehouse said.

Ernest shrugged his shoulders whimsically and accepted a cup of tea.

The Bishop bowed and gave me precedence.

'You foment class hatred,' I said. 'I consider it wrong and criminal to appeal to all that is narrow and brutal in the working class. Class hatred is anti-social, and it seems to me, anti-socialistic.'

'Not guilty,' he answered. 'Class hatred is neither in the text nor in the spirit of anything I have ever written.'

'Oh!' I cried reproachfully, and reached for his book and opened it.

He sipped his tea and smiled at me while I ran over the pages.

'Page one hundred and thirty-two,' I read aloud: ' " The class struggle, therefore, presents itself in the present stage of social development between the wage-paying and the wage-paid classes." '

I looked at him triumphantly.

'No mention there of class hatred,' he smiled back.

'But,' I answered, 'you say " class struggle." '

'A different thing from class hatred,' he replied. 'And, believe me, we foment no hatred. We say that the class struggle is a law of social development. We are not responsible for it. We do not make the class struggle. We merely explain it, as Newton explained gravitation. We explain the nature of the conflict of interest that produces the class struggle.'

'But there should be no conflict of interest!' I cried.

'I agree with you heartily,' he answered. 'That is what we socialists are trying to bring about—the abolition of the conflict of interest. Pardon me. Let me read an extract.' He took his book and turned back several pages. 'Page one hundred and twenty-six: "The cycle of class struggles which began with the dissolution of rude, tribal communism and the rise of private property will end with the passing of private property in the means of social existence." '

'But I disagree with you,' the Bishop interposed, his pale, ascetic face betraying by a faint glow the intensity of his feelings. 'Your premise is wrong. There is no such thing as a conflict of interest between labour and capital—or, rather, there ought not to be.'

'Thank you,' Ernest said gravely. 'By that last statement you have given me back my premise.'

'But why should there be a conflict?' the Bishop demanded warmly.

Ernest shrugged his shoulders. 'Because we are so made, I guess.'

'But we are not so made!' cried the other.

'Are you discussing the ideal man?' Ernest asked, ' —unselfish and godlike, and so few in numbers as to be practically non-existent, or are you discussing the common and ordinary average man?'

'The common and ordinary man,' was the answer.

'Who is weak and fallible, prone to error?'

Bishop Morehouse nodded.

'And petty and selfish?'

Again he nodded.

'Watch out!' Ernest warned. 'I said " selfish." '

'The average man is selfish,' the Bishop affirmed valiantly.

'Wants all he can get?'

'Wants all he can get—true, but deplorable.'

'Then I've got you.' Ernest's jaw snapped like a trap. 'Let me show you. Here is a man who works on the street railways.'

'He couldn't work if it weren't for capital,' the Bishop interrupted.

'True, and you will grant that capital would perish if there were no labour to earn the dividends.'

The Bishop was silent.

' Won't you?' Ernest insisted.

The Bishop nodded.

' Then our statements cancel each other,' Ernest said in a matter-of-fact tone, ' and we are where we were. Now to begin again. The working men on the street railway furnish the labour. The stockholders furnish the capital. By the joint effort of the working men and the capital, money is earned.[3] They divide between them this money that is earned. Capital's share is called " dividends ". Labours' share is called " wages." '

' Very good,' the Bishop interposed. ' And there is no reason that the division should not be amicable.'

' You have already forgotten what we had agreed upon,' Ernest replied. ' We agreed that the average man is selfish. He is the man that is. You have gone up in the air and are arranging a division between the kind of men that ought to be but are not. But to return to the earth, the working man, being selfish, wants all he can get in the division. The capitalist, being selfish, wants all he can get in the division. When there is only so much of the same thing, and when two men want all they can get of the same thing, there is a conflict of interest. This is the conflict of interest between labour and capital. And it is an irreconcilable conflict. As long as working men and capitalists exist, they will continue to quarrel over the division. If you were in San Francisco this afternoon, you'd have to walk. There isn't a street car running.'

' Another strike![4] the Bishop queried with alarm.

' Yes, they're quarrelling over the division of the earnings of the street railways.'

Bishop Morehouse became excited.

' It is wrong!' he cried. ' It is so short-sighted on the part of the working men. How can they hope to keep our sympathy—'

---

[3] In those days, groups of predatory individuals controlled all the means of transportation, and for the use of same levied toll upon the public.

[4] These quarrels were very common in those irrational and anarchic times. Sometimes the labourers refused to work. Sometimes the capitalists refused to let the labourers work. In the violence and turbulence of such disagreements much property was destroyed and many lives lost. All this is inconceivable to us—as inconceivable as another custom of that time, namely, the habit the men of the lower classes had of breaking the furniture when they quarrelled with their wives.

'When we are compelled to walk,' Ernest said slyly.

But Bishop Morehouse ignored him and went on:

'Their outlook is too narrow. Men should be men, not brutes. There will be violence and murder now, and sorrowing widows and orphans. Capital and labour should be friends. They should work hand in hand and to their mutual benefit.'

'Ah, now you are up in the air again,' Ernest remarked dryly. 'Come back to earth. Remember, we agreed that the average man is selfish.'

'But he ought not to be!' the Bishop cried.

'And there I agree with you,' was Ernest's rejoinder. 'He ought not to be selfish, but he will continue to be selfish as long as he lives in a social system that is based on pig-ethics.'

The Bishop was aghast, and my father chuckled.

'Yes, pig-ethics,' Ernest went on remorselessly. 'That is the meaning of the capitalist system. And that is what your Church is standing for, what you are preaching for every time you get in the pulpit. Pig-ethics! There is no other name for it.'

Bishop Morehouse turned appealingly to my father, but he laughed and nodded his head.

'I'm afraid Mr Everhard is right,' he said. '*Laissez-faire,* the let-alone policy of each for himself and devil take the hindmost. As Mr Everhard said the other night, the function you churchmen perform is to maintain the established order of society, and society is established on that foundation.'

'But that is not the teaching of Christ!' cried the Bishop.

'The Church is not teaching Christ these days,' Ernest put in quickly. 'That is why the working men will have nothing to do with the Church. The Church condones the frightful brutality and savagery with which the capitalist class treats the working class.'

'The Church does not condone it,' the Bishop objected.

'The Church does not protest against it,' Ernest replied. 'And in so far as the Church does not protest, it condones, for remember the Church is supported by the capitalist class.'

'I have not looked at it in that light,' the Bishop said naïvely. 'You must be wrong. I know that there is much that is sad and wicked in this world. I know that the Church has lost the—what you call the proletariat.'[5]

'You never had the proletariat,' Ernest cried. 'The proletariat has grown up outside the Church and without the
Church.'

'I do not follow you,' the Bishop said faintly.

'Then let me explain. With the introduction of machinery
and the factory system in the latter part of the eighteenth
century, the great mass of the working people was separated
from the land. The old system of labour was broken down.
The working people were driven from their villages and
herded in factory towns. The mothers and children were put
to work at the new machines. Family life ceased. The conditions were frightful. It is a tale of blood.'

'I know, I know,' Bishop Morehouse interrupted with an
agonised expression on his face. 'It was terrible. But it
occurred a century and a half ago.'

'And there, a century and a half ago, originated the
modern proletariat,' Ernest continued. 'And the Church
ignored it. While a slaughter-house was made of the nation
by the capitalists, the Church was dumb. It did not protest,
as today it does not protest. As Austin Lewis[6] says, speaking
of that time, those to whom the command 'Feed My lambs'
had been given, saw those lambs sold into slavery and worked
to death without a protest.[7] The Church was dumb then,
and before I go on I want you either flatly to agree with me
or flatly to disagree with me. Was the Church dumb then?'

Bishop Morehouse hesitated. Like Dr Hammerfield, he
was unused to this fierce 'infighting', as Ernest called it.

'The history of the eighteenth century is written,' Ernest
prompted. 'If the Church was not dumb, it will be found not
dumb in the books.'

[5] *Proletariat.* Derived originally from the Latin *proletarii,* the
name given in the census of Servius Tullius to those who were of
value to the state only as the rearers of offspring (*proles*); in other
words, they were of no importance either for wealth, or position,
or exceptional ability.

[6] Candidate for Governor of California on the Socialist ticket in
the fall election of 1906 Christian Era. An Englishman by birth,
a writer of many books on political economy and philosophy, and
one of the socialist leaders of the times.

[7] There is no more horrible page in history than the treatment of
the child and women slaves in the English factories in the latter
half of the eighteenth century of the Christian Era. In such industrial hells arose some of the proudest fortunes of that day.

' I am afraid the Church was dumb,' the Bishop confessed.

' And the Church is dumb today.'

' There I disagree,' said the Bishop.

Ernest paused, looked at him searchingly, and accepted the challenge.

' All right,' he said. ' Let us see. In Chicago there are women who toil all the week for ninety cents. Has the Church protested?'

' This is news to me,' was the answer. ' Ninety cents per week! It is horrible!'

' Has the Church protested?' Ernest insisted.

' The Church does not know.' The Bishop was struggling hard.

' Yet the command to the Church was, " Feed My lambs," ' Ernest sneered. And then, the next moment, ' Pardon my sneer, Bishop. But can you wonder that we lose patience with you? When have you protested to your capitalistic congregations at the working of children in the Southern cotton mills?[8]

' Children, six and seven years of age, working every night at twelve-hour shifts? They never see the blessed sunshine. They die like flies. The dividends are paid out of their blood. And out of the dividends magnificent churches are builded in New England, wherein your kind preaches pleasant platitudes to the sleek, full-bellied recipients of those dividends.'

' I did not know,' the Bishop murmured faintly. His face

---

[8] Everhard might had drawn a better illustration from the Southern Church's outspoken defence of chattel slavery prior to what is known as the ' War of the Rebellion.' Several such illustrations, culled from the documents of the times, are here appended. In A.D. 1835, the General Assembly of the Presbyterian Church resolved that ' *slavery is recognised in both the Old and New Testaments, and is not condemned by the authority of God.*' The Charleston Baptist Association issued the following, in an address in A.D. 1835: ' *The right of masters to dispose of the time of their slaves has been distinctly recognised by the Creator of all things, who is surely at liberty to vest the right of property over any object whomsoever He pleases.*' The Rev. E. D. Simon, Doctor of Divinity and professor in the Randolph-Macon Methodist College of Virginia, wrote: ' *Extracts from Holy Writ unequivocally assert the right of property in slaves, together with the usual incidents to that right. The right to buy and sell is clearly stated. Upon the whole, then, whether we consult the Jewish policy instituted by God Himself, or the uniform opinion and practice of mankind in all ages, or the injunctions of the*

was pale, and he seemed suffering from nausea.

'Then you have not protested?'

The Bishop shook his head.

'Then the Church is dumb today, as it was in the eighteenth century?'

The Bishop was silent, and for once Ernest forbore to press the point.

'And do not forget, whenever a churchman does protest, that he is discharged.'

'I hardly think that is fair,' was the objection.

'Will you protest?' Ernest demanded.

'Show me evils, such as you mention, in our own community, and I will protest.'

'I'll show you,' Ernest said quietly. 'I am at your disposal. I will take you on a journey through hell.'

'And I shall protest.' The Bishop straightened himself in his chair, and over his gentle face spread the harshness of the warrior. 'The Church shall not be dumb!'

'You will be discharged,' was the warning.

'I shall prove the contrary,' was the retort. 'I shall prove, if what you say is so, that the Church has erred through ignorance. And, furthermore, I hold that whatever is horrible in industrial society is due to the ignorance of the capitalist class. It will mend all that is wrong as soon as it receives the message. And this message it shall be the duty of the Church to deliver.'

New Testament and the moral law, we are brought to the conclusion that slavery is not immoral. Having established the point that the first African slaves were legally brought into bondage, the right to detain their children in bondage follows as an indispensable consequence. Thus we see that the slavery that exists in America was founded in right.'

It is not at all remarkable that this same note should have been struck by the Church a generation or so later in relation to the defence of capitalistic property. In the great museum at Asgard there is a book entitled 'Essays in Application,' written by Henry Van Dyke. The book was published in 1905 of the Christian Era. From what we can make out, Van Dyke must have been a Churchman. The book is a good example of what Everhard would have called bourgeois thinking. Note the similarity between the utterance of the Charleston Baptist Association quoted above, and the following utterance of Van Dyke seventy years later:

The Bible teaches that God owns the world. He distributes to every man according to His own good pleasure, conformably to general laws.'

Ernest laughed. He laughed brutally, and I was driven to the Bishop's defence.

'Remember,' I said, 'you see but one side of the shield. There is much good in us, though you give us credit for no good at all. Bishop Morehouse is right. The industrial wrong, terrible as you say it is, is due to ignorance. The divisions of society have become too widely separated.'

'The wild Indian is not so brutal and savage as the capitalist class,' he answered; and in that moment I hated him.

'You do not know us,' I answered. 'We are not brutal and savage.'

'Prove it,' he challenged.

'How can I prove it . . . to you?' I was growing angry.

He shook his head. 'I do not ask you to prove it to me. I ask you to prove it to yourself.'

'I know,' I said.

'You know nothing,' was his rude reply.

'There, there, children,' father said soothingly.

'I don't care—' I began indignantly, but Ernest interrupted.

'I understand you have money, or your father has, which is the same thing—money invested in the Sierra Mills.'

'What has that to do with it?' I cried.

'Nothing much,' he began slowly, 'except that the gown you wear is stained with blood. The food you eat is a bloody stew. The blood of little children and of strong men is dripping from your very roof-beams. I can close my eyes, now, and hear it drip, drop, drip, drop, all about me.'

And suiting the action to the words, he closed his eyes and leaned back in his chair. I burst into tears of mortification and hurt vanity. I had never been so brutally treated in my life. Both the Bishop and my father were embarrassed and perturbed. They tried to lead the conversation away into easier channels; but Ernest opened his eyes, looked at me, and waved them aside. His mouth was stern, and his eyes too; and in the latter there was no glint of laughter. What he was about to say, what terrible castigation he was going to give me, I never knew; for at that moment a man, passing along the sidewalk, stopped and glanced in at us. He was a large man, poorly dressed, and on his back was a great load of rattan and bamboo stands, chairs, and screens. He looked at the house as if debating whether or not he should come in and try to sell some of his wares.

' That man's name is Jackson,' Ernest said.

' With that strong body of his he should be at work, and not peddling,'[9] I answered curtly.

' Notice the sleeve of his left arm,' Ernest said gently.

I looked, and saw that the sleeve was empty.

' It was some of the blood from that arm that I heard dripping from your roof-beams,' Ernest said with continued gentleness. ' He lost his arm in the Sierra Mills, and like a broken-down horse you turned him out on the highway to die. When I say " you ", I mean the superintendent and the officials that you and the other stockholders pay to manage the mills for you. It was an accident. It was caused by his trying to save the company a few dollars. The toothed drum of the picker caught his arm. He might have let the small flint that he saw in the teeth go through. It would have smashed out a double row of spikes. But he reached for the flint, and his arm was picked and clawed to shreds from the finger tips to the shoulder. It was at night. The mills were working overtime. They paid a fat dividend that quarter. Jackson had been working many hours, and his muscles had lost their resiliency and snap. They made his movements a bit slow. That was why the machine caught him. He had a wife and three children.'

' And what did the company do for him?' I asked.

' Nothing. Oh, yes, they did do something. They successfully fought the damage suit he brought when he came out of hospital. The company employs very efficient lawyers, you know.'

' You have not told the whole story,' I said with conviction. ' Or else you do not know the whole story. Maybe the man was insolent.'

' Insolent! Ha! ha!' His laughter was Mephistophelian. ' Great God! Insolent! And with his arm chewed off! Nevertheless he was a meek and lowly servant and there is no record of his having been insolent.'

' But the courts,' I urged. ' The case would not have been decided against him had there been no more to the affair than you have mentioned.'

[9] In that day there were many thousands of those poor merchants called *pedlars*. They carried their whole stock in trade from door to door. It was a most wasteful expenditure of energy. Distribution was as confused and irrational as the whole general system of society.

' Colonel Ingram is leading counsel for the company. He is a shrewd lawyer.' Ernest looked at me intently for a moment, then went on: ' I'll tell you what you do, Miss Cunningham. You investigate Jackson's case.'

' I had already determined to,' I said coldly.

' All right,' he beamed good-naturedly, ' and I'll tell you where to find him. But I tremble for you when I think of all you are to prove by Jackson's arm.'

And so it came about that both the Bishop and I accepted Ernest's challenges. They went away together, leaving me smarting with a sense of injustice that had been done me and my class. The man was a beast. I hated him, then, and consoled myself with the thought that his behaviour was what was to be expected from a man of the working class.

CHAPTER 3

Jackson's Arm

LITTLE DID I dream the fateful part Jackson's arm was to play in my life. Jackson himself did not impress me when I hunted him out. I found him in a crazy ramshackle[1] house down near the bay on the edge of the marsh. Pools of stagnant water stood around the house, their surfaces covered with a green and putrid-looking scum, while the stench that arose from them was intolerable.

I found Jackson the meek and lowly man he had been described. He was making some sort of rattan-work, and he toiled on stolidly while I talked with him. But in spite of his meekness and lowliness, I fancied I caught the first note of a nascent bitterness in him when he said:

'They might a-given me a job as watchman,[2] anyway.'

I got little out of him. He struck me as stupid, and yet the deftness with which he worked with his one hand seemed to belie his stupidity. This suggested an idea to me.

'How did you happen to get your arm caught in the machine?' I asked.

He looked at me in a slow and pondering way, and shook his head. 'I don't know. It just happened.'

'Carelessness?' I prompted.

'No,' he answered, 'I ain't for callin' it that. I was workin' overtime, an' I guess I was tired out some. I worked seven-

---

[1] An adjective descriptive of ruined and dilapidated houses in which great numbers of the working people found shelter in those days. They invariably paid rent, and, considering the value of such houses, enormous rent, to the landlords.

[2] In those days thievery was incredibly prevalent. Everybody stole property from everybody else. The lords of society stole legally or else legalised their stealing, while the poorer classes stole illegally. Nothing was safe unless guarded. Enormous numbers of men were employed as watchmen to protect property. The houses of the well-to-do were a combination of safe deposit, vault, and fortress. The appropriation of the personal belongings of others by our own children of today is looked upon as a rudimentary survival of the theft-characteristic that in those early times was universal.

teen years in them mills, an' I've took notice that most of
the accidents happens just before whistle-blow.[3] I'm willin'
to bet that more accidents happens in the hour before whistle-
blow than in all the rest of the day. A man ain't so quick
after workin' steady for hours. I've seen too many of 'em cut
up an' gouged an' chawed not to know.'

' Many of them?' I queried.

' Hundreds an' hundreds, an' children, too.'

With the exception of the terrible details, Jackson's story
of his accident was the same as that I had already heard.
When I asked him if he had broken some rule of working the
machinery, he shook his head.

' I chucked off the belt with my right hand,' he said, ' an'
made a reach for the flint with my left, I didn't stop to see
if the belt was off. I thought my right hand had done it—only
it didn't. I reached quick, and the belt wasn't all the way off.
And then my arm was chewed off.'

' It must have been painful,' I said sympathetically.

' The crunchin' of the bones wasn't nice,' was his answer.

His mind was rather hazy concerning the damage suit.
Only one thing was clear to him, and that was that he had
not got any damages. He had a feeling that the testimony of
the foreman and the superintendent had brought about the
adverse decision of the court. Their testimony, as he put it,
' wasn't what it ought to have ben.' And to them I resolved
to go.

One thing was plain. Jackson's situation was wretched. His
wife was in ill health, and he was unable to earn, by his
rattan-work and peddling, sufficient food for the family. He
was back in his rent, and the oldest boy, a lad of eleven, had
started to work in the mills.

' They might a-given me that watchman's job,' were his
last words as I went away.

By the time I had seen the lawyer who had handled Jackson's case, and the two foremen and the superintendent at
the mills who had testified, I began to feel that there was
something after all in Ernest's contention.

He was a weak and inefficient-looking man, the lawyer, and
at sight of him I did not wonder that Jackson's case had been
lost. My first thought was that it had served Jackson right
for getting such a lawyer. But the next moment two of

[3] The labourers were called to work and dismissed by savage,
screaming, nerve-racking steam-whistles.

Ernest's statements came flashing into my consciousness:
' The company employs very efficient lawyers,' and ' Colonel
Ingram is a shrewd lawyer.' I did some rapid thinking. It
dawned upon me that of course the company could afford
finer legal talent than could a working man like Jackson. But
this was merely a minor detail. There was some very good
reason, I was sure, why Jackson's case had gone against
him. ' Why did you lose the case?' I asked.

The lawyer was perplexed and worried for a moment, and
I found it in my heart to pity the wretched little creature.
Then he began to whine. I do believe his whine was con-
genital. He was a man beaten at birth. He whined about the
testimony. The witnesses had given only the evidence that
helped the other side. Not one word could he get out of
them that would have helped Jackson. They knew which side
their bread was buttered on. Jackson was a fool. He had been
brow-beaten and confused by Colonel Ingram. Colonel
Ingram was brilliant at cross-examination. He had made
Jackson answer damaging questions.

' How could his answers be damaging if he had the right
on his side?' I demanded.

' What's right got to do with it?' he demanded back. ' You
see all those books.' He moved his hand over the array of
volumes on the walls of his tiny office. ' All my reading and
studying of them has taught me that law is one thing and
right is another thing. Ask any lawyer. You go to Sunday-
school to learn what is right. But you go to those books to
learn . . . law.'

' Do you mean to tell me that Jackson had the right on
his side and yet was beaten?' I queried tentatively. ' Do you
mean to tell me that there is no justice in Judge Caldwell's
court?'

The little lawyer glared at me a moment, and then the
belligerence faded out of his face.

' I hadn't a fair chance,' he began whining again. ' They
made a fool out of Jackson and out of me, too. What chance
had I? Colonel Ingram is a great lawyer. If he wasn't great,
would he have charge of the law business of the Sierra Mills,
of the Erston Land Syndicate, of the Berkeley Consolidated,
of the Oakland, San Leandro, and Pleasanton Electric? He's
a corporation lawyer, and corporation lawyers are not paid
for being fools.[4] What do you think the Sierra Mills alone

[4] The function of the corporation lawyer was to serve, by corrupt

give him twenty thousand dollars a year for? Because he's worth twenty thousand dollars a year to them, that's what for. I'm not worth that much. If I was, I wouldn't be on the outside, starving and taking cases like Jackson's. What do you think I'd have got if I'd won Jackson's case?'

' You'd have robbed him, most probably,' I answered.

' Of course I would,' he cried angrily. ' I've got to live, haven't I?'[5]

' He has a wife and children,' I chided.

' So have I a wife and children,' he retorted. ' And there's not a soul in this world except myself that cares whether they starve or not.'

His face suddenly softened, and he opened his watch and showed me a small photograph of a woman and two little girls pasted inside the case.

' There they are. Look at them. We've had a hard time, a hard time. I had hoped to send them away to the country if I'd won Jackson's case. They're not healthy here, but I can't afford to send them away.'

When I started to leave, he dropped back into his whine.

' I hadn't a ghost of a chance. Colonel Ingram and Judge Caldwell are pretty friendly. I'm not saying that if I'd got the right kind of testimony out of their witnesses on cross-examination, that friendship would have decided the case. And yet I must say that Judge Caldwell did a whole lot to prevent my getting that very testimony. Why, Judge Caldwell and Colonel Ingram belong to the same lodge and the same club. They live in the same neighbourhood—one I can't afford. And their wives are always in and out of each other's houses. They're always having whist parties and such things back and forth.'

---

methods, the money-grabbing propensities of the corporations. It is on record that Theodore Roosevelt, at that time President of the United States, said in A.D. 1905, in his address at Harvard Commencement: ' *We all know that, as things actually are, many of the most influential and most highly remunerated members of the Bar in every centre of wealth, make it their special task to work out bold and ingenious schemes by which their wealthy clients, individual or corporate, can evade the laws which were made to regulate, in the interests of the public, the uses of great wealth.*'

[5] A typical illustration of the internecine strife that permeated all society. Men preyed upon one another like ravening wolves. The big wolves ate the little wolves, and in the social pack Jackson was one of the least of the little wolves.

'And yet you think Jackson had the right of it?' I asked, pausing for the moment on the threshold.

'I don't think; I know it,' was his answer. 'And at first I thought he had some show, too. But I didn't tell my wife. I didn't want to disappoint her: she had her heart set on a trip to the country. Hard enough as it was.'

'Why did you not call attention to the fact that Jackson was trying to save the machinery from being injured?' I asked Peter Donnelly, one of the foremen who had testified at the trial.

He pondered a long time before replying. Then he cast an anxious look about him and said:

'Because I've a good wife an' three of the sweetest children ye ever laid eyes on, that's why.'

'I do not understand,' I said.

'In other words, because it wouldn't a-ben healthy,' he answered.

'You mean—' I began.

But he interrupted passionately.

'I mean what I said. It's long years I've worked in the mills. I began as a little lad on the spindles, I worked up ever since. It's by hard work I got to my present exalted position. I'm a foreman, if you please. An' I doubt me if there's a man in the mills that'd put out a hand to drag me from drownin'. I used to belong to the union. But I've stayed by the company through two strikes. They called me 'scab'. There's not a man among 'em today to take a drink with me if I asked him. D'ye see the scars on me head where I was struck with flying bricks? There ain't a child at the spindles but what would curse me name. Me only friend is the company. It's not me duty, but me bread and butter an' the life of me children to stand by the mills. That's why.'

'Was Jackson to blame?' I asked.

'He should a-got the damages. He was a good worker an' never made trouble.'

'Then you are not at liberty to tell the whole truth, as you had sworn to do?'

He shook his head.

'The truth, the whole truth, and nothing but the truth?' I said solemnly.

Again his face became impassioned, and he lifted it, not to me, but to heaven.

'I'd let me soul an' body burn in everlastin' hell for

them children of mine,' was his answer.

Henry Dallas, the superintendent, was a vulpine-faced creature who regarded me insolently and refused to talk. Not a word could I get from him concerning the trial and his testimony. But with the other foreman I had better luck. James Smith was a hard-faced man, and my heart sank as I encountered him. He, too, gave me the impression that he was not a free agent, and as we talked I began to see that he was mentally superior to the average of his kind. He agreed with Peter Donnelly that Jackson should have got damages, and he went further and called the action heartless and cold-blooded that had turned the worker adrift after he had been made helpless by the accident. Also, he explained that there were many accidents in the mills, and that the company's policy was to fight to the bitter end all consequent damage suits.

'It means hundreds of thousands a year to the stock-holders,' he said; and as he spoke I remembered the last divi-dend that had been paid my father, and the pretty gown for me and the books for him that had been bought out of that dividend. I remembered Ernest's charge that my gown was stained with blood, and my flesh began to crawl underneath my garments.

'When you testified at the trial, you didn't point out that Jackson received his accident through trying to save the machinery from damage?' I said.

'No, I did not,' was the answer, and his mouth set bitterly. 'I testified to the effect that Jackson injured himself by neg-lect and carelessness, and that the company was not in any way to blame or liable.'

'Was it carelessness?' I asked.

'Call it that, or anything you want to call it. The fact is, a man gets tired after he's been working for hours.'

I was becoming interested in the man. He certainly was of a superior kind.

'You are better educated than most working men,' I said.

'I went through high school,' he replied. 'I worked my way through doing janitor-work. I wanted to go through the university. But my father died, and I came to work in the mills.

'I wanted to become a naturalist,' he explained shyly, as though confessing a weakness. 'I love animals. But I came to work in the mills. When I was promoted to foreman I got married, then the family came, and . . . well, I wasn't my own boss any more.'

' What do you mean by that?' I asked.

' I was explaining why I testified at the trial the way I did—why I followed instructions.'

' Whose instructions?'

' Colonel Ingram. He outlined the evidence I was to give.'

' And it lost Jackson's case for him.'

He nodded, and the blood began to rise darkly in his face.

' And Jackson had a wife and two children dependent on him.'

' I know,' he said quietly, though his face was growing darker.

' Tell me,' I went on, ' was it easy to make yourself over from what you were, say in high school, to the man you must have become to do such a thing at the trial?'

The suddenness of his outburst startled and frightened me. He ripped[6] out a savage oath, and clenched his fist as though about to strike me.

' I beg your pardon,' he said the next moment. ' No, it was not easy. And now I guess you can go away. You've got all you wanted out of me. But let me tell you this before you go. It won't do you any good to repeat anything I've said. I'll deny it, and there are no witnesses. I'll deny every word of it; and if I have to, I'll do it under oath on the witness stand.'

After my interview with Smith I went to my father's office in the Chemistry Building and there encountered Ernest. It was quite unexpected, but he met me with his bold eyes and firm handclasp, and with that curious blend of his of awkwardness and ease. It was as though our last stormy meeting was forgotten; but I was not in the mood to have it forgotten.

' I have been looking up Jackson's case,' I said abruptly.

He was all interested attention, and waited for me to go

---

[6] It is interesting to note the virilities of language that were common speech in that day, as indicative of the life, ' red of claw and fang,' that was then lived. Reference is here made, of course, not to the oath of Smith, but to the verb *ripped* used by Avis Everhard.

on, though I could see in his eyes the certitude that my convictions had been shaken.

'He seems to have been badly treated,' I confessed. 'I—I —think some of his blood is dripping from our roof-beams.'

'Of course,' he answered. 'If Jackson and all his fellows were treated mercifully the dividends would not be so large.'

'I shall never be able to take pleasure in pretty gowns again,' I added.

I felt humble and contrite, and was aware of a sweet feeling that Ernest was a sort of father confessor. Then, as ever after, his strength appealed to me. It seemed to radiate a promise of peace and protection.

'Nor will you be able to take pleasure in sackcloth,' he said gravely. 'There are the jute mills, you know, and the same thing goes on there. It goes on everywhere. Our boasted civilisation is based upon blood, soaked in blood, and neither you nor I nor any of us can escape the scarlet stain. The men you talked with—who were they?'

I told him all that had taken place.

'And not one of them was a free agent,' he said. 'They were all tied to the merciless industrial machine. And the pathos of it and the tragedy is that they are tied by their heart-strings. Their children—always the young life that it is their instinct to protect. This instinct is stronger than any ethic they possess. My father! He lied, he stole, he did all sorts of dishonourable things to put bread into my mouth and into the mouths of my brothers and sisters. He was a slave to the industrial machine, and it stamped his life out, worked him to death.'

'But you,' I interjected. 'You are surely a free agent.'

'Not wholly,' he replied. 'I am not tied by my heart-strings. I am often thankful that I have no children, and I dearly love children. Yet if I married I should not dare to have any.'

'That surely is bad doctrine,' I cried.

'I know it is,' he said sadly. 'But it is expedient doctrine. I am a revolutionist, and it is a perilous vocation.'

I laughed incredulously.

'If I tried to enter your father's house at night to steal his dividends from the Sierra Mills, what would he do?'

'He sleeps with a revolver on the stand by the bed,' I answered. 'He would most probably shoot you.'

'And if I and a few others should lead a million and a

half of men[7] into the houses of all the well-to-do, there would be a great deal of shooting, wouldn't there?'

'Yes, but you are not doing that,' I objected.

'It is precisely what I am doing. And we intend to take, not the mere wealth in the houses, but all the sources of that wealth, all the mines, and railroads, and factories, and banks and stores. That is the revolution. It is truly perilous. There will be more shooting, I am afraid, than even I dream of. But as I was saying, no one today is a free agent. We are all caught up in the wheels and cogs of the industrial machine. You found that you were, and that the men you talked with were. Talk with more of them. Go and see Colonel Ingram. Look up the reporters that kept Jackson's case out of the papers, and the editors that run the papers. You will find them all slaves of the machine.'

A little later in our conversation I asked him a simple little question about the liability of working men to accidents, and received a statistical lecture in return.

'It is all in the books,' he said. 'The figures have been gathered, and it has been proved conclusively that accidents rarely occur in the first hours of the morning work, but that they increase rapidly in the succeeding hours as the workers grow tired and slower in both their muscular and mental processes.

'Why, do you know that your father has three times as many chances for safety of life and limb as has a working man? He has. The insurance[8] companies know. They will charge him four dollars and twenty cents a year on a thousand-dollar accident policy, and for the same policy they will charge a labourer fifteen dollars.'

'And you?' I asked; and in the moment of asking I was

---

[7] This reference is to the socialist vote cast in the United States in 1910. The rise of this vote clearly indicates the swift growth of the party of revolution. Its voting strength in the United States in 1888 was 2,068; in 1902, 127,713; in 1904, 435,040; in 1908, 1,108,427; and in 1910, 1,688,211.

[8] In the terrible wolf-struggle of those centuries, no man was permanently safe, no matter how much wealth he amassed. Out of fear for the welfare of their families men devised the scheme of insurance. To us, in this intelligent age, such a device is laughably absurd and primitive. But in that age insurance was a very serious matter. The amusing part of it is that the funds of the insurance companies were frequently plundered and wasted by the very officials who were entrusted with the management of them.

aware of a solicitude that was something more than slight.

'Oh, as a revolutionist, I have about eight chances to the working man's one of being injured or killed,' he answered carelessly. 'The insurance companies charge the highly trained chemists that handle explosives eight times what they charge the working men. I don't think they'd insure me at all. Why did you ask?'

My eyes fluttered, and I could feel the blood warm in my face. It was not that he had caught me in my solicitude, but that I had caught myself, and in his presence.

Just then my father came in and began making preparations to depart with me. Ernest returned some books he had borrowed, and went away first. But just as he was going, he turned and said:

'Oh, by the way, while you are ruining your own peace of mind and I am ruining the Bishop's, you'd better look up Mrs Wickson and Mrs Pertonwaithe. Their husbands, you know, are the two principal stockholders in the Mills. Like all the rest of humanity, those two women are tied to the machine, but they are so tied that they sit on top of it.'

CHAPTER 4

Slaves of the Machine

THE MORE I thought of Jackson's arm, the more shaken I was. I was confronted by the concrete. For the first time I was seeing life. My university life, and study and culture, had not been real. I had learned nothing but theories of life and society that looked all very well on the printed page, but now I had seen life itself. Jackson's arm was a fact of life. 'The fact, man, the irrefragable fact!' of Ernest's was ringing in my consciousness.

It seemed monstrous, impossible, that our whole society was based upon blood. And yet there was Jackson. I could not get away from him. Constantly my thought swung back to him as the compass to the Pole. He had been monstrously treated. His blood had not been paid for, in order that a larger dividend might be paid. And I knew a score of happy, complacent families that had received those dividends, and by that much had profited by Jackson's blood. If one man could be so monstrously treated and society move on its way unheeding, might not many men be so monstrously treated? I remembered Ernest's women of Chicago who toiled for ninety cents a week, and the child slaves of the Southern cotton mills he had described. And I could see their wan white hands, from which the blood had been pressed, at work upon the cloth out of which had been made my gown. And then I thought of the Sierra Mills and the dividends that had been paid, and I saw the blood of Jackson upon my gown as well. Jackson I could not escape. Always my meditations led me back to him.

Down in the depths of me I had a feeling that I stood on the edge of a precipice. It was as though I were about to see a new and awful revelation of life. And not I alone. My whole world was turning over. There was my father. I could see the effect Ernest was beginning to have on him. And then there was the Bishop. When I had last seen him he had looked a sick man. He was at high nervous tension, and in his eyes there was unspeakable horror. From the little I learned I knew that Ernest had been keeping his promise of taking him through hell. But what scenes of hell the Bishop's eyes had seen, I knew not, for he seemed too stunned to speak about them.

Once, the feeling strong upon me that my little world and all the world was turning over, I thought of Ernest as the cause of it; and also I thought, 'We were so happy and peaceful before he came!' And the next moment I was aware that the thought was a treason against truth, and Ernest rose before me transfigured, the apostle of truth, with shining brows and the fearlessness of one of God's own angels, battling for the truth and the right, and battling for the succour of the poor and lonely and oppressed. And then there arose before me another figure, the Christ! He, too, had taken the part of the lowly and oppressed, and against all the established power of priest and pharisee. And I remembered His end upon the cross, and my heart contracted with a pang as I thought of Ernest. Was he, too, destined for a cross?—he, with his clarion call and war-noted voice, and all the fine man's vigour of him.

And in that moment I knew that I loved him, and that I was melting with desire to comfort him. I thought of his life. A sordid, harsh, and meagre life it must have been. And I thought of his father who had lied and stolen for him and been worked to death. And he himself had gone into the mills when he was ten! All my heart seemed bursting with desire to fold my arms around him, and to rest his head on my breast—his head that must be weary with so many thoughts; and to give him rest—just rest—and easement and forgetfulness for a tender space.

I met Colonel Ingram at a church reception. Him I knew well and had known well for many years. I trapped him behind large palms and rubber plants, though he did not know he was trapped. He met me with the conventional gaiety and gallantry. He was ever a graceful man, diplomatic, tactful, and considerate. And as for appearance, he was the most distinguished-looking man in our society. Beside him even the venerable head of the university looked tawdry and small.

And yet I found Colonel Ingram situated the same as the unlettered mechanics. He was not a free agent. He, too, was bound upon the wheel. I shall never forget the change in him when I mentioned Jackson's case. His smiling good-nature vanished like a ghost. A sudden, frightful expression distorted his well-bred face. I felt the same alarm that I had felt when James Smith broke out. But Colonel Ingram did not curse. That was the slight difference that was left between the working man and him. He was famed as a wit, but he had no wit now. And, unconsciously, this way and that he glanced for avenues of escape. But he was trapped amid the palms and rubber trees.

Oh, he was sick of the sound of Jackson's name. Why had I brought the matter up? He did not relish my joke. It was poor taste on my part, and very inconsiderate. Did I not know that in his profession personal feelings did not count? He left his personal feelings at home when he went down to the office. At the office he had only professional feelings.

'Should Jackson have received damages?' I asked.

'Certainly,' he answered. 'That is, personally, I have a feeling that he should. But that has nothing to do with the legal aspects of the case.'

He was getting his scattered wits slightly in hand.

'Tell me, has right anything to do with the law?' I asked.

'You have used the wrong initial consonant,' he smiled in answer.

'Might?' I queried; and he nodded his head. 'And yet we are supposed to get justice by means of the law?'

'That is the paradox of it,' he countered. 'We do get justice.'

'You are speaking professionally now, are you not?' I asked.

Colonel Ingram blushed, actually blushed, and again he looked anxiously about him for a way of escape. But I blocked his path and did not offer to move.

'Tell me,' I said, 'when one surrenders his personal feelings to his professional feelings, may not the action be defined as a sort of spiritual mayhem?'

I did not get an answer. Colonel Ingram had ingloriously bolted, overturning a palm in his flight.

Next I tried the newspapers. I wrote a quiet, restrained, dispassionate account of Jackson's case. I made no charges against the men with whom I had talked, nor, for that matter, did I even mention them. I gave the actual facts of the case, the long years Jackson had worked in the mills, his effort to save the machinery from damage and the consequent accident, and his own present wretched and starving condition. The three local newspapers rejected my communication, likewise did the two weeklies.

I got hold of Percy Layton. He was a graduate of the university, had gone in for journalism, and was then serving his apprenticeship as reporter on the most influential of the three newspapers. He smiled when I asked him the reason the newspapers suppressed all mention of Jackson or his case.

'Editorial policy,' he said. 'We have nothing to do with that. It's up to the editors.'

'But why is it policy?' I asked.

'We're all solid with the corporations,' he answered. 'If you paid advertising rates, you couldn't get any such matter into the papers. A man who tried to smuggle it in would lose his job. You couldn't get it in if you paid ten times the regular advertising rates.'

'How about your own policy?' I questioned. 'It would seem your function is to twist truth at the command of your employers, who, in turn, obey the behests of the corporations.'

'I haven't anything to do with that.' He looked uncomfortable for the moment, then brightened as he saw his way out. 'I, myself, do not write untruthful things. I keep square all right with my own conscience. Of course, there's lots that's repugnant in the course of the day's work. But then, you see, that's all part of the day's work,' he wound up, boyishly.

'Yet you expect to sit at an editor's desk some day and conduct a policy.'

'I'll be case-hardened by that time,' was his reply.

'Since you are not yet case-hardened, tell me what you think right now about the general editorial policy.'

'I don't think,' he answered quickly. 'One can't kick over the ropes if he's going to succeed in journalism. I've learned that much, at any rate.'

And he nodded his young head sagely.

'But the right?' I persisted.

'You don't understand the game. Of course it's all right, because it comes out all right, don't you see?'

'Delightfully vague,' I murmured; but my heart was aching for the youth of him and I felt that I must either scream or burst into tears.

I was beginning to see through the appearances of the society in which I had always lived, and to find the frightful realities that were beneath. There seemed a tacit conspiracy against Jackson, and I was aware of a thrill of sympathy for the whining lawyer who had ingloriously fought his case. But this tacit conspiracy grew large. Not alone was it aimed against Jackson. It was aimed against every working man who was maimed in the mills. And if against every man in the mills, why not against every man in all the other mills and factories? In fact, was it not true of all the industries?

And if this was so, then society was a lie. I shrank back from my own conclusions. It was too terrible and awful to be true. But there was Jackson, and Jackson's arm, and the blood that stained my gown and dripped from my own roof-beams. And there were many Jacksons—hundreds of them in the mills alone, as Jackson himself had said. Jackson I could not escape.

I saw Mr Wickson and Mr Pertonwaithe, the two men who held most of the stock in the Sierra Mills. But I could not shake them as I had shaken the mechanics in their employ. I discovered that they had an ethic superior to that of the rest of society. It was what I may call the aristocratic ethic or the master ethic.[1] They talked in large ways of policy, and they identified policy and right. And to me they talked in fatherly ways, patronising my youth and inexperience. They were the most hopeless of all I had encountered in my quest. They believed absolutely that their conduct was right. There was no question about it, no discussion. They were convinced that they were the saviours of society, and that it was they who made happiness for the many. And they drew pathetic pictures of what would be the sufferings of the working class were it not for the employment that they, and they alone, by their wisdom, provided for it.

Fresh from these two masters, I met Ernest and related my experience. He looked at me with a pleased expression, and said:

' Really, this is fine. You are beginning to dig truth for yourself. It is your own empirical generalisation, and it is correct. No man in the industrial machine is a free-will agent, except the large capitalist, and he isn't, if you'll pardon the Irishism.[2] You see the masters are quite sure that they are

[1] Before Avis Everhard was born, John Stuart Mill, in his essay, *On Liberty*, wrote: 'Wherever there is an ascendant class, a large portion of the morality emanates from its class interests and its class feelings of superiority.'
[2] Verbal contradictions, called *bulls*, were long an amiable weakness of the ancient Irish.

right in what they are doing. That is the crowning absurdity of the whole situation. They are so tied by their human nature that they can't do a thing unless they think it is right. They must have a sanction for their acts.

'When they want to do a thing, in business of course, they must wait till there arises in their brains, somehow, a religious, or ethical, or scientific, or philosophic, concept that the thing is right. And then they go ahead and do it, unwitting that one of the weaknesses of the human mind is that the wish is parent to the thought. No matter what they want to do, the sanction always comes. They are superficial casuists. They are Jesuitical. They even see their way to doing wrong that right may come of it. One of the pleasant and axiomatic fictions they have created is that they are superior to the rest of mankind in wisdom and efficiency. Therefrom comes their sanction to manage the bread and butter of the rest of mankind. They have even resurrected the theory of the divine right of kings—commercial kings in their case.[3]

'The weakness in their position lies in that they are merely business men. They are not philosophers. They are not biologists nor sociologists. If they were, of course all would be well. A business man who was also a biologist and a sociologist would know, approximately, the right thing to do for humanity. But, outside the realm of business, these men are stupid. They know only business. They do not know mankind nor society, and yet they set themselves up as arbiters of the fates of the hungry millions and all the other millions thrown in. History, some day, will have an excruciating laugh at their expense.'

I was not surprised when I had my talk out with Mrs Wickson and Mrs Pertonwaithe. They were society women.[4]

---

[3] The newspapers, in 1902 of that era, credited the president of the Anthracite Coal Trust, George F. Baer, with the enunciation of the following principle: *'The rights and interests of the labouring man will be protected by the Christian men to whom God in His infinite wisdom has given the property interests of the country.'*

[4] *Society* is here used in a restricted sense, a common usage of the times to denote the gilded drones that did no labour, but only glutted themselves at the honey-vats of the workers. Neither the business men nor the labourers had time or opportunity for *society*. *Society* was the creation of the idle rich who toiled not and who in this way played.

Their homes were palaces. They had many homes scattered over the country, in the mountains, on lakes, and by the sea. They were tended by armies of servants, and their social activities were bewildering. They patronised the university and the churches, and the pastors especially bowed at their knees in meek subservience.[5] They were powers, these two women, what of the money that was theirs. The power of subsidisation of thought was theirs to a remarkable degree, as I was soon to learn under Ernest's tuition.

They aped their husbands, and talked in the same large ways about policy, and the duties and responsibilities of the rich. They were swayed by the same ethic that dominated their husbands—the ethic of their class; and they uttered glib phrases that their own ears did not understand.

Also, they grew irritated when I told them of the deplorable condition of Jackson's family, and when I wondered that they had made no voluntary provision for the man. I was told that they thanked no one for instructing them in their social duties. When I asked them flatly to assist Jackson, they as flatly refused. The astounding thing about it was that they refused in almost identically the same language, and this in face of the fact that I interviewed them separately and that one did not know that I had seen or was going to see the other. Their common reply was that they were glad of the opportunity to make it perfectly plain that no premium would ever be put on carelessness by them; nor would they, by paying for accidents, tempt the poor to hurt themselves in the machinery.[6]

And they were sincere, these two women. They were drunk with conviction of the superiority of their class and of themselves. They had a sanction, in their own class-ethic, for every act they performed. As I drove away from Mrs Pertonwaithe's great house, I looked back at it, and I remembered Ernest's expression that they were bound to the machine, but that they were so bound that they sat on top of it.

[5] 'Bring on your tainted money,' was the expressed sentiment of the Church during this period.
[6] In the files of the *Outlook,* a critical weekly of the period, in the number dated August 18, 1906, is related the circumstance of a working man losing his arm, the details of which are quite similar to those of Jackson's case as related by Avis Everhard.

CHAPTER 5

The Philomaths

E R N E S T W A S often at the house. Nor was it my father, merely, nor the controversial dinners, that drew him there. Even at that time I flattered myself that I played some part in causing his visits, and it was not long before I learned the correctness of my surmise. For never was there such a lover as Ernest Everhard. His gaze and his hand-clasp grew firmer and steadier, if that were possible; and the question that had grown from the first in his eyes, grew only the more imperative.

My impression of him, the first time I saw him, had been unfavourable. Then I had found myself attracted towards him. Next came my repulsion, when he so savagely attacked my class and me. After that, as I saw that he had not maligned my class, and that the harsh and bitter things he said about it were justified, I had drawn closer to him again. He became my oracle. For me he tore the sham from the face of society, and gave me glimpses of reality that were as unpleasant as they were undeniably true.

As I have said, there was never such a lover as he. No girl could live in a university town till she was twenty-four and not have love experiences. I had been made love to by beardless sophomores and grey professors, and by the athletes and the football giants. But not one of them made love to me as Ernest did. His arms were around me before I knew. His lips were on mine before I could protest or resist. Before his earnestness conventional maiden dignity was ridiculous. He swept me off my feet by the splendid invincible rush of him. He did not propose. He put his arms around me and kissed me and took it for granted that we should be married. There was no discussion about it. The only discussion—and that arose afterwards—was when we should be married.

It was unprecedented. It was unreal. Yet, in accordance with Ernest's test of truth, it worked. I trusted my life to it. And fortunate was the trust. Yet during those first days of our love, fear of the future came often to me when I thought of the violence and impetuosity of his love-making. Yet such

fears were groundless. No woman was ever blessed with
a gentler, tenderer husband. This gentleness and violence
on his part was a curious blend similar to the one in his carriage of awkwardness and ease. That slight awkwardness! He
never got over it, and it was delicious. His behaviour in our
drawing-room reminded me of a careful bull in a china
shop.[1]

It was at this time that vanished my last doubt of the com-
pleteness of my love for him (a subconscious doubt, at most).
It was at the Philomath Club—a wonderful night of battle,
wherein Ernest bearded the masters in their lair. Now the
Philomath Club was the most select on the Pacific Coast. It
was the creation of Miss Brentwood, an enormously wealthy
old maid; and it was her husband, and family, and toy. Its
members were the wealthiest in the community, and the
strongest-minded of the wealthy, with, of course, a sprinkling
of scholars to give it intellectual tone.

The Philomath had no club house. It was not that kind
of a club. Once a month its members gathered at some one
of their private houses to listen to a lecture. The lecturers
were usually, though not always, hired. If a chemist in New
York made a new discovery in say radium, all his expenses
across the continent were paid, and as well he received a
princely fee for his time. The same with a returning explorer
from the polar regions or the latest literary or artistic success.
No visitors were allowed, while it was the Philomath's policy
to permit none of its discussions to get into the papers. Thus
great statesmen—and there had been such occasions—were
able fully to speak their minds.

I spread before me a wrinkled letter, written to me by
Ernest twenty years ago, and from it I copy the following:

'Your father is a member of the Philomath, so you are
able to come. Therefore come next Tuesday night. I promise
you that you will have the time of your life. In your recent
encounters, you failed to shake the masters. If you come, I'll
shake them for you. I'll make them snarl like wolves. You
merely questioned their morality. When their morality is

[1] In those days it was still the custom to fill the living rooms with
bric-à-brac. They had not discovered simplicity of living. Such
rooms were museums, entailing endless labour to keep clean. The
dust-demon was the lord of the household. There were a myriad
devices for catching dust, and only a few devices for getting rid
of it.

questioned, they grow only the more complacent and superior. But I shall menace their money-bags. That will shake them to the roots of their primitive natures. If you can come, you will see the cave-man, in evening dress, snarling and snapping over a bone. I promise you a great caterwauling and an illuminating insight into the nature of the beast.

'They've invited me in order to tear me to pieces. This is the idea of Miss Brentwood. She clumsily hinted as much when she invited me. She's given them that kind of fun before. They delight in getting trustful-souled, gentle reformers before them. Miss Brentwood thinks I am as mild as a kitten and as good-natured and stolid as the family cow. I'll not deny that I helped to give her that impression. She was very tentative at first, until she divined my harmlessness. I am to receive a handsome fee—two hundred and fifty dollars—as befits the man who, though a Radical, once ran for governor. Also, I am to wear evening dress. This is compulsory. I never was so apparelled in my life. I suppose I'll have to hire one somewhere. But I'd do more than that to get a chance at the Philomaths.'

Of all places, the Club gathered that night at the Pertonwaithe house. Extra chairs had been brought into the great drawing-room, and in all there must have been two hundred Philomaths that sat down to hear Ernest. They were truly lords of society. I amused myself with running over in my mind the sum of the fortunes represented, and it ran well into the hundreds of millions. And the possessors were not of the idle rich. They were men of affairs who took most active parts in industrial and political life.

We were all seated when Miss Brentwood brought Ernest in. They moved at once to the head of the room, from where he was to speak. He was in evening dress, and, what of his broad shoulders and kingly head, he looked magnificent. And then there was that faint and unmistakable touch of awkwardness in his movements. I almost think I could have loved him for that alone. And as I looked at him I was aware of a great joy. I felt again the pulse of his palm on mine, the touch of his lips; and such pride was mine that I felt I must rise up and cry out to the assembled company: 'He is mine! He has held me in his arms, and I, mere I, have filled that mind of his to the exclusion of all his multitudinous and kingly thoughts!'

At the head of the room, Miss Brentwood introduced him to Colonel Van Gilbert, and I knew that the latter was to preside. Colonel Van Gilbert was a great corporation lawyer. In addition, he was immensely wealthy. The smallest fee he would deign to notice was a hundred thousand dollars. He was a master of law. The law was a puppet with which he played. He moulded it like clay, twisted and distorted it like a Chinese puzzle into any design he chose. In appearance and rhetoric he was old-fashioned, but in imagination and knowledge and resource he was as young as the latest statute. His first prominence had come when he broke the Shardwell will.[2] His fee for this one act was five hundred thousand dollars. From then on he had risen like a rocket. He was often called the greatest lawyer in the country—corporation lawyer, of course; and no classification of the three greatest lawyers in the United States could have excluded him.

He arose and began, in a few well-chosen phrases that carried an undertone of faint irony, to introduce Ernest. Colonel Van Gilbert was subtly facetious in his introduction of the social reformer and member of the working class, and the audience smiled. It made me angry, and I glanced at Ernest. The sight of him made me doubly angry. He did not seem to resent the delicate slurs. Worse than that, he did not seem to be aware of them. There he sat, gentle, and stolid, and somnolent. He really looked stupid. And for a moment the thought rose in my mind, What if he were over-awed by this imposing array of power and brains? Then I smiled. He couldn't fool me. But he fooled the others, just as he had fooled Miss Brentwood. She occupied a chair right up at the front, and several times she turned her head towards one or another of her confrères and smiled her appreciation of the remarks.

[2] This breaking of wills was a peculiar feature of the period. With the accumulation of vast fortunes, the problem of disposing of these fortunes after death was a vexing one to the accumulators. Will-making and will-breaking became complementary trades, like armour-making and gun-making. The shrewdest will-making lawyers were called in to make wills that could not be broken. But these wills were always broken, and very often by the very lawyers that had drawn them up. Nevertheless the delusion persisted in the wealthy class that an absolutely unbreakable will could be cast; and so, through the generations, clients and lawyers pursued the illusion. It was a pursuit like unto that of the Universal Solvent of the medieval alchemists.

Colonel Van Gilbert done, Ernest arose and began to speak. He began in a low voice, haltingly and modestly, and with an air of evident embarrassment. He spoke of his birth in the working class, and of the sordidness and wretchedness of his environment, where flesh and spirit were alike starved and tormented. He described his ambitions and ideals, and his conception of the paradise wherein lived the people of the upper classes. As he said:

' Up above me, I knew, were unselfishness of the spirit, clean and noble thinking, keen intellectual living. I knew all this because I read *Seaside Library*[3] novels, in which, with the exception of the villains and adventuresses, all men and women thought beautiful thoughts, spoke a beautiful tongue, and performed glorious deeds. In short, as I accepted the rising of the sun, I accepted that up above me was all that was fine and noble and gracious, all that gave decency and dignity to life, all that made life worth living and that remunerated one for his travail and misery.'

He went on and traced his life in the mills, the learning of the horseshoeing trade, and his meeting with the socialists. Among them, he said, he had found keen intellects and brilliant wits, ministers of the Gospel who had been broken because their Christianity was too wide for any congregation of mammon-worshippers, and professors who had been broken on the wheel of university subservience to the ruling class. The socialists were revolutionists, he said, struggling to overthrow the irrational society of the present and out of the material to build the rational society of the future. Much more he said that would take too long to write, but I shall never forget how he described the life among the revolutionists. All halting utterance vanished. His voice grew strong and confident, and it glowed as he glowed, and as the thoughts glowed that poured out from him. He said:

' Amongst the revolutionists I found, also, warm faith in the human, ardent idealism, sweetnesses of unselfishness, renunciation, and martyrdom—all the splendid, stinging things of the spirit. Here life was clean, noble, and alive. I was in touch with great souls who exalted flesh and spirit over dollars and cents, and to whom the thin wail of the starved slum child meant more than all the pomp and circumstance of commercial expansion and world empire. All

[3] A curious and amazing literature that served to make the working class utterly misapprehend the nature of the leisure class.

about me were nobleness of purpose and heroism of effort, and my days and nights were sunshine and starshine, all fire and dew, with before my eyes, ever burning and blazing, the Holy Grail, Christ's own Grail, the warm human, long-suffering and maltreated but to be rescued and saved at the last.'

As before I had seen him transfigured, so now he stood transfigured before me. His brows were bright with the divine that was in him, and brighter yet shone his eyes from the midst of the radiance that seemed to envelop him as a mantle. But the others did not see this radiance, and I assumed that it was due to the tears of joy and love that dimmed my vision. At any rate, Mr Wickson, who sat behind me, was unaffected, for I heard him sneer aloud, ' Utopian '.[4]

Ernest went on to his rise in society, till at last he came in touch with members of the upper classes and rubbed shoulders with the men who sat in the high places. Then came his disillusionment, and this disillusionment he described in terms that did not flatter his audience. He was surprised at the commonness of the clay. Life proved not to be fine and gracious. He was appalled by the selfishness he encountered, and what had surprised him even more than that was the absence of intellectual life. Fresh from his revolutionists, he was shocked by the intellectual stupidity of the master class. And then, in spite of their magnificent churches and well-paid preachers, he had found the masters, men and women, grossly material. It was true that they prattled sweet little ideals and dear little moralities, but in spite of their prattle the dominant key of the life they lived was materialistic. And they were without real morality—for instance, that which Christ had preached but which was no longer preached.

' I met men,' he said, ' who invoked the name of the Prince

---

[4] The people of that age were phrase slaves. The abjectness of their servitude is incomprehensible to us. There was a magic in words greater than the conjurer's art. So befuddled and chaotic were their minds that the utterance of a single word could negative the generalisations of a lifetime of serious research and thought. Such a word was the adjective *Utopian*. The mere utterance of it could damn any scheme, no matter how sanely conceived, of economic amelioration or regeneration. Vast populations grew frenzied over such phrases as ' an honest dollar,' and ' a full dinner pail.' The coinage of such phrases was considered strokes of genius.

of Peace in their diatribes against war and who put rifles in
the hands of Pinkertons[5] with which to shoot down strikers in
their own factories. I met men incoherent with indignation
at the brutality of prize-fighting, and who, at the same time,
were parties to the adulteration of food that killed each year
more babes than even red-handed Herod had killed.

' This delicate, aristocratic-featured gentleman was a
dummy director and a tool of corporations that secretly
robbed widows and orphans. This gentleman, who collected
fine editions and was a patron of literature, paid blackmail
to a heavy-jowled, black-browed boss of a municipal machine.
This editor, who published patent medicine advertisements,
called me a scoundrelly demagogue because I dared him to
print in his papers the truth about patent medicines.[6] This
man, talking soberly and earnestly about the beauties of
idealism and the goodness of God, had just betrayed his
comrades in a business deal. This man, a pillar of the church
and heavy contributor to foreign missions, worked his shop
girls ten hours a day on a starvation wage and thereby directly
encouraged prostitution. This man, who endowed chairs in
universities and erected magnificent chapels, perjured himself
in courts of law over dollars and cents. This railroad mag-
nate broke his word as a citizen, as a gentleman, and as a
Christian, when he granted a secret rebate, and he granted
many secret rebates. This senator was the tool and the slave,
the little puppet, of a brutal uneducated machine boss;[7] so
was this governor and this supreme court judge; and all
three rode on railroad passes; and also, this sleek capitalist
owned the machine, the machine boss, and the railroads that
issued the passes.

' And so it was, instead of in paradise, that I found my-

[5] Originally, they were private detectives; but they quickly became
hired fighting men of the capitalists, and ultimately developed into
the Mercenaries of the Oligarchy.

[6] *Patent medicines* were patent lies, but, like the charms and indul-
gences of the Middle Ages, they deceived the people. The only
difference lay in that the patent medicines were more harmful and
more costly.

[7] Even as late as A.D. 1912, the great mass of the people still
persisted in the belief that they ruled the country by virtue of
their ballots. In reality the country was ruled by what were called
political machines. At first the machine bosses charged the master
capitalists extortionate tolls for legislation; but in a short time
the master capitalists found it cheaper to own the political
machines themselves and to hire the machine bosses.

self in the arid desert of commercialism. I found nothing but
stupidity, except for business. I found none clean, noble, and
alive, though I found many who were alive—with rottenness.
What I did find was monstrous selfishness and heartlessness,
and a gross, gluttonous, practised, and practical materialism.'

Much more Ernest told them of themselves and of his disillusionment. Intellectually they had bored him; morally and
spiritually they had sickened him; so that he was glad to go
back to his revolutionists, who were clean, noble, and alive,
and all that the capitalists were not.

'And now,' he said, 'let me tell you about that revolution.'

But first I must say that his terrible diatribe had not
touched them. I looked about me at their faces and saw that
they remained complacently superior to what he had charged.
And I remembered what he had told me: that no indictment
of their morality could shake them. However, I could see that
the boldness of his language had affected Miss Brentwood.
She was looking worried and apprehensive.

Ernest began by describing the army of revolution, and
as he gave the figures of its strength (the votes cast in the
various countries), the assemblage began to grow restless.
Concern showed in their faces and I noticed a tightening of
lips. At last the gage of battle had been thrown down. He
described the international organisation of the socialists that
united the million and a half in the United States with the
twenty-three millions and a half in the rest of the world.

'Such an army of revolution,' he said, 'twenty-five
millions strong, is a thing to make rulers and ruling classes
pause and consider. The cry of this army is: "No quarter!
We want all that you possess. We will be content with nothing
less than all that you possess. We want in our hands the reins
of power and the destiny of mankind. Here are our hands.
They are strong hands. We are going to take your government, your palaces, and all your purpled ease away from you,
and in that day you shall work for your bread even as the
peasant in the field or the starved and runty clerk in your
metropolises. Here are our hands. They are strong hands!"'

And as he spoke he extended from his splendid shoulders
his two great arms, and the horseshoer's hands were clutching the air like eagle's talons. He was the spirit of regnant
labour as he stood there, his hands outreaching to rend and
crush his audience. I was aware of a faintly perceptible

shrinking on the part of the listeners before this figure of revolution, concrete, potential, and menacing. That is, the women shrank, and fear was in their faces. Not so with the men. They were of the active rich, and not the idle, and they were fighters. A low, throaty rumble arose, lingered on the air a moment, and ceased. It was the forerunner of the snarl, and I was to hear it many times that night—the token of the brute in man, the earnest of his primitive passions. And they were unconscious that they had made this sound. It was the growl of the pack, mouthed by the pack, and mouthed in all unconsciousness. And in that moment, as I saw the harshness form in their faces and saw the fight-light flashing in their eyes, I realised that not easily would they let their lordship of the world be wrested from them.

Ernest proceeded with his attack. He accounted for the existence of the million and a half of revolutionists in the United States by charging the capitalist class with having mismanaged society. He sketched the economic condition of the cave-man and of the savage peoples of today, pointing out that they possessed neither tools nor machines, and possessed only a natural efficiency of one in producing power. Then he traced the development of machinery and social organisation so that today the producing power of civilised man was a thousand times greater than that of the savage.

'Five men,' he said, 'can produce bread for a thousand. One man can produce cotton cloth for two hundred and fifty people, woollens for three hundred, and boots and shoes for a thousand. One would conclude from this that under a capable management of society modern civilised man would be a great deal better off than the cave-man. But is he? Let us see. In the United States today there are fifteen million[8] people living in poverty; and by poverty is meant that condition in life in which, through lack of food and adequate shelter, the mere standard of working efficiency cannot be maintained. In the United States today, in spite of all your so-called labour legislation, there are three millions of child labourers.[9] In twelve years their numbers have been doubled.

[8] Robert Hunter, in 1906, in a book entitled "Poverty," pointed out that at that time there were ten millions in the United States living in poverty.
[9] In the United States Census of 1900 (the last census the figures of which were made public), the number of child labourers was placed at 1,752,187.

And in passing I will ask you managers of society why you did not make public the census figures of 1910? And I will answer for you, that you were afraid. The figures of misery would have precipitated the revolution that even now is gathering.

'But to return to my indictment. If modern man's producing power is a thousand times greater than that of the caveman, why then, in the United States today, are there fifteen million people who are not properly sheltered and properly fed? Why then, in the United States today, are there three million child labourers? It is a true indictment. The capitalist class has mismanaged. In face of the facts that modern man lives more wretchedly than the cave-man, and that his producing power is a thousand times greater than that of the cave-man, no other conclusion is possible than that the capitalist class has mismanaged, that you have mismanaged, my masters, that you have criminally and selfishly mismanaged. And on this count you cannot answer me here tonight, face to face, any more than can your whole class answer the million and a half of revolutionists in the United States. You cannot answer. I challenge you to answer. And furthermore, I dare to say to you now that when I have finished you will not answer. On that point you will be tongue-tied, though you will talk wordily enough about other things.

'You have failed in your management. You have made a shambles of civilisation. You have been blind and greedy. You have risen up (as you today rise up), shamelessly, in our legislative halls, and declared that profits were impossible without the toil of children and babes. Don't take my word for it. It is all in the records against you. You have lulled your conscience to sleep with prattle of sweet ideals and dear moralities. You are fat with power and possession, drunken with success; and you have no more hope against us than have the drones, clustered about the honey-vats, when the worker-bees spring upon them to end their rotund existence. You have failed in your management of society, and your management is to be taken away from you. A million and a half of the men of the working class say that they are going to get the rest of the working class to join with them and take the management away from you. This is the revolution, my masters. Stop it if you can.'

For an appreciable lapse of time Ernest's voice continued to ring through the great room. Then arose the throaty rumble I had heard before, and a dozen men were on their feet clamouring for recognition from Colonel Van Gilbert. I noticed Miss Brentwood's shoulders moving convulsively, and for the moment I was angry, for I thought that she was laughing at Ernest. And then I discovered that it was not laughter, but hysteria. She was appalled by what she had done in bringing this firebrand before her blessed Philomath Club.

Colonel Van Gilbert did not notice the dozen men, with passion-wrought faces, who strove to get permission from him to speak. His own face was passion-wrought. He sprang to his feet, waving his arms, and for a moment could utter only incoherent sounds. Then speech poured from him. But it was not the speech of a one-hundred-thousand-dollar lawyer, nor was the rhetoric old-fashioned.

'Fallacy upon fallacy!' he cried. 'Never in all my life have I heard so many fallacies uttered in one short hour. And besides, young man, I must tell you that you have said nothing new. I learned all that at college before you were born. Jean Jacques Rousseau enunciated your socialist theory nearly two centuries ago. A return to the soil, forsooth! Reversion! Our biology teaches the absurdity of it. It has been truly said that a little learning is a dangerous thing, and you have exemplified it tonight with your madcap theories. Fallacy upon fallacy! I was never so nauseated in my life with overplus of fallacy. That for your immature generalisations and childish reasonings!'

He snapped his fingers contemptuously and proceeded to sit down. There were lip-exclamations of approval on the part of the women, and hoarser notes of confirmation came from the men. As for the dozen men who were clamouring for the floor, half of them began speaking at once. The confusion and babel was indescribable. Never had Mrs Pertonwaithe's spacious walls beheld such a spectacle. These, then, were the cool captains of industry and lords of society, these snarling, growling savages in evening clothes. Truly Ernest had shaken them when he stretched out his hands for their money-bags, his hands that had appeared in their eyes as the hands of the fifteen hundred thousand revolutionists.

But Ernest never lost his head in a situation. Before Colonel Van Gilbert had succeeded in sitting down, Ernest was on his feet and had sprung forward.

'One at a time!' he roared at them.

The sound arose from his great lungs and dominated the human tempest. By sheer compulsion of personality he commanded silence.

'One at a time,' he repeated softly. 'Let me answer Colonel Van Gilbert. After that the rest of you can come at me—but one at a time, remember. No mass-plays here. This is not a football field.

'As for you,' he went on, turning towards Colonel Van Gilbert, 'you have replied to nothing I have said. You have merely made a few excited and dogmatic assertions about my mental calibre. That may serve you in your business, but you can't talk to me like that. I am not a working man, cap in hand, asking you to increase my wages or to protect me from the machine at which I work. You cannot be dogmatic with truth when you deal with me. Save that for dealing with your wage-slaves. They will not dare reply to you because you hold their bread and butter, their lives, in your hands.

'As for this return to Nature that you say you learned at college before I was born, permit me to point out that on the face of it you cannot have learned anything since. Socialism has no more to do with the state of Nature than has differential calculus with a Bible class. I have called your class stupid when outside the realm of business. You, sir, have brilliantly exemplified my statement.'

This terrible castigation of her hundred-thousand-dollar lawyer was too much for Miss Brentwood's nerves. Her hysteria became violent, and she was helped, weeping and laughing, out of the room. It was just as well, for there was worse to follow.

'Don't take my word for it,' Ernest continued, when the interruption had been led away. 'Your own authorities with one unanimous voice will prove you stupid. Your own hired purveyors of knowledge will tell you that you are wrong. Go to your meekest little assistant instructor of sociology and ask him what is the difference between Rousseau's theory of the return to Nature and the theory of socialism; ask your greatest orthodox bourgeois political economists and sociologists; question through the pages of every textbook written on the subject and stored on the shelves of your subsidised libraries; and from one and all the answer will be that there is nothing congruous between the return to Nature and socialism. On the other hand the unanimous affirmative answer will be that the return to Nature and socialism are diametrically opposed to each other. As I say, don't take my word for it. The record of your stupidity is there in the books, your own books that you never read. And so far as your stupidity is concerned, you are but the exemplar of your class.

'You know law and business, Colonel Van Gilbert. You know how to serve corporations and increase dividends by twisting the law. Very good. Stick to it. You are quite a figure. You are a very good lawyer, but you are a poor historian, you know nothing of sociology, and your biology is contemporaneous with Pliny.'

Here Colonel Van Gilbert writhed in his chair. There was perfect quiet in the room. Everybody sat fascinated—paralysed, I may say. Such fearful treatment of the great Colonel Van Gilbert was unheard of, undreamed of, impossible to believe—the great Colonel Van Gilbert before whom judges trembled when he arose in court. But Ernest never gave quarter to an enemy.

'This is, of course, no reflection on you,' Ernest said. 'Every man to his trade. Only you stick to your trade and I'll stick to mine. You have specialised. When it comes to a knowledge of the law, of how best to evade the law or make new law for the benefit of thieving corporations, I am down in the dirt at your feet. But when it comes to sociology—my trade—you are down in the dirt at my feet. Remember that. Remember also, that your law is the stuff of a day, and that you are not versatile in the stuff of more than a day. Therefore your dogmatic assertions and rash generalisations on things historical and sociological are not worth the breath you waste on them.'

Ernest paused for a moment and regarded him thoughtfully, noting his face dark and twisted with anger, his panting chest, his writhing body, and his slim white hands nervously clenching and unclenching.

'But it seems you have breath to use, and I'll give you a chance to use it. I indicted your class. Show me that my indictment is wrong. I pointed out to you the wretchedness of modern man—three million child slaves in the United States, without whose labour profits would not be possible, and fifteen million under-fed, ill-clothed, and worse-housed people. I pointed out that modern man's producing power through social organisation and the use of machinery was a thousand times greater than that of the cave-man. And I stated that from these two facts no other conclusion was possible than that the capitalist class had mismanaged. This was my indictment, and I specifically and at length challenged you to answer it. Nay, I did more. I prophesied that you would not answer. It remained for your breath to smash my prophecy. You called my speech fallacy. Show the fallacy, Colonel Van Gilbert. Answer the indictment that I and my fifteen hundred thousand comrades have brought against your class and you.'

Colonel Van Gilbert quite forgot that he was presiding, and that in courtesy he should permit the other clamourers to speak. He was on his feet, flinging his arms, his rhetoric, and his control to the winds, alternately abusing Ernest for his youth and demagoguery, and savagely attacking the working class, elaborating its inefficiency and worthlessness.

'For a lawyer, you are the hardest man to keep to a point I ever saw,' Ernest began his answer to the tirade. 'My youth has nothing to do with what I have enunciated. Nor has the worthlessness of the working class. I charged the capitalist class with having mismanaged society. You have not answered. You have made no attempt to answer. Why? Is it because you have no answer? You are the champion of this whole audience. Every one here, except me, is hanging on your lips for that answer because they have no answer themselves. As for me, as I said before, I know that you not only cannot answer but that you will not attempt an answer.'

'This is intolerable!' Colonel Van Gilbert cried out. 'This is insult!'

'That you should not answer is intolerable,' Ernest replied gravely. 'No man can be intellectually insulted. Insult, in its very nature, is emotional. Recover yourself. Give me an intellectual answer to my intellectual charge that the capitalist class has mismanaged society.'

Colonel Van Gilbert remained silent, a sullen, superior expression on his face, such as will appear on the face of a man who will not bandy words with a ruffian.

'Do not be downcast,' Ernest said. 'Take consolation in the fact that no member of your class has ever yet answered that charge.' He turned to the other men who were anxious to speak. 'And now it's your chance. Fire away, and do not forget that I here challenge you to give the answer that Colonel Van Gilbert has failed to give.'

It would be impossible for me to write all that was said

in the discussion. I never realised before how many words could be spoken in three short hours. At any rate, it was glorious. The more his opponents grew excited, the more Ernest deliberately excited them. He had an encyclopaedic command of the field of knowledge, and by a word or a phrase, by delicate rapier thrusts, he punctured them. He named the points of their illogic. This was a false syllogism, that conclusion had no connexion with the premise, while that next premise was an impostor because it had cunningly hidden in it the conclusion that was being attempted to be proved. This was an error, that was an assumption, and the next was an assertion contrary to ascertained truth as printed in all the textbooks.

And so it went. Sometimes he exchanged the rapier for the club and went smashing amongst their thoughts right and left. And always he demanded facts and refused to discuss theories. And his facts made for them a Waterloo. When they attacked the working class, he always retorted, ' The pot calling the kettle black; that is no answer to the charge that your own face is dirty.' And to one and all he said: ' Why have you not answered the charge that your class has mismanaged? You have talked about other things and things concerning other things, but you have not answered. Is it because you have no answer?'

It was at the end of the discussion that Mr Wickson spoke. He was the only one that was cool, and Ernest treated him with a respect he had not accorded the others.

' No answer is necessary,' Mr Wickson said with slow deliberation. ' I have followed the whole discussion with amazement and disgust. I am disgusted with you gentlemen, members of my class. You have behaved like foolish little schoolboys, what with intruding ethics and the thunder of the common politician into such a discussion. You have been outgeneralled and outclassed. You have been very wordy, and all you have done is buzz. You have buzzed like gnats about a bear. Gentlemen, there stands the bear ' (he pointed at Ernest), ' and your buzzing has only tickled his ears.

' Believe me, the situation is serious. That bear reached out his paws tonight to crush us. He has said there are a million and a half of revolutionists in the United States. That is a fact. He has said that it is their intention to take away from us our governments, our palaces, and all our purpled ease. That, also, is a fact. A change, a great change, is coming in society; but, happily, it may not be the change the bear anticipates. The bear has said that he will crush us. What if we crush the bear?'

The throat-rumble arose in the great room, and man nodded to man with endorsement and certitude. Their faces were set hard. They were fighters, that was certain.

'But not by buzzing will we crush the bear,' Mr Wickson went on coldly and dispassionately. 'We will hunt the bear. We will not reply to the bear in words. Our reply shall be couched in terms of lead. We are in power. Nobody will deny it. By virtue of that power we shall remain in power.'

He turned suddenly upon Ernest. The moment was dramatic.

'This, then, is our answer. We have no words to waste on you. When you reach out your vaunted strong hands for our palaces and purpled ease, we will show you what strength is. In roar of shell and shrapnel and in whine of machine-guns will our answer be couched.[10] We will grind you revolutionists down under our heel, and we shall walk upon your faces. The world is ours, we are its lords, and ours it shall remain. As for the host of labour, it has been in the dirt since history began, and I read history aright. And in the dirt it shall remain so long as I and mine and those that come after us have the power. There is the word. It is the king of words —Power. Not God, not Mammon, but Power. Pour it over your tongue till it tingles with it. Power.'

'I am answered,' Ernest said quietly. 'It is the only answer that could be given. Power. It is what we of the working class preach. We know, and well we know by bitter experience, that no appeal for the right, for justice, for humanity, can ever touch you. Your hearts are hard as your heels with which you tread upon the faces of the poor. So we have preached power. By the power of our ballots on election day will we take your government away from you—'

'What if you do get a majority, a sweeping majority, on election day,' Mr Wickson broke in to demand. 'Suppose we refuse to turn the government over to you after you have captured it at the ballot-box?'

[10] To show the tenor of thought, the following definition is quoted from 'The Cynic's Word Book' (A.D. 1906), written by one Ambrose Bierce, an avowed and confirmed misanthrope of the period: 'Grape-shot, n. *An argument which the future is preparing in answer to the demands of American socialism.*'

'That, also, have we considered,' Ernest replied. 'And we shall give you an answer in terms of lead. Power, you have proclaimed the king of words. Very good. Power it shall be. And in the day that we sweep to victory at the ballot-box, and you refuse to turn over to us the government we have constitutionally and peacefully captured, and you demand what we are going to do about it—in that day, I say, we shall answer you; and in roar of shell and shrapnel and in whine of machine-guns shall our answer be couched.

'You cannot escape us. It is true that you have read history aright. It is true that labour has from the beginning of history been in the dirt. And it is equally true that so long as you and yours and those that come after you have power, that labour shall remain in the dirt. I agree with you. I agree with all that you have said. Power will be the arbiter, as it always has been the arbiter. It is a struggle of classes. Just as your class dragged down the old feudal nobility, so shall it be dragged down by my class, the working class. If you will read your biology and your sociology as clearly as you do your history, you will see that this end I have described is inevitable. It does not matter whether it is in one year, ten, or a thousand—your class shall be dragged down. And it shall be done by power. We of the labour hosts have conned that word over till our minds are all a-tingle with it. Power. It is a kingly word.'

And so ended the night with the Philomaths.

CHAPTER 6

Adumbrations

IT WAS about this time that the warnings of coming events began to fall around us thick and fast.

Ernest had already questioned father's policy of having socialists and labour leaders at his house, and of openly attending socialist meetings; and father had only laughed at him for his pains. As for myself, I was learning much from this contact with the working-class leaders and thinkers. I was seeing the other side of the shield. I was delighted with the unselfishness and high idealism I encountered, though I was appalled by the vast philosophic and scientific literature of socialism that was opened up to me. I was learning fast, but I learned not fast enough to realise then the peril of our position.

There were warnings, but I did not heed them. For instance, Mrs Pertonwaithe and Mrs Wickson exercised tremendous social power in the university town, and from them emanated the sentiment that I was a too-forward and self-assertive young woman, with a mischievous penchant for officiousness and interference in other persons' affairs. This I thought no more than natural, considering the part I had played in investigating the case of Jackson's arm. But the effect of such a sentiment, enunciated by two such powerful social arbiters, I underestimated.

True, I noticed a certain aloofness on the part of my general friends, but this I ascribed to the disapproval that was prevalent in my circles of my intended marriage with Ernest. It was not till some time afterward that Ernest pointed out to me clearly that this general attitude of my class was something more than spontaneous, that behind it were the hidden springs of an organised conduct. 'You have given shelter to an enemy of your class,' he said. 'And not alone shelter, for you have given your love, yourself. This is treason to your class. Think not that you will escape being penalised.'

But it was before this that father returned one afternoon. Ernest was with me, and we could see that father was angry

—philosophically angry. He was rarely really angry; but a certain measure of controlled anger he allowed himself. He called it a tonic. And we could see that he was tonic-angry when he entered the room.

'What do you think?' he demanded. 'I had luncheon with Wilcox.'

Wilcox was the superannuated president of the university, whose withered mind was stored with generalisations that were young in 1870, and which he had since failed to revise.

'I was invited,' father announced. 'I was sent for.'

He paused, and we waited.

'Oh, it was done very nicely, I'll allow; but I was reprimanded. I! And by that old fossil!'

'I'll wager I know what you were reprimanded for,' Ernest said.

'Not in three guesses,' father laughed.

'One guess will do,' Ernest retorted. 'And it won't be a guess. It will be a deduction. You were reprimanded for your private life.'

'The very thing!' father cried. 'How did you guess?'

'I knew it was coming. I warned you before about it.'

'Yes, you did,' father meditated. 'But I couldn't believe it. At any rate, it is only so much more clinching evidence for my book.'

'It is nothing to what will come,' Ernest went on, 'if you persist in your policy of having these socialists and Radicals of all sorts at your house, myself included.'

'Just what old Wilcox said. And of all unwarranted things! He said it was in poor taste, utterly profitless, anyway, and not in harmony with university traditions and policy. He said much more of the same vague sort, and I couldn't pin him down to anything specific. I made it pretty awkward for him, and he could only go on repeating himself and telling me how much he honoured me, and all the world honoured me, as a scientist. It wasn't an agreeable task for him. I could see he didn't like it.'

'He was not a free agent,' Ernest said. 'The leg-bar[1] is not always worn graciously.'

'Yes. I got that much out of him. He said the university

---

[1] *Leg-bar*—the African slaves were so manacled; also criminals. It was not until the coming of the Brotherhood of Man that the leg-bar passed out of use.

needed ever so much more money this year than the state was willing to furnish; and that it must come from wealthy personages who could not but be offended by the swerving of the university from its high ideal of the passionless pursuit of passionless intelligence. When I tried to pin him down to what my home life had to do with swerving the university from its high ideal, he offered me a two years' vacation, on full pay, in Europe, for recreation and research. Of course, I couldn't accept it under the circumstances.'

'It would have been far better if you had,' Ernest said gravely.

'It was a bribe,' father protested; and Ernest nodded.

'Also, the beggar said that there was talk, tea-table gossip and so forth about my daughter being seen in public with so notorious a character as you, and that it was not in keeping with university tone and dignity. Not that he personally objected—oh, no; but that there was talk and that I would understand.'

Ernest considered this announcement for a moment, and then said, and his face was very grave, withal there was a sombre wrath in it:

'There is more behind this than a mere university ideal. Somebody has put pressure on President Wilcox.'

'Do you think so?' father asked, and his face showed that he was interested rather than frightened.

'I wish I could convey to you the conception that is dimly forming in my own mind,' Ernest said. 'Never in the history of the world was society in so terrific flux as it is right now. The swift changes in our industrial system are causing equally swift changes in our religious, political, and social structures. An unseen and fearful revolution is taking place in the fibre and structure of society. One can only dimly feel these things. But they are in the air, now, today. One can feel the loom of them—things vast, vague, and terrible. My mind recoils from contemplation of what they may crystallise into. You heard Wickson talk the other night. Behind what he said were the same nameless, formless things that I feel. He spoke out of a superconscious apprehension of them.'

'You mean . . .?' father began, then paused.

'I mean that there is a shadow of something colossal and menacing that even now is beginning to fall across the land. Call it the shadow of an oligarchy, if you will; it is the nearest I dare approximate it. What its nature may be I refuse to imagine.[2] But what I wanted to say was this: You are in a perilous position—a peril that my own fear enhances because I am not able even to measure it. Take my advice and accept the vacation.'

'But it would be cowardly,' was the protest.

'Not at all. You are an old man. You have done your work in the world, and a great work. Leave the present battle to youth and strength. We young fellows have our work yet to do. Avis will stand by my side in what is to come. She will be your representative in the battle front.'

'But they can't hurt me,' father objected. 'Thank God I am independent. Oh, I assure you, I know the frightful persecution they can wage on a professor who is economically dependent on his university. But I am independent. I have not been a professor for the sake of my salary. I can get along very comfortably on my own income, and the salary is all they can take away from me.'

'But you do not realise,' Ernest answered. 'If all that I fear be so, your private income, your principal itself, can be taken from you just as easily as your salary.'

Father was silent for a few minutes. He was thinking deeply, and I could see the lines of decision forming in his face. At last he spoke.

'I shall not take the vacation.' He paused again. 'I shall go on with my book.[3] You may be wrong, but whether you

---

[2] Though, like Everhard, they did not dream of the nature of it, there were men, even before his time, who caught glimpses of the shadow. John C. Calhoun said: '*A power has risen up in the Government greater than the people themselves, consisting of many and various and powerful interests, combined into one mass, and held together by the cohesive power of the vast surplus in the banks.*' And that great humanist, Abraham Lincoln, said, just before his assassination: '*I see in the near future a crisis approaching that unnerves me and causes me to tremble for the safety of my country. . . . Corporations have been enthroned, an era of corruption in high places will follow, and the money-power of the country will endeavour to prolong its reign by working upon the prejudices of the people until the wealth is aggregated in a few hands and the Republic is destroyed.*'

[3] This book, 'Economics and Education,' was published in that year. Three copies of it are extant; two at Ardis, and one at Asgard. It dealt, in elaborate detail, with one factor in the persistence of the established, namely, the capitalistic bias of the universities and common schools. It was a logical and crushing indictment of the whole system of education that developed in the minds of the students only such ideas as were favourable to the

are wrong or right, I shall stand by my guns.'

'All right,' Ernest said. 'You are travelling the same path that Bishop Morehouse is, and towards a similar smash-up. You'll both be proletarians before you're done with it.'

The conversation turned upon the Bishop, and we got Ernest to explain what he had been doing with him.

'He is soul-sick from the journey through hell I have given him. I took him through the homes of a few of our factory workers. I showed him the human wrecks cast aside by the industrial machine, and he listened to their life stories. I took him through the slums of San Francisco, and in drunkenness, prostitution, and criminality he learned a deeper cause than innate depravity. He is very sick, and, worse than that, he has got out of hand. He is too ethical. He has been too severely touched. And, as usual, he is un-practical. He is up in the air with all kinds of ethical delu-sions and plans for mission work among the cultured. He feels it is his bounden duty to resurrect the ancient spirit of the Church and to deliver its message to the masters. He is overwrought. Sooner or later he is going to break out, and then there's going to be a smash-up. What form it will take I can't even guess. He is a pure, exalted soul, but he is so unpractical. He's beyond me. I can't keep his feet on the earth. And through the air he is rushing on to his Gethsemane. And after this his crucifixion. Such high souls are made for crucifixion.'

'And you?' I asked; and beneath my smile was the serious-ness of the anxiety of love.

'Not I,' he laughed back. 'I may be executed or assassi-nated, but I shall never be crucified. I am planted too solidly and stolidly upon the earth.'

'But why should you bring about the crucifixion of the Bishop?' I asked. 'You will not deny that you are the cause of it.'

'Why should I leave one comfortable soul in comfort when there are millions in travail and misery?' he demanded back.

'Then why did you advise father to accept the vacation?'

'Because I am not a pure, exalted soul,' was the answer. 'Because I am solid and stolid and selfish. Because I love you and, like Ruth of old, thy people are my people. As for

capitalistic régime, to the exclusion of all ideas that were inimical and subversive. This book created a furore, and was promptly suppressed by the Oligarchy.

the Bishop, he has no daughter. Besides, no matter how small the good, nevertheless his little inadequate wail will be productive of some good in the revolution, and every little bit counts.'

I could not agree with Ernest. I knew well the noble nature of Bishop Morehouse, and I could not conceive that his voice raised for righteousness would be no more than a little inadequate wail. But I did not yet have the harsh facts of life at my fingers' ends as Ernest had. He saw clearly the futility of the Bishop's great soul, as coming events were soon to show as clearly to me.

It was shortly after this day that Ernest told me, as a good story, the offer he had received from the Government, namely, an appointment as United States Commissioner of Labour. I was overjoyed. The salary was comparatively large, and would make safe our marriage. And then it surely was congenial work for Ernest, and, furthermore, my jealous pride in him made me hail the proffered appointment as a recognition of his abilities.

Then I noticed the twinkle in his eyes. He was laughing at me.

'You are not going to . . . to decline?' I quavered.

'It is a bribe,' he said. 'Behind it is the fine hand of Wickson, and behind him the hands of greater men than he. It is an old trick, old as the class struggle is old—stealing the captains from the army of labour. Poor betrayed labour! If you but knew how many of its leaders have been bought out in similar ways in the past. It is cheaper, so much cheaper, to buy a general than to fight him and his whole army. There was—but I'll not call any names. I'm bitter enough over it as it is. Dear heart, I am a captain of labour. I could not sell out. If for no other reason, the memory of my poor old father and the way he was worked to death would prevent.'

The tears were in his eyes, this great, strong hero of mine. He never could forgive the way his father had been malformed—the sordid lies and the petty thefts he had been compelled to, in order to put food in his children's mouths.

'My father was a good man,' Ernest once said to me. 'The soul of him was good, and yet it was twisted, and maimed, and blunted by the savagery of his life. He was made into a broken-down beast by his masters, the arch-beasts. He should be alive today, like your father. He had a strong constitution. But he was caught in the machine and worked to death for profit. Think of it. For profit—his life-blood transmuted into a wine-supper, or a jewelled gewgaw, or some similar sense-orgy of the parasitic and idle rich, his masters, the arch-beasts.'

CHAPTER 7

The Bishop's Vision

'THE BISHOP is out of hand,' Ernest wrote me. 'He is clear up in the air. Tonight he is going to begin putting to rights this very miserable world of ours. He is going to deliver his message. He has told me so, and I cannot dissuade him. Tonight he is chairman of the I.P.H., and he will embody his message in his introductory remarks.

'May I bring you to hear him? Of course, he is fore-doomed to futility. It will break your heart—it will break his; but for you it will be an excellent object-lesson. You know, dear heart, how proud I am because you love me. And be-cause of that I want you to know my fullest value, I want to redeem, in your eyes, some small measure of my un-worthiness. And so it is that my pride desires that you shall know my thinking is correct and right. My views are harsh; the futility of so noble a soul as the Bishop will show you the compulsion for such harshness. So come tonight. Sad though this night's happening will be, I feel that it will but draw you more closely to me.'

The I.P.H.[1] held its convention that night in San Fran-cisco.[2] This convention had been called to consider public immorality and the remedy for it. Bishop Morehouse pre-sided. He was very nervous as he sat on the platform, and I could see the high tension he was under. By his side were Bishop Dickinson; H. H. Jones, the head of the ethical department in the University of California; Mrs W. W. Hurd, the great charity organiser; Philip Ward, the equally great philanthropist; and several lesser luminaries in the field of morality and charity. Bishop Morehouse arose and abruptly began:

'I was in my brougham, driving through the streets. It was night-time. Now and then I looked through the car-

---

[1] There is no clue to the name of the organisation for which these initials stand.
[2] It took but a few minutes to cross by ferry from Berkeley to San Francisco. These, and the other bay cities, practically composed one community.

riage windows, and suddenly my eyes seemed to be opened, and I saw things as they really are. At first I covered my eyes with my hands to shut out the awful sight, and then, in the darkness the question came to me: What is to be done? What is to be done? A little later the question came to me in another way: What would the Master do? And with the question a great light seemed to fill the place, and I saw my duty sun-clear, as Saul saw his on the way to Damascus.

'I stopped the carriage, got out, and, after a few minutes' conversation, persuaded two of the public women to get into the brougham with me. If Jesus was right, then these two unfortunates were my sisters, and the only hope of their purification was in my affection and tenderness.

'I live in one of the loveliest localities in San Francisco. The house in which I live cost a hundred thousand dollars, and its furnishings, books, and works of art cost as much more. The house is a mansion. No, it is a palace, wherein there are many servants. I never knew what palaces were good for. I had thought they were made to live in. But now I know. I took the two women of the street to my palace, and they are going to stay with me. I hope to fill every room in my palace with such sisters as they.'

The audience had been growing more and more restless and unsettled, and the faces of those that sat on the platform had been betraying greater and greater dismay and consternation. And at this point Bishop Dickinson arose, and, with an expression of disgust on his face, fled from the platform and the hall. But Bishop Morehouse, oblivious to all, his eyes filled with his vision, continued:

'Oh, sisters and brothers, in this act of mine I find the solution of all my difficulties. I didn't know what broughams were made for, but now I know. They are made to carry the weak, the sick, and the aged; they are made to show honour to those who have lost the sense even of shame.

'I did not know what palaces were made for, but now I have found a use for them. The palaces of the Church should be hospitals and nurseries for those who have fallen by the wayside and are perishing.'

He made a long pause, plainly overcome by the thought that was in him, and nervous how best to express it.

'I am not fit, dear brethren, to tell you anything about morality. I have lived in shame and hypocrisies too long to be able to help others; but my action with those women, sisters

of mine, shows me that the better way is easy to find. To
those who believe in Jesus and His Gospel there can be no
other relation between man and man than the relation of
affection. Love alone is stronger than sin—stronger than
death. I therefore say to the rich among you that it is their
duty to do what I have done and am doing. Let each one
of you who is prosperous take into his house some thief and
treat him as his brother, some unfortunate and treat her as
his sister, and San Francisco will need no police force and
no magistrates; the prisons will be turned into hospitals, and
the criminal will disappear with his crime.

'We must give ourselves and not our money alone. We
must do as Christ did; that is the message of the Church
today. We have wandered far from the Master's teaching.
We are consumed in our own flesh-pots. We have put mammon in the place of Christ. I have here a poem that tells the
whole story. I should like to read it to you. It was written by
an erring soul who yet saw clearly.[3] It must not be mistaken
for an attack upon the Catholic Church. It is an attack upon
all churches, upon the pomp and splendour of all churches
that have wandered from the Master's path and hedged themselves in from His lambs. Here it is:

'The silver trumpets rang across the Dome;
    The people knelt upon the ground with awe;
    And borne upon the necks of men I saw,
Like some great God, the Holy Lord of Rome.

'Priest-like, he wore a robe more white than foam,
    And, king-like, swathed himself in royal red,
    Three crowns of gold rose high upon his head;
In splendour and in light the Pope passed home.

'My heart stole back across wide wastes of years
    To One who wandered by a lonely sea;
And sought in vain for any place of rest:
"Foxes have holes, and every bird its nest,
    I, only I, must wander wearily,
And bruise my feet and drink wine salt with tears." '

The audience was agitated, but unresponsive. Yet Bishop
Morehouse was not aware of it. He held steadily on his
way.

[3] Oscar Wilde, one of the lords of language of the nineteenth
century of the Christian era.

'And so I say to the rich among you, and to all the rich, that bitterly you oppress the Master's lambs. You have hardened your hearts. You have closed your ears to the voices that are crying in the land—the voices of pain and sorrow that you will not hear, but that some day will be heard. And so I say—'

But at this point, H. H. Jones and Philip Ward, who had already risen from their chairs, led the Bishop off the platform, while the audience sat breathless and shocked.

Ernest laughed harshly and savagely when he had gained the street. His laughter jarred upon me. My heart seemed ready to burst with suppressed tears.

'He has delivered his message,' Ernest cried. 'The manhood and the deep-hidden, tender nature of their Bishop burst out, and his Christian audience, that loved him, concluded that he was crazy! Did you see them leading him so solicitously from the platform? There must have been laughter in hell at the spectacle.'

'Nevertheless, it will make a great impression, what the Bishop did and said tonight,' I said.

'Think so?' Ernest queried mockingly.

'It will make a sensation,' I asserted. 'Didn't you see the reporters scribbling like mad while he was speaking?'

'Not a line of which will appear in tomorrow's papers.'

'I can't believe it,' I cried.

'Just wait and see,' was the answer. 'Not a line, not a thought that he uttered. The daily press? The daily suppressage!'

'But the reporters,' I objected. 'I saw them.'

'Not a word that he uttered will see print. You have forgotten the editors. They draw their salaries for the policy they maintain. Their policy is to print nothing that is a vital menace to the established. The Bishop's utterance was a violent assault upon the established morality. It was heresy. They led him from the platform to prevent him from uttering more heresy. The newspapers will purge his heresy in the oblivion of silence. The press of the United States? It is a parasitic growth that battens on the capitalist class. Its function is to serve the established by moulding public opinion, and right well it serves it.

'Let me prophesy. Tomorrow's papers will merely mention that the Bishop is in poor health, that he has been working too hard, and that he broke down last night. The next mention, some days hence, will be to the effect that he is suffering from nervous prostration and has been given a vacation by his grateful flock. After that, one of two things will happen: either the Bishop will see the error of his way and return from his vacation a well man in whose eyes there are no more visions, or else he will persist in his madness, and then you may expect to see in the papers, couched pathetically and tenderly, the announcement of his insanity. After that he will be left to gibber his visions to padded walls.'

'Now there you go too far!' I cried out.

'In the eyes of society it will truly be insanity,' he replied. 'What honest man, who is not insane, would take lost women and thieves into his house to dwell with him sisterly and brotherly? True, Christ died between two thieves, but that is another story. Insanity? The mental processes of the man with whom one disagrees are always wrong. Therefore the mind of the man is wrong. Where is the line between wrong mind and insane mind? It is inconceivable that any sane man can radically disagree with one's most sane conclusions.

'There is a good example of it in this evening's paper. Mary M'Kenna lives south of Market Street. She is a poor but honest women. She is also patriotic. But she has erroneous ideas concerning the American flag and the protection it is supposed to symbolise. And here's what happened to her. Her husband had an accident and was laid up in hospital three months. In spite of taking in washing, she got behind in her rent. Yesterday they evicted her. But first, she hoisted an American flag, and from under its folds she announced that by virtue of its protection they could not turn her out on to the cold street. What was done? She was arrested and arraigned for insanity. Today she was examined by the regular insanity experts. She was found insane. She was consigned to the Napa Asylum.'

'But that is far-fetched,' I objected. 'Suppose I should disagree with everybody about the literary style of a book. They wouldn't send me to an asylum for that.'

'Very true,' he replied. 'But such divergence of opinion would constitute no menace to society. Therein lies the difference. The divergence of opinion on the parts of Mary M'Kenna and the Bishop do menace society. What if all the poor people should refuse to pay rent and shelter themselves under the American flag? Landlordism would go crumbling.

The Bishop's views are just as perilous to society. Ergo, to the asylum with him.'

But still I refused to believe.

'Wait and see,' Ernest said, and I waited.

Next morning I sent out for all the papers. So far Ernest was right. Not a word that Bishop Morehouse had uttered was in print. Mention was made in one or two of the papers that he had been overcome by his feelings. Yet the platitudes of the speakers that followed him were reported at length.

Several days later the brief announcement was made that he had gone away on a vacation to recover from the effects of overwork. So far so good, but there had been no hint of insanity, nor even of nervous collapse. Little did I dream the terrible road the Bishop was destined to travel—the Gethsemane and crucifixion that Ernest had pondered about.

CHAPTER 8

The Machine-breakers

I T W A S just before Ernest ran for Congress, on the Socialist ticket, that father gave what he privately called his 'Profit and Loss' dinner. Ernest called it the dinner of the Machine Breakers. In point of fact, it was merely a dinner for business men—small business men, of course. I doubt if one of them was interested in any business the total capitalisation of which exceeded a couple of hundred thousand dollars. They were truly representative middle-class business men.

There was Owen, of Silverberg, Owen & Company—a large grocery firm with several branch stores. We bought our groceries from them. There were both partners of the big drug firm of Kowalt & Washburn, and Mr Asmunsen, the owner of a large granite quarry in Contra Costa County. And there were many similar men, owners or part-owners in small factories, small businesses, and small industries—small capitalists, in short.

They were shrewd-faced, interesting men, and they talked with simplicity and clearness. Their unanimous complaint was against the corporations and trusts. Their creed was, 'Bust the trusts'. All oppression originated in the trusts, and one and all told the same tale of woe. They advocated Government ownership of such trusts as the railroads and telegraphs, and excessive income taxes, graduated with ferocity, to destroy large accumulations. Likewise they advocated, as a cure for local ills, municipal ownership of such public utilities as water, gas, telephones, and street railways.

Especially interesting was Mr Asmunsen's narrative of his tribulations as a quarry owner. He confessed that he never made any profits out of his quarry, and this in spite of the enormous volume of business that had been caused by the destruction of San Francisco by the big earthquake. For six years the rebuilding of San Francisco had been going on, and his business had quadrupled and octupled, and yet he was no better off.

'The railroad knows my business just a little bit better than I do,' he said. 'It knows my operating expenses to a cent, and it knows the terms of my contracts. How it knows these things I can only guess. It must have spies in my employ, and it must have access to the parties to all my contracts. For look you, when I place a big contract, the terms of which favour me a goodly profit, the freight rate from my quarry to market is promptly raised. No explanation is made. The railroad gets my profit. Under such circumstances I have never succeeded in getting the railroad to reconsider its raise. On the other hand, when there have been accidents, increased expenses of operating, or contracts with less profitable terms, I have always succeeded in getting the railroad to lower its rate. What is the result? Large or small, the railroad always gets my profits.'

'What remains to you over and above,' Ernest interrupted to ask, 'would roughly be the equivalent of your salary as a manager did the railroad own the quarry.'

'The very thing,' Mr Asmunsen replied. 'Only a short time ago I had my books gone through for the past ten years. I discovered that for those ten years my gain was just equivalent to a manager's salary. The railroad might just as well have owned my quarry and hired me to run it.'

'But with this difference,' Ernest laughed; 'the railroad would have had to assume all the risk which you so obligingly assumed for it.'

'Very true,' Mr Asmunsen answered sadly.

Having let them have their say, Ernest began asking questions right and left. He began with Mr Owen.

'You started a branch store here in Berkeley about six months ago?'

'Yes,' Mr Owen answered.

'And since then I've noticed that three little corner groceries have gone out of business. Was your branch store the cause of it?'

Mr Owen affirmed with a complacent smile. 'They had no chance against us.'

'Why not?'

'We had greater capital. With a large business there is always less waste and greater efficiency.'

'And your branch store absorbed the profits of the three small ones. I see. But tell me, what became of the owners of the three stores?'

'One is driving a delivery wagon for us. I don't know what happened to the other two.'

Ernest turned abruptly on Mr Kowalt.

'You sell a great deal of cut-rates.[1] What has become of the owners of the small drug stores that you forced to the wall?'

'One of them, Mr Haasfurther, has charge now of our prescription department,' was the answer.

'And you absorbed the profits they had been making?'

'Surely. That is what we are in business for.'

'And you?' Ernest said suddenly to Mr Asmunsen. 'You are disgusted because the railroad has absorbed your profits?'

Mr Asmunsen nodded.

'What you want is to make profits yourself?'

Again Mr Asmunsen nodded.

'Out of others?'

There was no answer.

'Out of others?' Ernest insisted.

'That is the way profits are made,' Mr Asmunsen replied curtly.

'Then the business game is to make profits out of others, and to prevent others from making profits out of you. That's it, isn't it?'

Ernest had to repeat his question before Mr Asmunsen gave an answer, and then he said:

'Yes, that's it, except that we do not object to the others making profits so long as they are not extortionate.'

'By extortionate you mean large; yet you do not object to making large profits yourself? ... Surely not?'

And Mr Asmunsen amiably confessed to the weakness. There was one other man who was quizzed by Ernest at this juncture, a Mr Calvin, who had once been a great dairy-owner.

'Some time ago you were fighting the Milk Trust,' Ernest said to him; 'and now you are in Grange politics.[2] How did it happen?'

'Oh, I haven't quit the fight,' Mr Calvin answered, and

---

[1] A lowering of selling price to cost, and even to less than cost. Thus, a large company could sell at a loss for a longer period than a small company, and so drive the small company out of business. A common device of competition.

[2] Many efforts were made during this period to organise the perishing farmer class into a political party, the aim of which was to destroy the trusts and corporations by drastic legislation. All such attempts ended in failure.

he looked belligerent enough. 'I'm fighting the trust on the only field where it is possible to fight—the political field. Let me show you. A few years ago we dairymen had everything our own way.'

'But you competed among yourselves?' Ernest interrupted.

'Yes, that was what kept the profits down. We did try to organise, but independent dairymen always broke through us. Then came the Milk Trust.'

'Financed by surplus capital from Standard Oil,'[3] Ernest said.

'Yes,' Mr Calvin acknowledged. 'But we did not know it at the time. Its agents approached us with a club. "Come in and be fat", was their proposition, "or stay out and starve." Most of us came in. Those that didn't starved. Oh, it paid us . . . at first. Milk was raised a cent a quart. One-quarter of this cent came to us. Three-quarters of it went to the trust. Then milk was raised another cent, only we didn't get any of that cent. Our complaints were useless. The trust was in control. We discovered that we were pawns. Finally the additional quarter of a cent was denied us. Then the trust began to squeeze us out. What could we do? We were squeezed out. There were no dairymen, only a Milk Trust.'

'But with milk two cents higher, I should think you could have competed,' Ernest suggested slyly.

'So we thought. We tried it.' Mr Calvin paused a moment. 'It broke us. The trust could put milk upon the market more cheaply than we. It could sell still at a slight profit when we were selling at actual loss. I dropped fifty thousand dollars in that venture. Most of us went bankrupt.[4] The dairymen were wiped out of existence.'

'So the trust took your profits away from you,' Ernest said, 'and you've gone into politics in order to legislate the trust out of existence and get the profits back?'

Mr Calvin's face lighted up. 'That is precisely what I say in my speeches to the farmers. That's our whole idea in a nutshell.'

'And yet the trust produces milk more cheaply than could

---

[3] The first successful great trust—almost a generation in advance of the rest.

[4] Bankruptcy—a peculiar institution that enabled an individual, who had failed in competitive industry, to forgo paying his debts. The effect was to ameliorate the too savage conditions of the fang-and-claw social struggle.

the independent dairymen?' Ernest queried.

'Why shouldn't it, with the splendid organisation and new machinery its large capital makes possible?'

'There is no discussion,' Ernest answered. 'It certainly should, and, furthermore, it does.'

Mr Calvin here launched out into a political speech in exposition of his views. He was warmly followed by a number of the others, and the cry of all was to destroy the trusts.

'Poor simple folk,' Ernest said to me in an undertone. 'They see clearly as far as they see, but they see only to the ends of their noses.'

A little later he got the floor again, and in his characteristic way controlled it for the rest of the evening.

'I have listened carefully to all of you,' he began, 'and I see plainly that you play the business game in the orthodox fashion. Life sums itself up to you in profits. You have a firm and abiding belief that you were created for the sole purpose of making profits. Only there is a hitch. In the midst of your own profit-making along comes the trust and takes your profits away from you. This is a dilemma that interferes somehow with the aim of creation, and the only way out, as it seems to you, is to destroy that which takes from you your profits.

'I have listened carefully, and there is only one name that will epitomise you. I shall call you that name. You are machine-breakers. Do you know what a machine-breaker is? Let me tell you. In the eighteenth century, in England, men and women wove cloth on hand-looms in their own cottages. It was a slow, clumsy, and costly way of weaving cloth, this cottage system of manufacture. Along came the steam-engine and labour-saving machinery. A thousand looms assembled in a large factory, and driven by a central engine, wove cloth vastly more cheaply than could the cottage weavers on their hand-looms. Here in the factory was combination, and before it competition faded away. The men and women who had worked the hand-looms for themselves now went into the factories and worked the machine-looms, not for themselves, but for the capitalist owners. Furthermore, little children went to work on the machine-looms, at lower wages, and displaced the men. This made hard times for the men. Their standard of living fell. They starved. And they said it was all the fault of the machines. Therefore they proceeded to break the machines. They did not succeed, and they were very stupid.

'Yet you have not learned their lesson. Here are you, a century and a half later, trying to break machines. By your own confession the trust machines do the work more efficiently and more cheaply than you can. That is why you cannot compete with them. And yet you would break those machines. You are even more stupid than the stupid workmen of England. And while you maunder about restoring competition, the trusts go on destroying you.

'One and all you tell the same story—the passing away of competition and the coming on of combination. You, Mr Owen, destroyed competition here in Berkeley when your branch store drove the three small groceries out of business. Your combination was more effective. Yet you feel the pressure of other combinations on you, the trust combinations, and you cry out. It is because you are not a trust. If you were a grocery trust for the whole United States, you would be singing another song. And the song would be, " Blessed are the trusts." And yet again, not only is your small combination not a trust, but you are aware yourself of its lack of strength. You are beginning to divine your own end. You feel yourself and your branch stores a pawn in the game. You see the powerful interests rising and growing more powerful day by day; you feel their mailed hands descending upon your profits and taking a pinch here and a pinch there—the railroad trust, the oil trust, the steel trust, the coal trust; and you know that in the end they will destroy you, take away from you the last per cent of your little profits.

'You, sir, are a poor gamester. When you squeezed out the three small groceries here in Berkeley by virtue of your superior combination, you swelled out your chest, talked about efficiency and enterprise, and sent your wife to Europe on the profits you had gained by eating up the three small groceries. It is dog eat dog, and you ate them up. But, on the other hand, you are being eaten up in turn by the bigger dogs, wherefore you squeal. And what I say to you is true of all of you at this table. You are all squealing. You are all playing the losing game, and you are all squealing about it.

'But when you squeal you don't state the situation flatly, as I have stated it. You don't say that you like to squeeze profits out of others, and that you are making all the row because others are squeezing your profits out of you. No, you are too cunning for that. You say something else. You make small-capitalist political speeches such as Mr Calvin made. What did he say? Here are a few of his phrases I caught: " Our original principles are all right." " What this country requires is a return to fundamental American methods—free opportunity for all," " The spirit of liberty in which this nation was born," " Let us return to the principles of our fore-fathers."

' When he says " free opportunity for all," he means free opportunity to squeeze profits, which freedom of opportunity is now denied him by the great trusts. And the absurd thing about it is that you have repeated these phrases so often that you believe them. You want opportunity to plunder your fellowmen in your own small way, but you hypnotise yourselves into thinking you want freedom. You are piggish and acquisitive, but the magic of your phrases leads you to believe that you are patriotic. Your desire for profits, which is sheer selfishness, you metamorphose into altruistic solicitude for suffering humanity. Come on now, right here amongst ourselves, and be honest for once. Look the matter in the face and state it in direct terms.'

There were flushed and angry faces at the table, and withal a measure of awe. They were a little frightened at this smooth-faced young fellow, and the swing and smash of his words, and his dreadful trait of calling a spade a spade. Mr Calvin promptly replied:

' And why not?' he demanded. ' Why can we not return to the ways of our fathers when this republic was founded? You have spoken much truth. Mr Everhard, unpalatable though it has been. But here amongst ourselves let us speak out. Let us throw off all disguise and accept the truth as Mr Everhard has flatly stated it. It is true that we smaller capitalists are after profits, and that the trusts are taking our profits away from us. It is true that we want to destroy the trusts in order that our profits may remain to us. And why can we not do it? Why not? I say, why not?'

' Ah, now we come to the gist of the matter,' Ernest said with a pleased expression. ' I'll try to tell you why not, though the telling will be rather hard. You see, you fellows have studied business, in a small way, but you have not studied social evolution at all. You are in the midst of a transition stage now in economic evolution, but you do not understand it, and that's what causes all the confusion. Why cannot you return? Because you can't. You can no more cause the tide of economic evolution to flow back in its channel along the way it came than you can make water run uphill. Joshua made the sun stand still upon Gibeon, but you would outdo Joshua. You would make the sun go backward in the sky. You would have time retrace its steps from noon to morning.

'In a face of labour-saving machinery, of organised production, of the increased efficiency of combination, you would set the economic sun back a whole generation or so to the time when there were no great capitalists, no great machinery, no railroads—a time when a host of little capitalists warred with each other in economic anarchy, and when production was primitive, wasteful, unorganised, and costly. Believe me, Joshua's task was easier, and he had Jehovah to help him. But God has forsaken you small capitalists. The sun of the small capitalists is setting. It will never rise again. Nor is it in your power even to make it stand still. You are perishing, and you are doomed to perish utterly from the face of society.

'This is the fiat of evolution. It is the word of God. Combination is stronger than competition. Primitive man was a puny creature hiding in the crevices of the rocks. He combined and made war upon his carnivorous enemies. They were competitive beasts. Primitive man was a combinative beast, and because of it he rose to primacy over all the animals. And man has been achieving greater and greater combinations ever since. It is combination *versus* competition, a thousand centuries long struggle, in which competition has always been worsted. Whoso enlists on the side of competition perishes.'

'But the trusts themselves arose out of competition,' Mr Calvin interrupted.

'Very true,' Ernest answered. 'And the trusts themselves destroyed competition. That, by your own word, is why you are no longer in the dairy business.'

The first laughter of the evening went around the table, and even Mr Calvin joined in the laugh against himself.

'And now, while we are on the trusts,' Ernest went on, 'let us settle a few things. I shall make certain statements, and if you disagree with them, speak up. Silence will mean agreement. Is it not true that a machine-loom will weave more cloth and weave more cheaply than a hand-loom?' He paused, but nobody spoke up. 'Is it not then highly irrational to break the machine-loom and go back to the clumsy and more costly hand-loom method of weaving?' Heads nodded in acquiescence. 'Is it not true that that combination known as a trust produces more efficiently and cheaply than can a thousand competing small concerns?' Still no one objected. 'Then is it not irrational to destroy that cheap and efficient combination?'

No one answered for a long time. Then Mr Kowalt spoke.

'What are we to do, then?' he demanded. 'To destroy the trusts is the only way we can see to escape their domination.'

Ernest was all fire and aliveness on the instant.

'I'll show you another way!' he cried. 'Let us not destroy those wonderful machines that produce efficiently and cheaply. Let us control them. Let us profit by their efficiency and cheapness. Let us run them for ourselves. Let us oust the present owners of the wonderful machines, and let us own the wonderful machines ourselves. That, gentlemen, is socialism, a greater combination than the trusts, a greater economic and social combination than any that has as yet appeared on the planet. It is in line with evolution. We meet combination with greater combination. It is the winning side. Come on over with us socialists and play on the winning side.'

Here arose dissent. There was a shaking of heads, and muttering arose.

'All right, then, you prefer to be anachronisms,' Ernest laughed. 'You prefer to play atavistic rôles. You are doomed to perish as all atavisms perish. Have you ever asked what will happen to you when greater combinations than even the present trusts arise? Have you ever considered where you will stand when the great trusts themselves combine into the combination of combinations—into the social, economic, and political trust?'

He turned abruptly and irrelevantly upon Mr Calvin.

'Tell me,' Ernest said, 'if this is not true. You are compelled to form a new political party because the old parties are in the hands of the trusts. The chief obstacle to your Grange propaganda is the trusts. Behind every obstacle you encounter, every blow that smites you, every defeat that you receive, is the hand of the trusts. Is this not so? Tell me.'

Mr Calvin sat in uncomfortable silence.

'Go ahead,' Ernest encouraged.

'It is true,' Mr Calvin confessed. 'We captured the state

legislature of Oregon and put through splendid protective legislation, and it was vetoed by the governor, who was a creature of the trusts. We elected a governor of Colorado, and the legislature refused to permit him to take office. Twice we have passed a national income tax, and each time the supreme court smashed it as unconstitutional. The courts are in the hands of the trusts. We, the people, do not pay our judges sufficiently. But there will come a time—'

'When the combination of the trusts will control all legislation, when the combination of the trusts will itself be the Government,' Ernest interrupted.

'Never! never!' were the cries that arose. Everybody was excited and belligerent.

'Tell me,' Ernest demanded, 'what will you do when such a time comes?'

'We will rise in our strength!' Mr Asmunsen cried, and many voices backed his decision.

'That will be civil war,' Ernest warned them.

'So be it civil war,' was Mr Asmunsen's answer, with the cries of all the men at the table behind him. 'We have not forgotten the deeds of our forefathers. For our liberties we are ready to fight and die.'

Ernest smiled.

'Do not forget,' he said, 'that we had tacitly agreed that liberty in your case, gentlemen, means liberty to squeeze profits out of others.'

The table was angry, now, fighting angry; but Ernest controlled the tumult and made himself heard.

'One more question. When you rise in your strength, remember, the reason for your rising will be that the Government is in the hands of the trusts. Therefore, against your strength the Government will turn the regular army, the navy, the militia, the police—in short, the whole organised war machinery of the United States. Where will your strength be then?'

Dismay sat on their faces, and before they could recover, Ernest struck again.

'Do you remember, not so long ago, when our regular army was only fifty thousand? Year by year it has been increased until today it is three hundred thousand.'

Again he struck.

'Nor is that all. While you diligently pursued that favourite phantom of yours, called profits, and moralised about that

favourite fetish of yours, called competition, even greater
and more direful things have been accomplished by combination. There is the militia.'

'It is our strength!' cried Mr Kowalt. 'With it we
would repel the invasion of the regular army.'

'You would go into the militia yourself,' was Ernest's
retort, 'and be sent to Maine, or Florida, or the Philippines,
or anywhere else, to drown in blood your own comrades
civil-warring for their liberties. While from Kansas, or Wis-
consin, or any other state, your own comrades would go into
the militia and come here to California to drown in blood
your own civil-warring.'

Now they were really shocked, and they sat wordless, until
Mr Owen murmured:

'We would not go into the militia. That would settle it.
We would not be so foolish.'

Ernest laughed outright.

'You do not understand the combination that has been
effected. You could not help yourself. You would be drafted
into the militia.'

'There is such a thing as civil law,' Mr Owen insisted.

'Not when the Government suspends civil law. In that
day when you speak of rising in your strength, your strength
would be turned against yourself. Into the militia you would
go, willy-nilly. *Habeas corpus,* I heard some one mutter
just now. Instead of *habeas corpus* you would get post mor-
tems. If you refused to go into the militia, or to obey after
you were in, you would be tried by drumhead court martial
and shot down like dogs. It is the law.'

'It is not the law!' Mr Calvin asserted positively. 'There
is no such law. Young man, you have dreamed all this. Why,
you spoke of sending the militia to the Philippines. That is
unconstitutional. The Constitution especially states that the
militia cannot be sent out of the country.'

'What's the Constitution got to do with it?' Ernest
demanded. 'The courts interpret the Constitution, and the
courts, as Mr Asmunsen agreed, are the creatures of the
trusts. Besides, it is, as I have said, the law. It has been the
law for years, for nine years, gentlemen.'

'That we can be drafted into the militia?' Mr Calvin
asked incredulously. 'That they can shoot us by drumhead
court martial if we refuse.'

'Yes,' Ernest answered, 'precisely that.'

'How is it that we have never heard of this law?' my father asked, and I could see that it was likewise new to him.

'For two reasons,' Ernest said. 'First, there has been no need to enforce it. If there had, you'd have heard of it soon enough. And secondly, the law was rushed through Congress and the Senate secretly, with practically no discussion. Of course, the newspapers made no mention of it. But we socialists knew about it. We published it in our papers. But you never read our papers.'

'I still insist you are dreaming,' Mr Calvin said, stubbornly. 'The country would never have permitted it.'

'But the country did permit it,' Ernest replied.

'And as for my dreaming—' he put his hand in his pocket and drew out a small pamphlet—'tell me if this looks like dream-stuff.'

He opened it and began to read:

'"Section One, be it enacted, and so forth, and so forth, that the militia shall consist of every able-bodied male citizen of the respective states, territories, and District of Columbia, who is more than eighteen and less than forty-five years of age."

'"Section Seven, that any officer or enlisted man"—remember Section One, gentlemen, you are all enlisted men—"that any enlisted man of the militia who shall refuse or neglect to present himself to such mustering officer upon being called forth as herein prescribed, shall be subject to trial by court martial, and shall be punished as such court martial shall direct."

'"Section Eight, that courts martial, for the trial of officers or men of the militia, shall be composed of militia officers only."

'"Section Nine, that the militia, when called into the actual service of the United States, shall be subject to the same rules and articles of war as the regular troops of the United States."

'There you are, gentlemen, American citizens, and fellow militiamen. Nine years ago we socialists thought that law was aimed against labour. But it would seem that it was aimed against you too. Congressman Wiley, in the brief discussion that was permitted, said that the bill " provided for a reserve force to take the mob by the throat "—you're the mob, gentlemen—" and protect at all hazards life, liberty, and property." And in the time to come, when you rise in your strength, remember that you will be rising against the property of the trusts, and the liberty of the trusts, according to the law, to squeeze you. Your teeth are pulled, gentlemen. Your claws are trimmed. In the day you rise in your strength, toothless and clawless, you will be as harmless as an army of clams.'

' I don't believe it!' Kowalt cried. ' There is no such law. It is a canard got up by you socialists.'

' This bill was introduced in the House of Representatives on July 30, 1902,' was the reply. ' It was introduced by Representative Dick of Ohio. It was rushed through. It was passed unanimously by the Senate on January 14, 1903. And just seven days afterwards was approved by the President of the United States.'[5]

---

[5] Everhard was right in the essential particulars, though his date of the introduction of the bill is in error. The bill was introduced on June 30, and not on July 30. The *Congressional Record* is here in Ardis, and a reference to it shows mention of the bill on the following dates: June 30, December 9, 15, 16, and 17, 1902, and January 7 and 14, 1903. The ignorance evidenced by the business men at the dinner was nothing unusual. Very few people knew of the existence of this law. E. Untermann, a revolutionist, in July 1903, published a pamphlet at Girard, Kansas, on the 'Militia Bill.' This pamphlet had a small circulation among working men; but already had the segregation of classes proceeded so far, that the members of the middle class never heard of the pamphlet at all, and so remained in ignorance of the law.

CHAPTER 9

The Mathematics of a Dream

I N T H E midst of the consternation his revelation had produced, Ernest began again to speak.

'You have said, a dozen of you tonight, that socialism is impossible. You have asserted the impossible, now let me demonstrate the inevitable. Not only is it inevitable that you small capitalists shall pass away, but it is inevitable that the large capitalists, and the trusts also, shall pass away. Remember, the tide of evolution never flows backwards. It flows on and on, and it flows from competition to combination, and from little combination to large combination, and from large combination to colossal combination, and it flows on to socialism, which is the most colossal combination of all.

'You tell me that I dream. Very good. I'll give you the mathematics of my dream; and here, in advance, I challenge you to show that my mathematics are wrong. I shall develop the inevitability of the breakdown of the capitalist system, and I shall demonstrate mathematically why it must break down. Here goes, and bear with me if at first I seem irrelevant.

'Let us, first of all, investigate a particular industrial process, and whenever I state something with which you disagree, please interrupt me. Here is a shoe factory. This factory takes leather and makes it into shoes. Here is one hundred dollars' worth of leather. It goes through the factory and comes out in the form of shoes, worth, let us say, two hundred dollars. What has happened? One hundred dollars has been added to the value of the leather. How was it added? Let us see.

'Capital and labour added this value of one hundred dollars. Capital furnished the factory, the machines, and paid all the expenses. Labour furnished labour. By the joint effort of capital and labour one hundred dollars of value was added. Are you all agreed so far?'

Heads nodded around the table in affirmation.

'Labour and capital having produced this one hundred dollars, now proceed to divide it. The statistics of this division are fractional; so let us, for the sake of convenience, make them roughly approximate. Capital takes fifty dollars as its share, and labour gets in wages fifty dollars as its share. We will not enter into the squabbling over the division.[1] No matter how much squabbling takes place, in one percentage or another the division is arranged. And take notice here, that what is true of this particular industrial process is true of all industrial processes. Am I right?'

Again the whole table agreed with Ernest.

'Now, suppose labour, having received its fifty dollars, wanted to buy back shoes. It could only buy back fifty dollars' worth. That's clear, isn't it?

'And now we shift from this particular process to the sum total of all industrial processes in the United States, which includes the leather itself, raw material, transportation, selling, everything. We will say, for the sake of round figures, that the total production of wealth in the United States in one year is four billion dollars. Then labour has received in wages, during the same period, two billion dollars. Four billion dollars has been produced. How much of this can labour buy back? Two billions. There is no discussion of this, I am sure. For that matter, my percentages are mild. Because of a thousand capitalistic devices, labour cannot buy back even half of the total product.

'But to return. We will say labour buys back two billions. Then it stands to reason that labour can consume only two billions. There are still two billions to be accounted for, which labour cannot buy back and consume.'

'Labour does not consume its two billions, even,' Mr Kowalt spoke up. 'If it did, it would not have any deposits in the savings banks.'

'Labour's deposits in the savings banks are only a sort of reserve fund that is consumed as fast as it accumulates. These deposits are saved for old age, for sickness and accident, and for funeral expenses. The savings bank deposit is simply a piece of the loaf put back on the shelf to be eaten

[1] Everhard here clearly develops the cause of all the labour troubles of that time. In the division of the joint-product, capital wanted all it could get, and labour wanted all it could get. This quarrel over the division was irreconcilable. So long as the system of capitalistic production existed, labour and capital continued to quarrel over the division of the joint-product. It is a ludicrous spectacle to us, but we must not forget that we have seven centuries' advantage over those that lived in that time.

next day. No, labour consumes all of the total product that its wages will buy back.

'Two billions are left to capital. After it has paid its expenses, does it consume the remainder? Does capital consume all of its two billions?'

Ernest stopped and put the question point blank to a number of the men. They shook their heads.

'I don't know,' one of them frankly said.

'Of course you do,' Ernest went on. 'Stop and think a moment. If capital consumed its share, the sum total of capital could not increase. It would remain constant. If you will look at the economic history of the United States, you will see that the sum total of capital has continually increased. Therefore capital does not consume its share. Do you remember when England owned so much of our railroad bonds? As the years went by, we bought back those bonds. What does that mean? That part of capital's unconsumed share brought back the bonds. What is the meaning of the fact that today the capitalists of the United States own hundreds and hundreds of millions of dollars of Mexican bonds, Russian bonds, Italian bonds, Grecian bonds? The meaning is that those hundreds and hundreds of millions were part of capital's share which capital did not consume. Furthermore, from the very beginning of the capitalist system, capital has never consumed all of its share.

'And now we come to the point. Four billion dollars of wealth is produced in one year in the United States. Labour buys back and consumes two billions. Capital does not consume the remaining two billions. There is a large balance left over unconsumed. What is done with this balance? What can be done with it? Labour cannot consume any of it, for labour has already spent all its wages. Capital will not consume this balance, because, already, according to its nature, it has consumed all it can. And still remains the balance. What can be done with it? What is done with it?'

'It is sold abroad,' Mr Kowalt volunteered.

'The very thing,' Ernest agreed. 'Because of this balance arises our need for a foreign market. This is sold abroad. It has to be sold abroad. There is no other way of getting rid of it. And that unconsumed surplus, sold abroad, becomes what we call our favourable balance of trade. Are we all agreed so far?'

'Surely it is a waste of time to elaborate these A B C's of

commerce,' Mr Calvin said tartly. 'We all understand them.'

'And it is by these A B C's I have so carefully elaborated that I shall confound you,' Ernest retorted. 'There's the beauty of it. And I'm going to confound you with them right now. Here goes.

'The United States is a capitalist country that has developed its resources. According to its capitalist system of industry, it has an unconsumed surplus that must be got rid of, and that must be got rid of abroad.[2] What is true of the United States is true of every other capitalist country with developed resources. Every one of such countries has an unconsumed surplus. Don't forget that they have already traded with one another, and that these surpluses yet remain. Labour in all these countries has spent its wages, and cannot buy any of the surpluses. Capital in all these countries has already consumed all it is able to according to its nature. And still remain the surpluses. They cannot dispose of these surpluses to one another. How are they going to get rid of them?'

'Sell them to countries with undeveloped resources,' Mr Kowalt suggested.

'The very thing. You see, my argument is so clear and simple that in your own minds you carry it on for me. And now for the next step. Suppose the United States disposes of its surplus to a country with undeveloped resources like, say, Brazil. Remember this surplus is over and above trade, which articles of trade have been consumed. What, then, does the United States get in return from Brazil?'

'Gold,' said Mr Kowalt.

'But there is only so much gold, and not much of it, in the world,' Ernest objected.

'Gold in the form of securities and bonds and so forth,'

[2] Theodore Roosevelt, President of the United States a few years prior to this time, made the following public declaration: '*A more liberal and extensive reciprocity in the purchase and sale of commodities is necessary, so that the over-production of the United States can be satisfactorily disposed of to foreign countries.*' Of course, this over-production he mentions was the profits of the capitalistic system over and beyond the consuming power of the capitalists. It was at this time that Senator Mark Hanna said: '*The production of wealth in the United States is one-third larger annually than its consumption.*' Also a fellow-Senator, Chauncey Depew, said: '*The American people produce annually two billions more wealth than they consume.*'

Mr Kowalt amended.

'Now you've struck it,' Ernest said. 'From Brazil the United States, in return for her surplus, gets bonds and securities. And what does that mean? It means that the United States is coming to own railroads in Brazil, factories, mines, and lands in Brazil. And what is the meaning of that in turn?'

Mr Kowalt pondered and shook his head.

'I'll tell you,' Ernest continued. 'It means that the resources of Brazil are being developed. And now, the next point. When Brazil, under the capitalist system, has developed her resources, she will herself have an unconsumed surplus. Can she get rid of this surplus to the United States? No, because the United States has herself a surplus. Can the United States do what she previously did—get rid of her surplus to Brazil? No, for Brazil now has a surplus too.

'What happens? The United States and Brazil must both seek out other countries with undeveloped resources, in order to unload the surpluses on them. But by the very process of unloading the surpluses, the resources of those countries are in turn developed. Soon they have surpluses, and are seeking other countries on which to unload. Now, gentlemen, follow me. The planet is only so large. There are only so many countries in the world. What will happen when every country in the world, down to the smallest and last, with a surplus in its hands, stands confronting every other country with surpluses in their hands?'

He paused and regarded his listeners. The bepuzzlement in their faces was delicious. Also, there was awe in their faces. Out of abstractions Ernest had conjured a vision and made them see it. They were seeing it then, as they sat there, and they were frightened by it.

'We started with A B C, Mr Calvin,' Ernest said slyly. 'I have now given you the rest of the alphabet. It is very simple. That is the beauty of it. You surely have the answer forthcoming. What, then, when every country in the world has an unconsumed surplus? Where will your capitalist system be then?'

But Mr Calvin shook a troubled head. He was obviously questing back through Ernest's reasoning in search of an error.

'Let me briefly go over the ground with you again,' Ernest said. 'We began with a particular industrial process, the shoe factory. We found that the division of the joint-product that took place there was similar to the division that took place in the sum total of all industrial processes. We found that labour could buy back with its wages only so much of the product, and that capital did not consume all of the remainder of the product. We found that when labour had consumed to the full extent of its wages, and when capital had consumed all it wanted, that there was still left an unconsumed surplus. We agreed that this surplus could only be disposed of abroad. We agreed, also, that the effect of unloading this surplus on another country would be to develop the resources of that country, and that in a short time that country would have an unconsumed surplus. We extended this process to all the countries on the planet, till every country was producing every year, and every day, an unconsumed surplus, which it could dispose of to no other country. And now I ask you again, What are we going to do with those surpluses?'

Still no one answered.

' Mr Calvin?' Ernest queried.

' It beats me,' Mr Calvin confessed.

' I never dreamed of such a thing,' Mr Asmunsen said. ' And yet it does seem clear as print.'

It was the first time I had ever heard Karl Marx's[3] doctrine of surplus value elaborated, and Ernest had done it so simply that I, too, sat puzzled and dumbfounded.

' I'll tell you a way to get rid of the surplus,' Ernest said. ' Throw it into the sea. Throw every year hundreds of millions of dollars' worth of shoes and wheat and clothing and all the commodities of commerce into the sea. Won't that fix it?'

' It will certainly fix it,' Mr Calvin answered. ' But it is absurd for you to talk that way.'

Ernest was upon him like a flash.

' Is it a bit more absurd than what you advocate, you machine-breaker, returning to the antediluvian ways of your forefathers? What do you propose in order to get rid of the

[3] Karl Marx—the great intellectual hero of socialism: A German Jew of the nineteenth century. A contemporary of John Stuart Mill. It seems incredible to us that whole generations should have elapsed after the enunciation of Marx's economic discoveries, in which time he was sneered at by the world's accepted thinkers and scholars. Because of his discoveries he was banished from his native country, and he died an exile in England.

surplus? You would escape the problem of the surplus by not producing any surplus. And how do you propose to avoid producing a surplus? By returning to a primitive method of production, so confused and disorderly and irrational, so wasteful and costly, that it will be impossible to produce a surplus.'

Mr Calvin swallowed. The point had been driven home. He swallowed again and cleared his throat.

' You are right,' he said. ' I stand convicted. It is absurd. But we've got to do something. It is a case of life and death for us of the middle class. We refuse to perish. We elect to be absurd and to return to the truly crude and wasteful methods of our forefathers. We will put back industry to its pretrust stage. We will break the machines. And what are you going to do about it?'

' But you can't break the machines,' Ernest replied. ' You cannot make the tide of evolution flow backward. Opposed to you are two great forces, each of which is more powerful than you of the middle class. The large capitalists, the trusts, in short, will not let you turn back. They don't want the machines destroyed. And greater than the trusts, and more powerful, is labour. It will not let you destroy the machines. The ownership of the world, along with the machines, lies between the trusts and labour. That is the battle alignment. Neither side wants the destruction of the machines. But each side wants to possess the machines. In this battle the middle class has no place. The middle class is a pygmy between two giants. Don't you see, you poor perishing middle class, you are caught between the upper and nether millstones, and even now has the grinding begun.

' I have demonstrated to you mathematically the inevitable breakdown of the capitalist system. When every country stands with an unconsumed and unsaleable surplus on its hands, the capitalist system will break down under the terrific structure of profits that it itself has reared. And in that day there won't be any destruction of the machines. The struggle then will be for the ownership of the machines. If labour wins, your way will be easy. The United States, and the whole world for that matter, will enter upon a new and tremendous era. Instead of being crushed by the machines, life will be made fairer, and happier, and nobler by them. You of the destroyed middle class, along with labour—there will be nothing but labour then; so you, and all the rest of labour, will participate in the equitable distribution of the products of the wonderful machines. And we, all of us, will make new and more wonderful machines. And there won't be any unconsumed surplus, because there won't be any profits.'

' But suppose the trusts win in this battle over the ownership of the machines and the world?' Mr Kowalt asked.

' Then,' Ernest answered, ' you, and labour, and all of us, will be crushed under the iron heel of a despotism as relentless and terrible as any despotism that has blackened the pages of the history of man. That will be a good name for that despotism, the Iron Heel.'[4]

There was a long pause, and every man at the table meditated in ways unwonted and profound.

' But this socialism of yours is a dream,' Mr Calvin said; and repeated, ' a dream.'

' I'll show you something that isn't a dream, then,' Ernest answered. ' And that something I shall call the Oligarchy. You call it the Plutocracy. We both mean the same thing, the large capitalists or the trusts. Let us see where the power lies today. And in order to do so, let us apportion society into its class divisions.

' There are three big classes in society. First comes the Plutocracy, which is composed of wealthy bankers, railway magnates, corporation directors, and trust magnates. Second is the middle class, your class, gentlemen, which is composed of farmers, merchants, small manufacturers, and professional men. And third and last comes my class, the proletariat, which is composed of the wage-workers.[5]

' You cannot but grant that the ownership of wealth constitutes essential power in the United States today. How is this wealth owned by these three classes? Here are the figures. The Plutocracy owns sixty-seven billions of wealth. Of the total number of persons engaged in occupations in the United States, only nine-tenths of one per cent. are from the Plutocracy, yet the Plutocracy owns seventy per cent. of the total wealth. The middle class owns twenty-four billions.

---

[4] The earliest known use of that name to designate the Oligarchy.
[5] This division of society made by Everhard is in accordance with that made by Lucien Sanial, one of the statistical authorities of that time. His calculation of the membership of these divisions by occupations, from the United States Census of 1900, is as follows: Plutocratic class, 250,251; Middle class, 8,429,845; and Proletariat class, 20,393,137.

Twenty-nine per cent. of those in occupations are from the middle class, and they own twenty-five per cent. of the total wealth. Remains the proletariat. It owns four billions. Of all persons in occupations, seventy per cent. come from the proletariat; and the proletariat owns four per cent. of the total wealth. Where does the power lie, gentlemen?'

'From your own figures, we of the middle class are more powerful than labour,' Mr Asmunsen remarked.

'Calling us weak does not make you stronger in the face of the strength of the Plutocracy,' Ernest retorted. 'And furthermore, I'm not done with you. There is a greater strength than wealth, and it is greater because it cannot be taken away. Our strength, the strength of the proletariat, is in our muscles, in our hands to cast ballots, in our fingers to pull triggers. This strength we cannot be stripped of. It is the primitive strength, it is the strength that is to life germane, it is the strength that is stronger than wealth, and that wealth cannot take away.

'But your strength is detachable. It can be taken away from you. Even now the Plutocracy is taking it away from you. In the end it will take it all away from you. And then you will cease to be the middle class. You will descend to us. You will become proletarians. And the beauty of it is that you will then add to our strength. We will hail you brothers, and we will fight shoulder to shoulder in the cause of humanity.

'You see, labour has nothing concrete of which to be despoiled. Its share of the wealth of the country consists of clothes and household furniture, with here and there, in very rare cases, an unencumbered home. But you have the concrete wealth, twenty-four billions of it, and the Plutocracy will take it away from you. Of course, there is the large likelihood that the proletariat will take it away first. Don't you see your position, gentlemen? The middle class is a wobbly little lamb between a lion and a tiger. If one doesn't get you, the other will. And if the Plutocracy gets you first, why, it's only a matter of time when the Proletariat gets the Plutocracy.

'Even your present wealth is not a true measure of your power. The strength of your wealth at this moment is only an empty shell. That is why you are crying out your feeble little battle-cry, 'Return to the ways of our fathers.' You are aware of your impotency. You know that your strength is an empty shell. And I'll show you the emptiness of it.

'What power have the farmers? Over fifty per cent. are thralls by virtue of the fact that they are merely tenants or are mortgaged. And all of them are thralls by virtue of the fact that the trusts already own or control (which is the same thing, only better)—own and control all the means of marketing the crops, such as cold storage, railroads, elevators, and steamship lines. And, furthermore, the trusts control the markets. In all this the farmers are without power. As regards their political and governmental power, I'll take that up later, along with the political and governmental power of the whole middle class.

'Day by day the trusts squeeze out the farmers as they squeezed out Mr Calvin and the rest of the dairymen. And day by day are the merchants squeezed out in the same way. Do you remember how, in six months, the Tobacco Trust squeezed out over four hundred cigar stores in New York City alone? Where are the old-time owners of the coal fields? You know today, without my telling you, that the Railroad Trust owns or controls the entire anthracite and bituminous coal fields. Doesn't the Standard Oil Trust[6] own a score of the ocean lines? And does it not also control copper, to say nothing of running a smelter trust as a little side enterprise? There are ten thousand cities in the United States tonight lighted by the companies owned or controlled by Standard Oil, and in as many cities all the electric transportation—urban, suburban, and interurban—is in the hands of Standard Oil. The small capitalists who were in these thousands of enterprises are gone. You know that. It's the same way that you are going.

'The small manufacturer is like the farmer; and small manufacturers and farmers today are reduced, to all intents and purposes, to feudal tenure. For that matter, the professional men and the artists are at this present moment villeins in every thing but name, while the politicians are henchmen. Why do you, Mr Calvin, work all your nights and days to organise the farmers, along with the rest of the middle class, into a new political party? Because the politicians of the old parties will have nothing to do with your atavistic ideas; and with your atavistic ideas they will have nothing to do because they are what I said they are, henchmen, retainers of the

[6] Standard Oil and Rockefeller—see footnote on page 108.

Plutocracy.

' I spoke of the professional men and the artists as villeins. What else are they? One and all, the professors, the preachers, and the editors, hold their jobs by serving the Plutocracy, and their service consists of propagating only such ideas as are either harmless to or commendatory of the Plutocracy. Whenever they propagate ideas that menace the Plutocracy, they lose their jobs, in which case, if they have not provided for the rainy day, they descend into the proletariat and either perish or become working-class agitators. And don't forget that it is the press, the pulpit, and the university that mould public opinion, set the thought-pace of the nation. As for the artists, they merely pander to the little less than ignoble tastes of the Plutocracy.

' But after all, wealth in itself is not the real power; it is the means of power, and power is governmental. Who controls the Government today? The proletariat with its twenty millions engaged in occupations? Even you laugh at the idea. Does the middle class, with its eight million occupied members? No more than the proletariat. Who, then, controls the Government? The Plutocracy, with its paltry quarter of a million of occupied members. But this quarter of a million does not control the Government, though it renders yeoman service. It is the brain of the Plutocracy that controls the Government, and this brain consists of seven[7] small and powerful groups of men. And do not forget that these groups are working today practically in unison.

' Let me point out the power of but one of them, the railroad group. It employs forty thousand lawyers to defeat the people in the courts. It issues countless thousands of free passes to judges, bankers, editors, ministers, university men,

[7] Even as late as 1907, it was considered that eleven groups dominated the country, but this number was reduced by the amalgamation of the five railroad groups into a supreme combination of all the railroads. These five groups so amalgamated, along with their financial and political allies, were (1) James J. Hill with his control of the North-west; (2) the Pennsylvania railway group, Schiff financial manager, with big banking firms of Philadelphia and New York; (3) Harriman, with Frick for counsel and Odell as political lieutenant, controlling the central continental, South-western and Southern Pacific Coast lines of transportation; (4) the Gould family railway interests; and (5) Moore, Reid, and Leeds, known as the ' Rock Island crowd.' These strong oligarchs arose out of the conflict of competition and travelled the inevitable road towards combination.

members of state legislatures, and of Congress. It maintains luxurious lobbies[8] at every state capital, and at the national capital; and in all the cities and towns of the land it employs an immense army of pettifoggers and small politicians whose business is to attend primaries, pack conventions, get on juries, bribe judges, and in every way to work for its interests.[9]

' Gentlemen, I have merely sketched the power of one of the seven groups that constitute the brain of the Plutocracy.[10]

---

[8] *Lobby*—a peculiar institution for bribing, bulldozing, and corrupting the legislators who were supposed to represent the people's interests.

[9] A decade before this speech of Everhard's the New York Board of Trade issued a report from which the following is quoted: ' *The railroads control absolutely the legislatures of a majority of the states of the Union; they make and unmake United States' Senators, congressmen, and governors, and are practically dictators of the governmental policy of the United States.*'

[10] Rockefeller began as a member of the proletariat and through thrift and cunning succeeded in developing the first perfect trust, namely, that known as Standard Oil. We cannot forbear giving the following remarkable page from the history of the times, to show how the need for reinvestment of the Standard Oil surplus crushed out small capitalists and hastened the breakdown of the capitalist system. David Graham Phillips was a Radical writer of the period, and the quotation, by him, is taken from a copy of the *Saturday Evening Post*, dated October 4, A.D. 1902. This is the only copy of this publication that has come down to us, and yet, from its appearance and content, we cannot but conclude that it was one of the popular periodicals with a large circulation. The quotation here follows:

' *About ten years ago Rockefeller's income was given as thirty millions by an excellent authority. He had reached the limit of profitable investment of profits in the oil industry. Here, then, were these enormous sums in cash pouring in—more than* $2,000,000 *a month for John Davison Rockefeller alone. The problem of reinvestment became more serious. It became a nightmare. The oil income was swelling, swelling, and the number of sound investments limited, even more limited than it is now. It was through no special eagerness for more gains that the Rockefellers began to branch out from oil into other things. They were forced, swept on by this inrolling tide of wealth which their monopoly magnet irresistibly attracted. They developed a staff of investment seekers and investigators. It is said that the chief of this staff has a salary of* $125,000 *a year.*

' *The first conspicuous excursion and incursion of the Rockefeller was into the railway field. By* 1895 *they controlled one-fifth of the railway mileage of the country. What do they own or, through dominant ownership, control today? They are powerful in all the*

Your twenty-four billions of wealth does not give you twenty-five cents' worth of governmental power. It is an empty shell, and soon even the empty shell will be taken away from you. The Plutocracy has all power in its hands today. It today makes the laws, for it owns the Senate, Congress, the courts, aand the state legislatures. And not only that. Behind law must be force to execute the law. Today the Plutocracy makes the law, and to enforce the law it has at its beck and call the police, the army, the navy, and, lastly, the militia, which is you, and me, and all of us.'

Little discussion took place after this, and the dinner soon broke up. All were quiet and subdued, and leave-taking was done with low voices. It seemed almost that they were scared by the vision of the times they had seen.

'The situation is, indeed, serious,' Mr Calvin said to Ernest. 'I have little quarrel with the way you have depicted it. Only I disagree with you about the doom of the middle class. We shall survive, and we shall overthrow the trusts.'

'And return to the ways of your fathers,' Ernest finished for him.

---

great railways of New York, north, east, and west, except one, where their share is only a few millions. They are in most of the great railways radiating from Chicago. They dominate in several of the systems that extend to the Pacific. It is their votes that make Mr Morgan so potent, though, it may be added, they need his brains more than he needs their votes—at present, and the combination of the two constitutes in large measure the " community of interest."

'But railways could not alone absorb rapidly enough these mighty floods of gold. Presently John D. Rockefeller's $2,500,000 a month had increased to four, to five, to six millions a month, to $75,000,000 a year. Illuminating oil was becoming all profit. The reinvestments of income were adding their mite of many annual millions.

'The Rockefellers went into gas and electricity when those industries had developed to the safe investment stage. And now a large part of the American people must begin to enrich the Rockefellers as soon as the sun goes down, no matter what form of illuminant they use. They went into farm mortgages. It is said that when prosperity a few years ago enabled the farmers to rid themselves of their mortgages, John D. Rockefeller was moved almost to tears; eight millions which he had thought taken care of for years to come at a good interest were suddenly dumped upon his doorstep and there set up a squawking for a new home. This unexpected addition to his worriments in finding places for the progeny of his petroleum and their progeny, and their progeny's

'Even so,' Mr Calvin answered gravely. 'I know it's a sort of machine-breaking, and that it is absurd. But then life seems absurd today, what of the machinations of the Plutocracy. And at any rate, our sort of machine-breaking is at least practical and possible, which your dream is not. Your socialistic dream is . . . well, a dream. We cannot follow you.'

'I only wish you fellows knew a little something about evolution and sociology,' Ernest said wistfully as they shook hands. 'We would be saved so much trouble if you did.'

---

progeny, was too much for the equanimity of a man without a digestion. . . .

'The Rockefellers went into mines—iron and coal and copper and lead; into other industrial companies; into street railways, into national, state, and municipal bonds; into steamships and steamboats and telegraphy; into real estate, into sky scrapers and residences and hotels and business blocks; into life insurance, into banking. There was soon literally no field of industry where their millions were not at work. . . .

'The Rockefeller bank—the National City Bank—is by itself far and away the biggest bank in the United States. It is exceeded in the world only by the Bank of England and the Bank of France. The deposits average more than one hundred millions a day; and it dominates the call loan market on Wall Street and the stock market. But it is not alone; it is the head of the Rockefeller chain of banks, which includes fourteen banks and trust companies in New York City, and banks of great strength and influence in every large money centre in the country.

'John° D. Rockefeller owns Standard Oil stock worth between four and five hundred millions at the market quotations. He has a hundred millions in the Steel Trust, almost as much in a single western railway system, half as much in a second, and so on and on and on until the mind wearies of the cataloguing. His income last year was about $100,000,000—it is doubtful if the incomes of all the Rothschilds together make a greater sum. And it is going up by leaps and bounds.'

CHAPTER 10

The Vortex

FOLLOWING LIKE thunder-claps upon the Business Men's dinner, occurred event after event of terrifying moment; and I, little I, who had lived so placidly all my days in the quiet university town, found myself and my personal affairs drawn into the vortex of the great world-affairs. Whether it was my love for Ernest, or the clear sight he had given me of the society in which I lived, that made me a revolutionist, I know not; but a revolutionist I became, and I was plunged into a whirl of happenings that would have been inconceivable three short months before.

The crisis in my own fortunes came simultaneously with great crisis in society. First of all, father was discharged from the university. Oh, he was not technically discharged. His resignation was demanded, that was all. This, in itself, did not amount to much. Father, in fact, was delighted. He was especially delighted because his discharge had been precipitated by the publication of his book, *Economics and Education*. It clinched his argument, he contended. What better evidence could be advanced to prove that education was dominated by the capitalist class?

But this proof never got anywhere. Nobody knew he had been forced to resign from the university. He was so eminent a scientist that such an announcement, coupled with the reason for his enforced resignation, would have created somewhat of a furore all over the world. The newspapers showered him with praise and honour, and commended him for having given up the drudgery of the lecture room in order to devote his whole time to scientific research.

At first father laughed. Then he became angry—tonic angry. Then came the suppression of his book. This suppression was performed secretly, so secretly that at first we could not comprehend. The publication of the book had immediately caused a bit of excitement in the country. Father had been politely abused in the capitalist press, the tone of the abuse being to the effect that it was a pity so great a scientist should leave his field and invade the realm of sociology about which he knew nothing, and wherein he had promptly become lost. This lasted for a week, while father chuckled and said the book had touched a sore spot on capitalism. And then, abruptly, the newspapers and the critical magazines ceased saying anything about the book at all. Also, and with equal suddenness, the book disappeared from the market. Not a copy was obtainable from any bookseller. Father wrote to the publishers, and was informed that the plates had been accidentally injured. An unsatisfactory correspondence followed. Driven finally to an unequivocal stand, the publishers stated that they could not see their way to putting the book into type again, but that they were quite willing to relinquish their rights in it.

'And you won't find another publishing house in the country to touch it,' Ernest said. 'And if I were you I'd hunt cover right now. You've merely got a foretaste of the Iron Heel.'

But father was nothing if not a scientist. He never believed in jumping to conclusions. A laboratory experiment was no experiment if it were not carried through in all its details. So he patiently went the round of the publishing houses. They gave a multitude of excuses, but not one house would consider the book.

When father became convinced that the book had actually been suppressed, he tried to get the fact into the newspapers; but his communications were ignored. At a political meeting of the socialists, where many reporters were present, father saw his chance. He arose and related the history of the suppression of the book. He laughed next day when he read the newspapers, and then he grew angry to a degree that eliminated all tonic qualities. The papers made no mention of the book, but they misreported him beautifully. They twisted his words and phrases away from the context, and turned his subdued and controlled remarks into a howling anarchistic speech. It was done artfully. One instance, in particular, I remember. He had used the phrase ' social revolution '. The reporter merely dropped out ' social '. This was sent out all over the country in an Associated Press dispatch, and from all over the country arose a cry of alarm. Father was branded as a nihilist and an anarchist, and in one cartoon that was copied widely he was portrayed waving a red flag at the head of a mob of long-haired, wild-eyed men who bore in their hands torches, knives, and dynamite bombs.

He was assailed terribly in the press, in long and abusive editorials, for his anarchy, and hints were made of mental breakdown on his part. This behaviour, on the part of the capitalist press, was nothing new, Ernest told us. It was the custom, he said, to send reporters to all the socialist meetings, for the express purpose of misreporting and distorting what was said, in order to frighten the middle class away from any possible affiliation with the proletariat. And repeatedly Ernest warned father to cease fighting and to take to cover.

The socialist press of the country took up the fight, however, and throughout the reading portion of the working class it was known that the book had been suppressed. But this knowledge stopped with the working class. Next, the 'Appeal to Reason', a big socialist publishing house, arranged with father to bring out the book. Father was jubilant, but Ernest was alarmed.

'I tell you we are on the verge of the unknown,' he insisted. 'Big things are happening secretly all around us. We can feel them. We do not know what they are, but they are there. The whole fabric of society is a-tremble with them. Don't ask me. I don't know myself. But out of this flux of society something is about to crystallise. It is crystallising now. The suppression of the book is a precipitation. How many books have been suppressed? We haven't the least idea. We are in the dark. We have no way of learning. Watch out next for the suppression of the socialist press and socialist publishing houses. I'm afraid it's coming. We are going to be throttled.'

Ernest had his hand on the pulse of events even more closely than the rest of the socialists, and within two days the first blow was struck. The *Appeal to Reason* was a weekly, and its regular circulation among the proletariat was seven hundred and fifty thousand. Also, it very frequently got out special editions of from two to five millions. These great editions were paid for and distributed by the small army of voluntary workers who had marshalled around the *Appeal*. The first blow was aimed at these special editions, and it was a crushing one. By an arbitrary ruling of the Post Office, these editions were decided to be not the regular circulation of the paper, and for that reason were denied admission to the mails.

A week later the Post Office Department ruled that the

paper was seditious, and barred it entirely from the mails. This was a fearful blow to the socialist propaganda. The *Appeal* was desperate. It devised a plan of reaching its subscribers through the express companies, but they declined to handle it. This was the end of the *Appeal*. But not quite. It prepared to go on with its book publishing. Twenty thousand copies of father's book were in the bindery, and the presses were turning off more. And then, without warning, a mob arose one night, and under a waving American flag, singing patriotic songs, set fire to the great plant of the *Appeal* and totally destroyed it.

Now Girard, Kansas, was a quiet, peaceable town. There had never been any labour troubles there. The *Appeal* paid union wages; and, in fact, was the backbone of the town, giving employment to hundreds of men and women. It was not the citizens of Girard that composed the mob. This mob had risen up out of the earth apparently, and to all intents and purposes, its work done, it had gone back into the earth. Ernest saw in the affair the most sinister import.

' The Black Hundreds[1] are being organised in the United States,' he said. ' This is the beginning. There will be more of it. The Iron Heel is getting bold.'

And so perished father's book. We were to see much of the Black Hundreds as the days went by. Week by week more of the socialist papers were barred from the mails, and in a number of instances the Black Hundreds destroyed the socialist presses. Of course, the newspapers of the land lived up to the reactionary policy of the ruling class, and the destroyed socialist press was misrepresented and vilified, while the Black Hundreds were represented as true patriots and saviours of society. So convincing was all this misrepresentation that even sincere ministers in the pulpit praised the Black Hundreds while regretting the necessity of violence.

History was making fast. The fall elections were soon to occur, and Ernest was nominated by the socialist party to run for Congress. His chance for election was most favourable. The street-car strike in San Francisco had been broken. And following upon it the teamsters' strike had been broken.

[1] The Black Hundreds were reactionary mobs organised by the perishing Autocracy in the Russian Revolution. These reactionary groups attacked the revolutionary groups and also, at needed moments, rioted and destroyed property so as to afford the Autocracy the pretext of calling out the Cossacks.

These two defeats had been very disastrous to organised labour. The whole Water Front Federation, along with its allies in the structural trades, had backed up the teamsters, and all had smashed down ingloriously. It had been a bloody strike. The police had broken countless heads with their riot clubs; and the death list had been augmented by the turning loose of a machine-gun on the strikers from the barns of the Marsden Special Delivery Company.

In consequence, the men were sullen and vindictive. They wanted blood, and revenge. Beaten on their chosen field, they were ripe to seek revenge by means of political action. They still maintained their labour organisation, and this gave them strength in the political struggle that was on. Ernest's chance for election grew stronger and stronger. Day by day unions and more unions voted their support to the socialists, until even Ernest laughed when the Undertakers' Assistants and the Chicken Pickers fell into line. Labour became mulish. While it packed the socialist meetings with mad enthusiasm, it was impervious to the wiles of the old-party politicians. The old-party orators were usually greeted with empty halls, though occasionally they encountered full halls where they were so roughly handled that more than once it was necessary to call out the police reserves.

History was making fast. The air was vibrant with things happening and impending. The country was on the verge of hard times,[2] caused by a series of prosperous years wherein the difficulty of disposing abroad of the unconsumed surplus had become increasingly difficult. Industries were working short time; many great factories were standing idle against the time when the surplus should be gone; and wages were being cut right and left.

Also, the great machinist strike had been broken. Two hundred thousand machinists, along with their five hundred thousand allies in the metal-working trades, had been defeated in as bloody a strike as had ever marred the United States. Pitched battles had been fought with the small armies of armed strike-breakers[3] put in the field by the employers'

---

[2] Under the capitalist régime these periods of hard times were as inevitable as they were absurd. Prosperity always brought calamity. This, of course, was due to the excess of unconsumed profits that was piled up.

[3] Strike-breakers—these were, in purpose and practice and everything except name, the private soldiers of the capitalists. They

associations; the Black Hundreds, appearing in scores of wide-scattered places, had destroyed property; and, in consequence, a hundred thousand regular soldiers of the United States had been called out to put a frightful end to the whole affair. A number of the labour leaders had been executed; many others had been sentenced to prison, while thousands of the rank and file of the strikers had been herded into bull-pens[4] and abominably treated by the soldiers.

The years of prosperity were now to be paid for. All markets were glutted; all markets were falling; and amidst the general crumble of prices the price of labour crumbled fastest of all. The land was convulsed with industrial dissensions. Labour was striking here, there, and everywhere; and where it was not striking, it was being turned out by the capitalists. The papers were filled with tales of violence and blood. And through it all the Black Hundreds played their part. Riot, arson, and wanton destruction of property was their function, and well they performed it. The whole regular army was in the field, called there by the actions of the Black Hundreds.[5] All cities and towns were like armed camps, and

---

were thoroughly organised and well armed, and they were held in readiness to be hurled in special trains to any part of the country where labour went out on strike or was locked out by the employers. Only those curious times could have given rise to the amazing spectacle of one Farley, a notorious commander of strike-breakers, who, in 1906, swept across the United States in special trains from New York to San Francisco with an army of twenty-five hundred men, fully armed and equipped, to break a strike of the San Francisco street carmen. Such an act was in direct violation of the laws of the land. The fact that this act, and thousands of similar acts, went unpunished, goes to show how completely the judiciary was the creature of the Plutocracy.

[4] *Bull-pen*—in a miners' strike in Idaho, in the latter part of the nineteenth century, it happened that many of the strikers were confined in a bull-pen by the troops. The practice and the name continued in the twentieth century.

[5] The name only, and not the idea, was imported from Russia. The Black Hundreds were a development out of the secret agents of the capitalists, and their use arose in the labour struggles of the nineteenth century. There is no discussion of this. No less an authority of the time than Carrol D. Wright, United States Commissioner of Labour, is responsible for the statement. From his book, entitled 'The Battles of Labour,' is quoted the declaration that '*in some of the great historic strikes the employers themselves have instigated acts of violence*'; that manufacturers have deliberately provoked strikes in order to get rid of surplus stock;

labourers were shot down like dogs. Out of the vast army of
the unemployed the strike-breakers were recruited; and when
the strike-breakers were worsted by the labour unions, the
troops always appeared and crushed the unions. Then there
was the militia. As yet, it was not necessary to have recourse
to the secret militia law. Only the regularly organised militia
was out, and it was out everywhere, and in this time of
terror the regular army was increased an additional hundred
thousand by the government.

Never had labour received such an all-round beating. The
great captains of industry, the oligarchs, had for the first time
thrown their full weight into the breach the struggling employers' associations had made. These associations were practically middle class affairs, and now, compelled by hard times
and crashing markets, and aided by the great captains of
industry, they gave organised labour an awful and decisive
defeat. It was an all-powerful alliance, but it was an alliance
of the lion and the lamb, as the middle class was soon to
learn.

Labour was bloody and sullen, but crushed. Yet its defeat
did not put an end to the hard times. The banks, themselves
constituting one of the most important forces of the Oligarchy, continued to call in credits. The Wall Street[6] group
turned the stock market into a maelstrom where the values of
all the land crumbled away almost to nothingness. And out
of all the rack and ruin rose the form of the nascent Oligarchy, imperturbable, indifferent, and sure. Its serenity and
certitude was terrifying. Not only did it use its own vast
power, but it used all the power of the United States Treasury
to carry out its plans.

The captains of industry had turned upon the middle class.
The employers' associations, that had helped the captains of
industry to tear and rend labour were now torn and rent by
their quondam allies. Amidst the crashing of the middle men,

---

and that freight cars have been burned by employers' agents during railroad strikes in order to increase disorder. It was out of
these secret agents of the employers that the Black Hundreds arose;
and it was they in turn, that later became that terrible weapon
of the Oligarchy, the agents-provocateurs.

[6] *Wall Street*—so named from a street in ancient New York,
where was situated the stock exchange, and where the irrational
organisation of society permitted under-handed manipulation of
all the industries of the country.

the small business men and manufacturers, the trusts stood
firm. Nay, the trusts did more than stand firm. They were
active. They sowed wind, and wind, and ever more wind;
for they alone knew how to reap the whirlwind and make a
profit out of it. And such profits! Colossal profits! Strong
enough themselves to weather the storm that was largely their
own brewing, they turned loose and plundered the wrecks
that floated about them. Values were pitifully and inconceivably shrunken, and the trusts added hugely to their holdings,
even extending their enterprises into many new fields—and
always at the expense of the middle class.

Thus the summer of 1912 witnessed the virtual death-
thrust to the middle class. Even Ernest was astounded at the
quickness with which it had been done. He shook his head
ominously, and looked forward without hope to the fall elections.

'It's no use,' he said. 'We are beaten. The Iron Heel is
here. I had hoped for a peaceable victory at the ballot-box.
I was wrong. Wickson was right. We shall be robbed of our
few remaining liberties; the Iron Heel will walk upon our
faces; nothing remains but a bloody revolution of the working
class. Of course we will win, but I shudder to think of it.'

And from then on Ernest pinned his faith on revolution.
In this he was in advance of his party. His fellow-socialists
could not agree with him. They still insisted that victory
could be gained through the elections. It was not that they
were stunned. They were too cool-headed and courageous
for that. They were merely incredulous, that was all. Ernest
could not get them seriously to fear the coming of the
Oligarchy. They were stirred by him, but they were too sure
of their own strength. There was no room in their theoretical
social evolution for an oligarchy, therefore the Oligarchy
could not be.

'We'll send you to Congress and it will be all right,' they
told him at one of our secret meetings.

'And when they take me out of Congress,' Ernest replied
coldly, 'and put me against a wall, and blow my brains out
—what then?'

'Then we'll rise in our might,' a dozen voices answered at
once.

'Then you'll welter in your gore,' was his retort. 'I've
heard that song sung by the middle class, and where is it
now in its might?'

CHAPTER 11

The Great Adventure

MR WICKSON did not send for father. They met by chance on the ferry boat to San Francisco, so that the warning he gave father was not premeditated. Had they not met accidentally, there would not have been any warning. Not that the outcome would have been different, however. Father came of stout old 'Mayflower'[1] stock, and the blood was imperative in him.

'Ernest was right,' he told me, as soon as he had returned home. 'Ernest is a very remarkable young man, and I'd rather see you his wife than the wife of Rockefeller himself or the King of England.'

'What's the matter?' I asked in alarm.

'The Oligarchy is about to tread upon our faces—yours and mine. Wickson as much as told me so. He was very kind —for an oligarch. He offered to reinstate me in the university. What do you think of that? He, Wickson, a sordid money-grabber, has the power to determine whether I shall or shall not teach in the university of the state. But he offered me even better than that—offered to make me president of some great college of physical sciences that is being planned—the Oligarchy must get rid of its surplus somehow, you see.

' "Do you remember what I told that socialist lover of your daughter's?" he said. "I told him that we would walk upon the faces of the working class. And so we shall. As for you, I have for you a deep respect as a scientist; but if you throw your fortunes in with the working class—well, watch out for your face, that is all." And then he turned and left me.'

'It means we'll have to marry earlier than you planned,' was Ernest's comment when we told him.

I could not follow his reasoning, but I was soon to learn

[1] One of the first ships that carried colonists to America, after the discovery of the New World. Descendants of these original colonists were for a while inordinately proud of their genealogy; but in time the blood became so widely diffused that it ran in the veins practically of all Americans.

it. It was at this time that the quarterly dividend of the Sierra Mills was paid—or, rather, should have been paid, for father did not receive his. After waiting several days, father wrote to the secretary. Promptly came the reply that there was no record on the books of father's owning any stock, and a polite request for more explicit information.

'I'll make it explicit enough, confound him,' father declared, and departed for the bank to get the stock in question from his safe-deposit box.

'Ernest is a very remarkable man,' he said when he got back and while I was helping him off with his overcoat. 'I repeat, my daughter, that young man of yours is a very remarkable young man.'

I had learned, whenever he praised Ernest in such fashion, to expect disaster.

'They have already walked upon my face,' father explained. 'There was no stock. The box was empty. You and Ernest will have to get married pretty quickly.'

Father insisted on laboratory methods. He brought the Sierra Mills into court, but he could not bring the books of the Sierra Mills into court. He did not control the courts, and the Sierra Mills did. That explained it all. He was thoroughly beaten by the law, and the barefaced robbery held good.

It is almost laughable now, when I look back on it, the way father was beaten. He met Wickson accidentally on the street in San Francisco, and he told Wickson that he was a damned scoundrel. And then father was arrested for attempted assault, fined in the police court, and bound over to keep the peace. It was all so ridiculous that when he got home he had to laugh himself. But what a furore was raised in the local papers! There was grave talk about the bacillus of violence that infected all men who embrace socialism; and father, with his long and peaceful life, was instanced as a shining example of how the bacillus of violence worked. Also, it was asserted by more than one paper that father's mind had weakened under the strain of scientific study, and confinement in a state asylum for the insane was suggested. Nor was this merely talk. It was an imminent peril. But father was wise enough to see it. He had the Bishop's experience to lesson from, and he lessoned well. He kept quiet, no matter what injustice was perpetrated on him, and really, I think, surprised his enemies.

There was the matter of the house—our home. A mortgage was foreclosed on it, and we had to give up possession. Of course there wasn't any mortgage, and never had been any mortgage. The ground had been bought outright, and the house had been paid for when it was built. And house and lot had always been free and unencumbered. Nevertheless there was the mortgage, properly and legally drawn up and signed, with a record of the payments of interest through a number of years. Father made no outcry. As he had been robbed of his money, so was he now robbed of his home. And he had no recourse. The machinery of society was in the hands of those who were bent on breaking him. He was a philosopher at heart, and he was no longer even angry.

' I am doomed to be broken,' he said to me; ' but that is no reason that I should not try to be shattered as little as possible. These old bones of mine are fragile, and I've learned my lesson. God knows I don't want to spend my last days in an insane asylum.'

Which reminds me of Bishop Morehouse, whom I have neglected for many pages. But first let me tell of my marriage. In the play of events, my marriage sinks into insignificance, I know, so I shall barely mention it.

' Now we shall become real proletarians,' father said, when we were driven from our home. ' I have often envied that young man of yours for his actual knowledge of the proletariat. Now I shall see and learn for myself.'

Father must have had strong in him the blood of adventure. He looked upon our catastrophe in the light of an adventure. No anger nor bitterness possessed him. He was too philosophic and simple to be vindictive, and he lived too much in the world of mind to miss the creature comforts we were giving up. So it was, when we moved to San Francisco into four wretched rooms in the slum, south of Market Street, that he embarked upon the adventure with the joy and enthusiasm of a child—combined with the clear sight and mental grasp of an extraordinary intellect. He really never crystallised mentally. He had no false sense of values. Conventional or habitual values meant nothing to him. The only values he recognised were mathematical and scientific facts. My father was a great man. He had the mind and the soul that only great men have. In ways he was even greater than Ernest, than whom I have known none greater.

Even I found some relief in our change of living. If nothing else, I was escaping from the organised ostracism that had been our increasing portion in the university town ever since the enmity of the nascent Oligarchy had been incurred. And the change was to me likewise adventure, and the greatest of all, for it was love-adventure. The change in our fortunes had hastened my marriage, and it was as a wife that I came to live in the four rooms in Pell Street, in the San Francisco slum.

And this out of all remains: I made Ernest happy. I came into his stormy life, not as a new perturbing force, but as one that made toward peace and repose. I gave him rest. It was the guerdon of my love for him. It was the one infallible token that I had not failed. To bring forgetfulness, or the light of gladness, into those poor tired eyes of his—what greater joy could have blessed me than that?

Those dear tired eyes. He toiled as few men ever toiled, and all his lifetime he toiled for others. That was the measure of his manhood. He was a humanist and a lover. And he, with his incarnate spirit of battle, his gladiator body and his eagle spirit—he was as gentle and tender to me as a poet. He was a poet. A singer in deeds. And all his life he sang the song of man. And he did it out of sheer love of man, and for man he gave his life and was crucified.

And all this he did with no hope of future reward. In his conception of things there was no future life. He, who fairly burnt with immortality, denied himself immortality—such was the paradox of him. He, so warm in spirit, was dominated by that cold and forbidding philosophy, materialistic monism. I used to refute him by telling him that I measured his immortality by the wings of his soul, and that I should have to live endless æons in order to achieve the full measurement. Whereat he would laugh, and his arms would leap out to me, and he would call me his sweet metaphysician; and the tiredness would pass out of his eyes, and into them would flood the happy lovelight that was in itself a new and sufficient advertisement of his immortality.

Also, he used to call me his dualist, and he would explain how Kant, by means of pure reason, had abolished reason, in order to worship God. And he drew the parallel and included me guilty of a similar act. And when I pleaded guilty, but defended the act as highly rational, he but pressed me closer and laughed as only one of God's own lovers could laugh. I was wont to deny that heredity and environment could explain his own originality and genius, any more than could the cold groping finger of science catch and analyse and classify that elusive essence that lurked in the constitution of life itself.

I held that space was an apparition of God, and that soul was a projection of the character of God; and when he called me his sweet metaphysician, I called him my immortal materialist. And so we loved and were happy; and I forgave him his materialism because of his tremendous work in the world, performed without thought of soul-gain thereby, and because of his so exceeding modesty of spirit that prevented him from having pride and regal consciousness of himself and his soul.

But he had pride. How could he have been an eagle and not have pride? His contention was that it was finer for a finite mortal speck of life to feel Godlike than for a god to feel godlike; and so it was that he exalted what he deemed his mortality. He was fond of quoting a fragment from a certain poem. He had never seen the whole poem, and he had tried vainly to learn its authorship. I here give the fragment, not alone because he loved it, but because it epitomised the paradox that he was in the spirit of him, and his conception of his spirit. For how can a man, with thrilling, and burning, and exaltation, recite the following and still be mere mortal earth, a bit of fugitive force, an evanescent form? Here it is:

' Joy upon joy and gain upon gain
   Are the destined rights of my birth,
 And I shout the praise of my endless days
   To the echoing edge of the earth.
 Though I suffer all deaths that a man can die
 To the uttermost end of time,
 I have deep-drained this, my cup of bliss,
 In every age and clime—
 The froth of Pride, the tang of Power,
 The sweet of Womanhood !
 I drain the lees upon my knees,
 For oh, the draught is good;
 I drink to Life, I drink to Death,
 And smack my lips with song,
 For when I die, another ' I ' shall pass the cup along.

' The man you drove from Eden's grove
     Was I, my Lord, was I,
 And I shall be there when the earth and the air
     Are rent from sea to sky;
 For it is my world, my gorgeous world,
     The world of my dearest woes,

From the first faint cry of the newborn I
    To the rack of the woman's throes.

' Packed with the pulse of an unborn race,
    Torn with a world's desire.
The surging flood of my wild young blood
    Would quench the judgment fire.
I am Man, Man, Man, from the tingling flesh
    To the dust of earthly goal,
From the nestling gloom of the pregnant womb
    To the sheen of my naked soul.
Bone of my bone and flesh of my flesh
    The whole world leaps to my will,
And the unslaked thirst of an Eden cursed
    Shall harrow the earth to its fill.
Almighty God, when I drain life's glass
    Of all its rainbow gleams,
The hapless plight of eternal night
    Shall be none too long for my dreams.

' The man you drove from Eden's grove
    Was I, my Lord, was I,
And I shall be there when the earth and the air
    Are rent from sea to sky;
For it is my world, my gorgeous world,
    The world of my dear delight,
From the brightest gleam of the Arctic stream
    To the dusk of my own love-night.' [2]

Ernest always overworked. His wonderful constitution kept
him up; but even that constitution could not keep the tired
look out of his eyes. His dear tired eyes! He never slept more
than four and one-half hours a night; yet he never found
time to do all the work he wanted to do. He never ceased
from his activities as a propagandist, and was always
scheduled long in advance for lectures to working-men's
organisations. Then there was the campaign. He did a man's
full work in that alone. With the suppression of the socialist
publishing houses, his meagre royalties ceased, and he was
hard-put to make a living; for he had to make a living in
addition to all his other labour. He did a great deal of translating for the magazines on scientific and philosophic subjects;
and, coming home late at night, worn out from the strain of
the campaign, he would plunge into his translating and toil
on well into the morning hours. And in addition to everything, there was his studying. To the day of his death he kept

[2] The authorship of this poem must remain for ever unknown.
This fragment is the only portion that has come down to us.

up his studies, and he studied prodigiously.

And yet he found time in which to love me and make me happy. But this was accomplished only through my merging my life completely into his. I learned shorthand and type-writing, and became his secretary. He insisted that I suc-ceeded in cutting his work in half; and so it was that I schooled myself to understand his work. Our interests became mutual and we worked together and played together.

And then there were our sweet stolen moments in the midst of our work—just a word, or caress, or flash of love-light; and our moments were sweeter for being stolen. For we lived on the heights, where the air was keen and sparkling, where the toil was for humanity, and where sordidness and selfish-ness never entered. We loved love, and our love was never smirched by anything less than the best. And this out of all remains: I did not fail. I gave him rest—he who worked so hard for others, my dear, tired-eyed mortalist.

CHAPTER 12

The Bishop

IT WAS after my marriage that I chanced upon Bishop Morehouse. But I must give the events in their proper sequence. After his outbreak at the I.P.H. Convention, the Bishop, being a gentle soul, had yielded to the friendly pressure brought to bear upon him, and had gone away on a vacation. But he returned more fixed than ever in his determination to preach the message of the Church. To the consternation of his congregation, his first sermon was quite similar to the address he had given before the Convention. Again he said, and at length and with distressing detail, that the Church had wandered away from the Master's teaching, and that Mammon had been instated in the place of Christ.

And the result was, willy-nilly, that he was led away to a private sanatorium for mental disease, while in the newspapers appeared pathetic accounts of his mental breakdown and of the saintliness of his character. He was held a prisoner in the sanitorium. I called repeatedly, but was denied access to him; and I was terribly impressed by the tragedy of a sane, normal, saintly man being crushed by the brutal will of society. For the Bishop was sane, and pure, and noble. As Ernest said, all that was the matter with him was that he had incorrect notions of biology and sociology, and because of his incorrect notions he had not gone about it in the right way to rectify matters.

What terrified me was the Bishop's helplessness. If he persisted in the truth as he saw it, he was doomed to an insane ward. And he could do nothing. His money, his position, his culture, could not save him. His views were perilous to society, and society could not conceive that such perilous views could be the product of a sane mind. Or, at least, it seems to me that such was society's attitude.

But the Bishop, in spite of the gentleness and purity of his spirit, was possessed of guile. He apprehended clearly his danger. He saw himself caught in the web, and he tried to escape from it. Denied help from his friends, such as father and Ernest and I could have given, he was left to battle for himself alone. And in the enforced solitude of the sanatorium he recovered. He became again sane. His eyes ceased to see visions; his brain was purged of the fancy that it was the duty of society to feed the Master's lambs.

As I say, he became well, quite well, and the newspapers and the church people hailed his return with joy. I went once to his church. The sermon was of the same order as the ones he had preached long before his eyes had seen visions. I was disappointed, shocked. Had society, then, beaten him into submission? Was he a coward? Had he been bull-dozed into recanting? Or had the strain been too great for him, and had he meekly surrendered to the Juggernaut of the established?

I called upon him in his beautiful home. He was woefully changed. He was thinner, and there were lines on his face which I had never seen before. He was manifestly distressed by my coming. He plucked nervously at his sleeve as we talked; and his eyes were restless, fluttering here, there, and everywhere, and refusing to meet mine. His mind seemed preoccupied, and there were strange pauses in his conversation, abrupt changes of topic, and an inconsecutiveness that was bewildering. Could this then, be the firm-poised, Christlike man I had known, with pure, limpid eyes, and a gaze steady and unfaltering as his soul? He had been manhandled; he had been cowed into subjection. His spirit was too gentle. It had not been mighty enough to face the organised wolf-pack of society.

I felt sad, unutterably sad. He talked ambiguously, and was so apprehensive of what I might say that I had not the heart to catechise him. He spoke in a far-away manner of his illness, and we talked disjointedly about the church, the alterations in the organ, and about petty charities; and he saw me depart with such evident relief that I should have laughed had not my heart been so full of tears.

The poor little hero. If I had only known! He was battling like a giant, and I did not guess it. Alone, all alone, in the midst of millions of his fellowmen, he was fighting his fight. Torn by his horror of the asylum and his fidelity to truth and the right, he clung steadfastly to truth and the right; but so alone was he that he did not dare to trust even me. He had learned his lesson well—too well.

But I was soon to know. One day the Bishop disappeared. He had told nobody that he was going away; and as the days went by and he did not reappear, there was much gossip to the effect that he had committed suicide while temporarily deranged. But this idea was dispelled when it was learned that he had sold all his possessions—his city mansion, his country house at Menlo Park, his paintings and collections, and even his cherished library. It was patent that he had made a clean and secret sweep of everything before he disappeared.

This happened during the time when calamity had overtaken us in our own affairs; and it was not till we were well settled in our new home that we had opportunity really to wonder and speculate about the Bishop's doings. And then everything was suddenly made clear. Early one evening, while it was yet twilight, I had run across the street and into the butcher-shop to get some chops for Ernest's supper. We called the last meal of the day ' supper ' in our new environment.

Just at the moment I came out of the butcher-shop, a man emerged from the corner grocery that stood alongside. A queer sense of familiarity made me look again. But the man had turned and was walking rapidly away. There was something about the slope of the shoulders and the fringe of silver hair between coat and collar and slouch hat that aroused vague memories. Instead of crossing the street, I hurried after the man. I quickened my pace, trying not to think the thoughts that formed unbidden in my brain. No, it was impossible. It could not be—not in those faded overalls, too long in the legs and frayed at the bottoms.

I paused, laughed at myself, and almost abandoned the chase. But the haunting familiarity of those shoulders and that silver hair! Again I hurried on. As I passed him I shot a keen look at his face; then I whirled around abruptly and confronted—the Bishop.

He halted with equal abruptness, and gasped. A large paper bag in his right hand fell to the sidewalk. It burst, and about his feet and mine bounced and rolled a flood of potatoes. He looked at me with surprise and alarm, then he seemed to wilt away; the shoulders drooped with dejection, and he uttered a deep sigh.

I held out my hand. He shook it, but his hand felt clammy. He cleared his throat in embarrassment, and I could see the sweat starting out on his forehead. It was evident that he was badly frightened.

' The potatoes,' he murmured faintly. ' They are precious.'

Between us we picked them up and replaced them in the broken bag, which he now held carefully in the hollow of his arm. I tried to tell him my gladness at meeting him and that he must come right home with me.

'Father will be rejoiced to see you,' I said. 'We live only a stone's throw away.'

'I can't,' he said. 'I must be going. Good-bye.'

He looked apprehensively about him, as though dreading discovery, and made an attempt to walk on.

'Tell me where you live, and I shall call later,' he said, when he saw that I walked beside him and that it was my intention to stick to him now that he was found.

'No,' I answered firmly. 'You must come now.'

He looked at the potatoes spilling on his arm, and at the small parcels on his other arm.

'Really, it is impossible,' he said. 'Forgive me for my rudeness. If you only knew.'

He looked as if he were going to break down, but the next moment he had himself in control.

'Besides, this food,' he went on. 'It is a sad case. It is terrible. She is an old woman. I must take it to her at once. She is suffering from want of it. I must go at once. You understand. Then I will return. I promise you.'

'Let me go with you,' I volunteered. 'Is it far?'

He sighed again, and surrendered.

'Only two blocks,' he said. 'Let us hasten.'

Under the Bishop's guidance I learned something of my own neighbourhood. I had not dreamed such wretchedness and misery existed in it. Of course, this was because I did not concern myself with charity. I had become convinced that Ernest was right when he sneered at charity as a poulticing of an ulcer. Remove the ulcer was his remedy; give to the worker his product; pension as soldiers those who grow honourably old in their toil, and there will be no need for charity. Convinced of this, I toiled with him at the revolution, and did not exhaust my energy in alleviating the social ills that continuously arose from the injustice of the system.

I followed the Bishop into a small room, ten by twelve, in a rear tenement. And there we found a little old German woman—sixty-four years old, the Bishop said. She was surprised at seeing me, but she nodded a pleasant greeting and went on sewing on the pair of man's trousers in her lap. Beside her, on the floor, was a pile of trousers. The Bishop discovered there was neither coal nor kindling, and went out to buy some.

I took up a pair of trousers and examined her work.

' Six cents, lady,' she said, nodding her head gently while she went on stitching. She stitched slowly, but never did she cease from stitching. She seemed mastered by the verb ' to stitch.'

' For all that work?' I asked. ' Is that what they pay? How long does it take you?'

' Yes,' she answered, ' that is what they pay. Six cents for finishing. Two hours' sewing on each pair.

' But the boss doesn't know that,' she added quickly, betraying a fear of getting him into trouble. ' I'm slow. I've got the rheumatism in my hands. Girls work much faster. They finish in half that time. The boss is kind. He lets me take the work home, now that I am old and the noise of the machine bothers my head. If it wasn't for his kindness, I'd starve.

' Yes, those who work in the shop get eight cents. But what can you do? There is not enough work for the young. The old have no chance. Often one pair is all I can get. Sometimes, like today, I am given eight pair to finish before night.'

I asked her the hours she worked, and she said it depended on the season.

' In the summer, when there is a rush order, I work from five in the morning to nine at night. But in the winter it is too cold. The hands do not early get over the stiffness. Then you must work later—till after midnight sometimes.

' Yes, it has been a bad summer. The hard times. God must be angry. This is the first work the boss has given me in a week. It is true one cannot eat much when there is no work. I am used to it. I have sewed all my life, in the old country and here in San Francisco—thirty-three years.

' If you are sure of the rent, it is all right. The houseman is very kind, but he must have his rent. It is fair. He only charges three dollars for this room. That is cheap. But it is not easy for you to find all of three dollars every month.'

She ceased talking, and, nodding her head, went on stitching.

' You have to be very careful as to how you spend your earnings,' I suggested.

She nodded emphatically.

'After the rent it's not so bad. Of course you can't buy meat. And there is no milk for the coffee. But always there is one meal a day, and often two.'

She said this last proudly. There was a smack of success in her words. But as she stitched on in silence, I noticed the sadness in her pleasant eyes and the droop of her mouth. The look in her eyes became faraway. She rubbed the dimness hastily out of them; it interfered with her stitching.

'No, it is not the hunger that makes the heart ache,' she explained. 'You get used to being hungry. It is for my child that I cry. It was the machine that killed her. It is true that she worked hard, but I cannot understand. She was strong. And she was young—only forty; and she worked only thirty years. She began young, it is true; but my man died. The boiler exploded down at the works. And what were we to do? She was ten, but she was very strong. But the machine killed her. Yes, it did. It killed her, and she was the fastest worker in the shop. I have thought about it often, and I know. That is why I cannot work in the shop. The machine bothers my head. Always I hear it saying, "I did it, I did it." And it says that all day long. And then I think of my daughter, and I cannot work.'

The moistness was in her old eyes again, and she had to wipe it away before she could go on stitching.

I heard the Bishop stumbling up the stairs, and I opened the door. What a spectacle he was. On his back he carried half a sack of coal, with kindling on top. Some of the coal dust had coated his face, and the sweat from his exertions was running in streaks. He dropped his burden in the corner by the stove and wiped his face on a coarse bandanna handkerchief. I could scarcely accept the verdict of my senses. The Bishop, black as a coal-heaver, in a working-man's cheap cotton shirt (one button was missing from the throat), and in overalls! That was the most incongruous of all—the overalls, frayed at the bottoms, dragged down at the heels, and held up by a narrow leather belt around the hips such as labourers wear.

Though the Bishop was warm, the poor, swollen hands of the old woman were already cramping with the cold; and before we left her, the Bishop had built the fire, while I had peeled the potatoes and put them on to boil. I was to learn, as time went by, that there were many cases similar to hers, and many worse, hidden away in the monstrous depths of the tenements in my neighbourhood.

We got back to find Ernest alarmed by my absence. After the first surprise of greeting was over, the Bishop leaned back in his chair, stretched out his overall-covered legs, and actually sighed a comfortable sigh. We were the first of his old friends he had met since his disappearance, he told us; and during the intervening weeks he must have suffered greatly from loneliness. He told us much, though he told us more of the joy he had experienced in doing the Master's bidding.

'For truly now,' he said, 'I am feeding his lambs. And I have learned a great lesson. The soul cannot be ministered to till the stomach is appeased. His lambs must be fed with bread and butter and potatoes and meat; after that, and only after that, are their spirits ready for more refined nourishment.'

He ate heartily of the supper I cooked. Never had he had such an appetite at our table in the old days. We spoke of it, and he said that he had never been so healthy in his life.

'I walk always now,' he said, and a blush was on his cheek at the thought of the time when he rode in his carriage, as though it were a sin not lightly to be laid.

'My health is better for it,' he added hastily. 'And I am very happy—indeed, most happy. At last I am a consecrated spirit.'

And yet there was in his face a permanent pain, the pain of the world that he was now taking to himself. He was seeing life in the raw, and it was a different life from what he had known within the printed books of his library.

'And you are responsible for all this, young man,' he said directly to Ernest.

Ernest was embarrassed and awkward.

'I—I warned you,' he faltered.

'No, you misunderstand,' the Bishop answered. 'I speak not in reproach, but in gratitude. I have you to thank for showing me my path. You led me from theories about life to life itself. You pulled aside the veils from the social shams. You were light in my darkness, but now I, too, see the light. And I am very happy, only . . .' he hesitated painfully, and in his eyes fear leaped large. 'Only the persecution. I harm no one. Why will they not let me alone? But it is not that. It is the nature of the persecution. I shouldn't mind if they cut my flesh with stripes, or burned me at the stake, or crucified me head-downward. But it is the asylum that frightens me. Think of it! Of me—in an asylum for the insane! It is revolting. I saw some of the cases at the sanatorium. They were violent. My blood chills when I think of it. And to be imprisoned for the rest of my life amid scenes of screaming madness! No! no! Not that! Not that!'

It was pitiful. His hands shook, his whole body quivered and shrank away from the picture he had conjured. But the next moment he was calm.

'Forgive me,' he said simply. 'It is my wretched nerves. And if the Master's work leads there, so be it. Who am I to complain?'

I felt like crying aloud as I looked at him: 'Great Bishop! O hero! God's hero!'

As the evening wore on, we learned more of his doings.

'I sold my house—my houses, rather,' he said, 'and all my other possessions. I knew I must do it secretly, else they would have taken everything away from me. That would have been terrible. I often marvel these days at the immense quantity of potatoes two or three hundred thousand dollars will buy, or bread, or meat, or coal and kindling.' He turned to Ernest. 'You are right, young man. Labour is dreadfully underpaid. I never did a bit of work in my life, except to appeal æsthetically to Pharisees—I thought I was preaching the message—and yet I was worth half a million dollars. I never knew what half a million dollars meant until I realised how much potatoes and bread and butter and meat it could buy. And then I realised something more. I realised that all those potatoes and that bread and butter and meat were mine, and that I had not worked to make them. Then it was clear to me someone else had worked and made them and been robbed of them. And when I came down amongst the poor I found those who had been robbed and who were hungry and wretched because they had been robbed.'

We drew him back to his narrative.

'The money? I have it deposited in many different banks under different names. It can never be taken away from me, because it can never be found. And it is so good, that money. It buys so much food. I never knew before what money was good for.'

'I wish we could get some of it for the propaganda,' Ernest said wistfully. 'It would do immense good.'

'Do you think so?' the Bishop said. 'I do not have much

faith in politics. In fact, I am afraid I do not understand politics.'

Ernest was delicate in such matters. He did not repeat his suggestion, though he knew only too well the sore straits the Socialist Party was in through lack of money.

'I sleep in cheap lodging-houses,' the Bishop went on. 'But I am afraid, and I never stay long in one place. Also, I rent two rooms in working-men's houses in different quarters of the city. It is a great extravagance, I know, but it is necessary. I make up for it in part by doing my own cooking, though sometimes I get something to eat in cheap coffee-houses. And I have made a discovery. Tamales[1] are very good when the air grows chilly late at night. Only they are so expensive. But I have discovered a place where I can get three for ten cents. They are not so good as the others, but they are very warming.

'And so I have at last found my work in the world, thanks to you, young man. It is the Master's work.' He looked at me, and his eyes twinkled. 'You caught me feeding his lambs, you know. And of course you will all keep my secret.'

He spoke carelessly enough, but there was real fear behind the speech. He promised to call upon us again. But a week later we read in the newspaper of the sad case of Bishop Morehouse, who had been committed to the Napa Asylum, and for whom there were still hopes held out. In vain we tried to see him, to have his case reconsidered or investigated. Nor could we learn anything about him except the reiterated statements that slight hopes were still held for his recovery.

'Christ told the rich young man to sell all he had,' Ernest said bitterly. 'The Bishop obeyed Christ's injunction and got locked up in a madhouse. Times have changed since Christ's day. A rich man today who gives all he has to the poor is crazy. There is no discussion. Society has spoken.'

---

[1] A Mexican dish, referred to occasionally in the literature of the times. It is supposed that it was warmly seasoned. No recipe of it has come down to us.

CHAPTER 13

The General Strike

O F   C O U R S E Ernest was elected to Congress in the great
socialist landslide that took place in the fall of 1912. One
great factor that helped to swell the socialist vote was the
destruction of Hearst.[1] This the Plutocracy found an easy
task. It cost Hearst eighteen million dollars a year to run his
various papers, and this sum, and more, he got back from
the middle class in payment for advertising. The source of his
financial strength lay wholly in the middle class. The trusts
did not advertise.[2] To destroy Hearst, all that was necessary
was to take away from him his advertising.

The whole middle class had not yet been exterminated.
The sturdy skeleton of it remained; but it was without power.
The small manufacturers and small business men who still
survived were at the complete mercy of the Plutocracy. They
had no economic nor political souls of their own. When the
fiat of the Plutocracy went forth, they withdrew their advertisements from the Hearst papers.

Hearst made a gallant fight. He brought his papers out
at a loss of a million and a half each month. He continued to
publish the advertisements for which he no longer received
pay. Again the fiat of the Plutocracy went forth, and the
small business men and manufacturers swamped him with a
flood of notices that he must discontinue running their old

[1] *William Randolph Hearst*—a young Californian millionaire who
became the most powerful newspaper owner in the country. His
newspapers were published in all the large cities, and they
appealed to the perishing middle class and to the proletariat. So
large was his following that he managed to take possession of the
empty shell of the old Democratic Party. He occupied an anoma-
lous position, preaching an emasculated socialism combined with
a nondescript sort of petty bourgeois capitalism. It was oil and
water, and there was no hope for him, though for a short period
he was a source of serious apprehension to the Plutocrats.

[2] The cost of advertising was amazing in those helter-skelter times.
Only the small capitalists competed, and therefore they did the
advertising. There being no competition where there was a trust,
there was no need for the trusts to advertise.

advertisements. Hearst persisted. Injunctions were served on him. Still he persisted. He received six months' imprisonment for contempt of court in disobeying the injunctions, while he was bankrupted by countless damage suits. He had no chance. The Plutocracy had passed sentence on him. The courts were in the hands of the Plutocracy to carry the sentence out. And with Hearst crashed also to destruction the Democratic Party that he had so recently captured.

With the destruction of Hearst and the Democratic Party, there were only two paths for his following to take. One was into the Socialist Party; the other was into the Republican Party. Then it was that we socialists reaped the fruit of Hearst's pseudo-socialistic preaching; for the great majority of his followers came over to us.

The expropriation of the farmers that took place at this time would also have swelled our vote had it not been for the brief and futile rise of the Grange Party. Ernest and the socialist leaders fought fiercely to capture the farmers; but the destruction of the socialist press and publishing houses constituted too great a handicap, while the mouth to mouth propaganda had not yet been perfected. So it was that politicians like Mr Calvin, who were themselves farmers long since expropriated, captured the farmers and threw their political strength away in a vain campaign.

' The poor farmers,' Ernest once laughed savagely; ' the trusts have them both coming and going.'

And that was really the situation. The seven great trusts, working together, had pooled their enormous surpluses and made a farm trust. The railroads, controlling rates, and the bankers and stock exchange gamesters, controlling prices, had long since bled the farmers into indebtedness. The bankers, and all the trusts for that matter, had likewise long since loaned colossal amounts of money to the farmers. The farmers were in the net. All that remained to be done was the drawing in of the net. This the Farm Trust proceeded to do.

The hard times of 1912 had already caused a frightful slump in the farm markets. Prices were now deliberately pressed down to bankruptcy, while the railroads, with extortionate rates, broke the back of the farmer-camel. Thus the farmers were compelled to borrow more and more, while they were prevented from paying back old loans. Then ensued the great foreclosing of mortgages and enforced collection of

notes. The farmers simply surrendered the land to the farm
trust. There was nothing else for them to do. And having
surrendered the land, the farmers next went to work for the
farm trust, becoming managers, superintendents, foremen,
and common labourers. They worked for wages. They became
villeins, in short—serfs bound to the soil by a living wage.
They could not leave their masters, for their masters composed the Plutocracy. They could not go to the cities, for
there, also, the Plutocracy was in control. They had but one
alternative—to leave the soil and become vagrants, in brief,
to starve. And even there they were frustrated, for stringent
vagrancy laws were passed and rigidly enforced.

Of course, here and there, farmers, and even whole com-
munities of farmers, escaped expropriation by virtue of
exceptional conditions. But they were merely strays and did
not count, and they were gathered in anyway during the
following year.[3]

Thus it was that in the fall of 1912 the socialist leaders,
with the exception of Ernest, decided that the end of capitalism had come. What of the hard times and the consequent
vast army of the unemployed; what of the destruction of the
farmers and the middle class; and what of the decisive defeat
administered all along the line to the labour unions; the
socialists were really justified in believing that the end of
capitalism had come and in themselves throwing down the
gauntlet to the Plutocracy.

Alas, how we underestimated the strength of the enemy!
Everywhere the socialists proclaimed their coming victory
at the ballot-box, while, in unmistakable terms, they stated
the situation. The Plutocracy accepted the challenge. It was

---

[3] The destruction of the Roman yeomanry proceeded far less
rapidly than the destruction of the American farmers and small
capitalists. There was momentum in the twentieth century, while
there was practically none in ancient Rome.

Numbers of the farmers, impelled by an insane lust for the
soil, and willing to show what beasts they could become, tried
to escape expropriation by withdrawing from any and all market-
dealing. They sold nothing. They bought nothing. Among themselves a primitive barter began to spring up. Their privation and
hardships were terrible, but they persisted. It became quite a
movement, in fact. The manner in which they were beaten was
unique and logical and simple. The Plutocracy, by virtue of its
possession of the government, raised their taxes. It was the weak
joint in their armour. Neither buying nor selling, they had no
money, and in the end their land was sold to pay the taxes.

the Plutocracy, weighing and balancing, that defeated us by dividing our strength. It was the Plutocracy, through its secret agents, that raised the cry that socialism was sacrilegious and atheistic; it was the Plutocracy that whipped the churches, and especially the Catholic Church, into line, and robbed us of a portion of the labour vote. And it was the Plutocracy, through its secret agents, of course, that encouraged the Grange Party and even spread it to the cities into the ranks of the dying middle class.

Nevertheless the socialist landslide occurred. But, instead of a sweeping victory with chief executive officers and majorities in all legislative bodies, we found ourselves in the minority. It is true, we elected fifty Congressmen; but when they took their seats in the spring of 1913 they found themselves without power of any sort. Yet they were more fortunate than the Grangers, who captured a dozen state governments, and who, in the spring, were not permitted to take possession of the captured offices. The incumbents refused to retire, and the courts were in the hands of the Oligarchy. But this is too far in advance of events. I have yet to tell of the stirring times of the winter of 1912.

The hard times at home had caused an immense decrease in consumption. Labour, out of work, had no wages with which to buy. The result was that the Plutocracy found a greater surplus than ever on its hands. This surplus it was compelled to dispose of abroad, and, what of its colossal plans, it needed money. Because of its strenuous efforts to dispose of the surplus in the world market, the Plutocracy clashed with Germany. Economic clashes were usually succeeded by wars, and this particular clash was no exception. The great German war-lord prepared, and so did the United States prepare.

The war-cloud hovered dark and ominous. The stage was set for a world-catastrophe, for in all the world were hard times, labour troubles, perishing middle classes, armies of unemployed, clashes of economic interests in the world-markets, and mutterings and rumblings of the socialist revolution.[4]

[4] For a long time these mutterings and rumblings had been heard. As far back as A.D. 1906, Lord Avebury, an Englishman, uttered the following in the House of Lords: ' *The unrest in Europe, the spread of socialism, and the ominous rise of Anarchism, are warnings to the governments and the ruling classes that the condition*

The Oligarchy wanted the war with Germany. And it wanted the war for a dozen reasons. In the juggling of events such a war would cause, in the reshuffling of the international cards and the making of new treaties and alliances, the Oligarchy had much to gain. And, furthermore, the war would consume many national surpluses, reduce the armies of unemployed that menaced all countries, and give the Oligarchy a breathing space in which to perfect its plans and carry them out. Such a war would virtually put the Oligarchy in possession of the world-market. Also, such a war would create a large standing army that need never be disbanded, while in the minds of the people would be substituted the issue, 'America *versus* Germany,' in place of 'Socialism *versus* Oligarchy.'

And truly the war would have done all these things had it not been for the socialists. A secret meeting of the Western leaders was held in our four tiny rooms in Pell Street. Here was first considered the stand the socialists were to take. It was not the first time we had put our foot down upon war,[5]

---

of the working classes in Europe is becoming intolerable, and that if a revolution is to be avoided some steps must be taken to increase wages, reduce the hours of labour, and lower the prices of the necessaries of life.' The Wall Street Journal, a stock gamesters' publication, in commenting upon Lord Avebury's speech, said: '*These words were spoken by an aristocrat and a member of the most conservative body in all Europe. That gives them all the more significance. They contain more valuable political economy than is to be found in most of the books. They sound a note of warning. Take heed, gentlemen, of the war and navy departments!*'

At the same time, Sydney Brooks, writing in America, in *Harper's Weekly,* said: '*You will not hear the socialists mentioned in Washington. Why should you? The politicians are always the last people in this country to see what is going on under their noses. They will jeer at me when I prophesy, and prophesy with the utmost confidence, that at the next presidential election the socialists will poll over a million votes.*'

[5] It was at the very beginning of the twentieth century A.D., that the international organisation of the socialists finally formulated their long-maturing policy on war. Epitomised, their doctrine was: *Why should the workingmen of one country fight with the workingmen of another country for the benefit of their capitalist masters?*

On May 21, A.D. 1905, when war threatened between Austria and Italy, the socialists of Italy, Austria, and Hungary held a conference at Trieste, and threatened a general strike of the working men of both countries in case war was declared. This was but it was the first time we had done so in the United States. After our secret meeting we got in touch with the national organisation, and soon our code cables were passing back and forth across the Atlantic between us and the International Bureau.

The German socialists were ready to act with us. There were over five million of them, many of them in the standing army, and, in addition, they were on friendly terms with the labour unions. In both countries the socialists came out in bold declaration against the war and threatened the general strike. And in the meantime they made preparation for the general strike. Furthermore, the revolutionary parties in all countries gave public utterance to the socialist principle of international peace that must be preserved at all hazards, even to the extent of revolt and revolution at home.

The general strike was the one great victory we American socialists won. On the 4th of December the American minister was withdrawn from the German capital. That night a German fleet made a dash on Honolulu, sinking three American cruisers and a revenue cutter, and bombarding the city. Next day both Germany and the United States declared war, and within an hour the socialists called the general strike in both countries.

For the first time the German war-lord faced the men of his empire who made his empire go. Without them he could not run his empire. The novelty of the situation lay in that their revolt was passive. They did not fight. They did nothing. And by doing nothing they tied their war-lord's hands. He would have asked for nothing better than an opportunity to loose his war-dogs on his rebellious proletariat. But this was denied him. He could not loose his war-dogs. Neither could he mobilise his army to go forth to war, nor could he punish his recalcitrant subjects. Not a wheel moved in his empire. Not a train ran, not a telegraphic message went over the wires, for the telegraphers and railroad men had ceased work along with the rest of the population.

And as it was in Germany, so it was in the United States. At last organised labour had learned its lesson. Beaten decisively on its own chosen field, it had abandoned that field and come over to the political field of the socialists; for the

---

repeated the following year, when the ' Morocco Affair ' threatened to involve France, Germany, and England.

general strike was a political strike. Besides, organised labour had been so badly beaten that it did not care. It joined in the general strike out of sheer desperation. The workers threw down their tools and left their tasks by the millions. Especially notable were the machinists. Their heads were bloody, their organisation had apparently been destroyed, yet out they came, along with their allies in the metal-working trades.

Even the common labourers and all unorganised labour ceased work. The strike had tied everything up so that nobody could work. Besides, the women proved to be the strongest promoters of the strike. They set their faces against the war. They did not want their men to go forth to die. Then, also, the idea of the general strike caught the mood of the people. It struck their sense of humour. The idea was infectious. The children struck in all the schools, and such teachers as came, went home again from deserted class-rooms. The general strike took the form of a great national picnic. And the idea of the solidarity of labour, so evidenced, appealed to the imagination of all. And, finally, there was no danger to be incurred by the colossal frolic. When everybody was guilty, how was anybody to be punished?

The United States was paralysed. No one knew what was happening. There were no newspapers, no letters, no dispatches. Every community was as completely isolated as though ten thousand miles of primeval wilderness stretched between it and the rest of the world. For that matter, the world had ceased to exist. And for a week this state of affairs was maintained.

In San Francisco we did not know what was happening even across the bay in Oakland or Berkeley. The effect on one's sensibilities was weird, depressing. It seemed as though some great cosmic thing lay dead. The pulse of the land had ceased to beat. Of a truth the nation had died. There were no wagons rumbling on the streets, no factory whistles, no hum of electricity in the air, no passing of street cars, no cries of newsboys—nothing but persons who at rare intervals went by like furtive ghosts, themselves oppressed and made unreal by the silence.

And during that week of silence the Oligarchy was taught its lesson. And well it learned the lesson. The general strike was a warning. It should never occur again. The Oligarchy would see to that.

At the end of the week, as had been prearranged, the telegraphers of Germany and the United States returned to their posts. Through them the socialist leaders of both countries presented their ultimatum to the rulers. The war should be called off, or the general strike would continue. It did not take long to come to an understanding. The war was declared off, and the populations of both countries returned to their tasks.

It was this renewal of peace that brought about the alliance between Germany and the United States. In reality, this was an alliance between the Emperor and the Oligarchy, for the purpose of meeting their common foe, the revolutionary proletariat of both countires. And it was this alliance that the Oligarchy afterward so treacherously broke when the German socialists rose and drove the war-lord from his throne. It was the very thing the Oligarchy had played for—the destruction of its great rival in the world-market. With the German Emperor out of the way, Germany would have no surplus to sell abroad. By the very nature of the socialist state, the German population would consume all that it produced. Of course, it would trade abroad certain things it produced for things it did not produce; but this would be quite different from an unconsumable surplus.

' I'll wager the Oligarchy finds justification,' Ernest said, when its treachery to the German Emperor became known. ' As usual, the Oligarchy will believe it has done right.'

And sure enough the Oligarchy's public defence for the act was that it had done it for the sake of the American people whose interest it was looking out for. It had flung its hated rival out of the world-market and enabled us to dispose of our surplus in that market.

' And the howling folly of it is that we are so helpless that such idiots really are managing our interests,' was Ernest's comment. ' They have enabled us to sell more abroad, which means that we'll be compelled to consume less at home.'

CHAPTER 14

The Beginning of the End

A S E A R L Y as January, 1913, Ernest saw the true trend of affairs, but he could not get his brother leaders to see the vision of the Iron Heel that had arisen in his brain. They were too confident. Events were rushing too rapidly to culmination. A crisis had come in world affairs. The American Oligarchy was practically in possession of the world-market, and scores of countries were flung out of that market with unconsumable and unsaleable surpluses on their hands. For such countries nothing remained but reorganisation. They could not continue their method of producing surpluses. The capitalistic system, so far as they were concerned, had hopelessly broken down.

The reorganisation of these countries took the form of revolution. It was a time of confusion and violence. Everywhere institutions and governments were crashing. Everywhere, with the exception of two or three countries, the erstwhile capitalist masters fought bitterly for their possessions. But the governments were taken away from them by the militant proletariat. At last was being realised Karl Marx's classic: ' The knell of private capitalist property sounds. The expropriators are expropriated.' And as fast as capitalistic governments crashed, co-operative commonwealths arose in their place.

' Why does the United States lag behind?'; ' Get busy, you American revolutionists!'; ' What's the matter with America?'—were the messages sent to us by our successful comrades in other lands. But we could not keep up. The Oligarchy stood in the way. Its bulk, like that of some huge monster, blocked our path.

' Wait till we take office in the spring,' we answered. ' Then you'll see.'

Behind this lay our secret. We had won over the Grangers, and in the spring a dozen states would pass into their hands by virtue of the elections of the preceding fall. At once would be instituted a dozen co-operative commonwealth states. After that, the rest would be easy.

' But what if the Grangers fail to get possession?' Ernest

demanded. And his comrades called him a calamity howler.

But this failure to get possession was not the chief danger that Ernest had in mind. What he foresaw was the defection of the great labour unions and the rise of the castes.

' Ghent has taught the oligarchs how to do it,' Ernest said. ' I'll wager they've made a text-book out of his *Benevolent Feudalism*.'[1]

Never shall I forget the night when, after a hot discussion with half a dozen labour leaders, Ernest turned to me and said quietly: ' That settles it. The Iron Heel has won. The end is in sight.'

This little conference in our home was unofficial; but Ernest, like the rest of his comrades, was working for assurances from the labour leaders that they would call out their men in the next general strike. O'Connor, the president of the Association of Machinists, had been foremost of the six leaders present in refusing to give such assurance.

' You have seen that you were beaten soundly at your old tactics of strike and boycott,' Ernest urged.

O'Connor and the others nodded their heads.

' And you saw what a general strike would do,' Ernest went on. ' We stopped the war with Germany. Never was there so fine a display of the solidarity and the power of labour. Labour can and will rule the world. If you continue to stand with us, we'll put an end to the reign of capitalism. It is your only hope. And what is more, you know it. There is no other way out. No matter what you do under your old tactics, you are doomed to defeat, if for no other reason because the masters control the courts.'[2]

---

[1] *Our Benevolent Feudalism*, a book published in A.D. 1902, by W. J. Ghent. It has always been insisted that Ghent put the idea of the Oligarchy into the minds of the great capitalists. This belief persists throughout the literature of the three centuries of the Iron Heel, and even in the literature of the first century of the Brotherhood of Man. Today we know better, but our knowledge does not overcome the fact that Ghent remains the most abused innocent man in all history.

[2] As a sample of the decisions of the courts averse to labour, the following instances are given. In the coalmining regions the employment of children was notorious. In A.D. 1905, labour succeeded in getting a law passed in Pennsylvania providing that proof of the age of the child and of certain educational qualifications must accompany the oath of the parent. This was promptly declared unconstitutional by the Luzerne County Court, on the ground that it violated the Fourteenth Amendment in that it discriminated

'You run ahead too fast,' O'Connor answered. 'You don't know all the ways out. There is another way out. We know what we're about. We're sick of strikes. They've got us beaten that way to a frazzle. But I don't think we'll ever need to call our men out again.'

'What is your way out?' Ernest demanded bluntly.

O'Connor laughed and shook his head. 'I can tell you this much: We've not been asleep. And we're not dreaming now.'

'There's nothing to be afraid of, or ashamed of, I hope,' Ernest challenged.

'I guess we know our business best,' was the retort.

'It's a dark business, from the way you hide it,' Ernest said with growing anger.

'We've paid for our experience in sweat and blood, and we've earned all that's coming to us,' was the reply. 'Charity begins at home.'

'If you're afraid to tell me your way out, I'll tell it to you.' Ernest's blood was up. 'You're going in for grab-sharing. You've made terms with the enemy, that's what you've done. You've sold out the cause of labour, of all labour. You are leaving the battle-field like cowards.'

'I'm not saying anything,' O'Connor answered sullenly. 'Only I guess we know what's best for us a little bit better than you do.'

'And you don't care a cent for what is best for the rest of labour. You kick it into the ditch.'

'I'm not saying anything,' O'Connor replied, 'except that I'm president of the Machinists' Association, and it's my business to consider the interests of the men I represent, that's all.'

---

between individuals of the same class—namely, children above fourteen years of age and children below. The state court sustained the decision. The New York Court of Special Sessions in A.D. 1905, declared unconstitutional the law prohibiting minors and women from working in factories after nine o'clock at night, the ground taken being that such a law was 'class legislation.' Again the bakers of that time were terribly overworked. The New York Legislature passed a law restricting work in bakeries to ten hours a day. In A.D. 1906, the Supreme Court of the United States declared this law to be unconstitutional. In part the decision read: *'There is no reasonable ground for interfering with the liberty of persons or the right of free contract by determining the hours of labour in the occupation of a baker.'*

And then, when the labour leaders had left, Ernest, with the calmness of defeat, outlined to me the course of events to come.

'The socialists used to foretell with joy,' he said, 'of the coming of the day when organised labour, defeated on the industrial field, would come over on to the political field. Well, the Iron Heel has defeated the labour unions on the industrial field and driven them over to the political field; and instead of this being joyful for us, it will be a source of grief. The Iron Heel learned its lesson. We showed it our power in the general strike. It has taken steps to prevent another general strike.'

'But how?' I asked.

'Simply by subsidising the great unions. They won't join in the next general strike. Therefore it won't be a general strike.'

'But the Iron Heel can't maintain so costly a programme for ever,' I objected.

'Oh, it hasn't subsidised all of the unions. That's not necessary. Here is what is going to happen. Wages are going to be advanced and hours shortened in the railroad unions, the iron and steel workers' unions, and the engineer and machinist unions. In these unions more favourable conditions will continue to prevail. Membership in these unions will become like seats in Paradise.'

'Still I don't see,' I objected. 'What is to become of the other unions? There are far more unions outside of this combination than in it.'

'The other unions will be ground out of existence—all of them. For, don't you see, the railway men, machinists and engineers, iron and steel workers, do all of the vitally essential work in our machine civilisation. Assured of their faithfulness, the Iron Heel can snap its fingers at all the rest of labour. Iron, steel, coal, machinery, and transportation constitute the backbone of the whole industrial fabric.'

'But coal?' I queried. 'There are nearly a million coal miners.'

'They are practically unskilled labour. They will not count. Their wages will go down and their hours will increase. They will be slaves like all the rest of us, and they will become about the most bestial of all of us. They will be compelled to work, just as the farmers are compelled to work now for the masters who robbed them of their land. And the same with all the other unions outside the combination. Watch them wobble and go to pieces, and their members become slaves driven to toil by empty stomachs and the law of the land.

' Do you know what will happen to Farley[3] and his strike-breakers? I'll tell you. Strike-breaking as an occupation will cease. There won't be any more strikes. In place of strikes will be slave revolts. Farley and his gang will be promoted to slave-driving. Oh, it won't be called that; it will be called enforcing the law of the land that compels the labourers to work. It simply prolongs the fight, this treachery of the big unions. Heaven only knows now where and when the Revolution will triumph.'

' But with such a powerful combination as the Oligarchy and the big unions, is there any reason to believe that the Revolution will ever triumph?' I queried. ' May not the combination endure for ever?'

He shook his head. ' One of our generalisations is that every system founded upon class and caste contains within itself the germs of its own decay. When a system is founded upon class, how can caste be prevented? The Iron Heel will not be able to prevent it, and in the end caste will destroy the Iron Heel. The oligarchs have already developed caste among themselves; but wait until the favoured unions develop caste. The Iron Heel will use all its power to prevent it, but it will fail.

' In the favoured unions are the flower of the American workingmen. They are strong, efficient men. They have become members of those unions through competition for place. Every fit workman in the United States will be possessed by the ambition to become a member of the favoured unions. The Oligarchy will encourage such ambition and the consequent competition. Thus will the strong men, who might else be revolutionists, be won away and their strength used to bolster the Oligarchy.

' On the other hand, the labour castes, the members of the favoured unions, will strive to make their organisations

[3] James Farley—a notorious strike-breaker of the period. A man more courageous than ethical, and of undeniable ability. He rose high under the rule of the Iron Heel and finally was translated into the oligarch class. He was assassinated in 1932 by Sarah Jenkins, whose husband, thirty years before, had been killed by Farley's strike-breakers.

into close corporations. And they will succeed. Membership in the labour castes will become hereditary. Sons will succeed fathers, and there will be no inflow of new strength from that eternal reservoir of strength, the common people. This will mean deterioration of the labour castes, and in the end they will become weaker and weaker. At the same time, as an institution, they will become temporarily all-powerful. They will be like the guards of the palace in old Rome, and there will be palace revolutions whereby the labour castes will seize the reins of power. And there will be counter-palace revolutions of the oligarchs, and sometimes the one, and sometimes the other, will be in power. And through it all the inevitable caste-weakening will go on, so that in the end the common people will come into their own.'

This foreshadowing of a slow social evolution was made when Ernest was first depressed by the defection of the great unions. I never agreed with him in it, and I disagree now, as I write these lines, more heartily than ever; for even now, though Ernest is gone, we are on the verge of the revolt that will sweep all oligarchies away. Yet I have here given Ernest's prophecy because it was his prophecy. In spite of his belief in it, he worked like a giant against it, and he, more than any man, has made possible the revolt that even now waits the signal to burst forth.[4]

'But if the Oligarchy persists,' I asked him that evening, 'what will become of the great surpluses that will fall to its share every year?'

'The surpluses will have to be expended somehow,' he answered; 'and trust the oligarchs to find a way. Magnificent roads will be built. There will be great achievements in science, and especially in art. When the oligarchs have completely mastered the people, they will have time to spare for other things. They will become worshippers of beauty. They will become art-lovers. And under their direction, and generously rewarded, will toil the artists. The result will be great art; for no longer, as up to yesterday, will the artists pander to the bourgeois taste of the middle class. It will be great art, I tell you, and wonder cities will arise that will make

[4] Everhard's social foresight was remarkable. As clearly as in the light of past events, he saw the defection of the favoured unions, the rise and the slow decay of the labour castes, and the struggle between the decaying oligarchs and labour castes for control of the great governmental machine.

tawdry and cheap the cities of old time. And in these cities will the oligarchs dwell and worship beauty.[5]

' Thus will the surplus be constantly expended while labour does the work. The building of these great works and cities will give a starvation ration to millions of common labourers, for the enormous bulk of the surplus will compel an equally enormous expenditure, and the oligarchs will build for a thousand years—ay, for ten thousand years. They will build as the Egyptians and the Babylonians never dreamed of building; and when the oligarchs have passed away, their great roads and their wonder cities will remain for the brotherhood of labour to tread upon and dwell within.[6]

' These things the oligarchs will do because they cannot help doing them. These great works will be the form their expenditure of the surplus will take, and in the same way that the ruling classes of Egypt of long ago expended the surplus they robbed from the people by the building of temples and pyramids. Under the oligarchs will flourish, not a priest class, but an artist class. And in place of the merchant class of bourgeoisie will be the labour castes. And beneath will be the abyss, wherein will fester and starve and rot, and ever renew itself, the common people, the great bulk of the population. And in the end, who knows in what day, the common people will rise up out of the abyss; the labour castes and the Oligarchy will crumble away; and then, at last, after the travail of the centuries, will it be the day of the common man. I had thought to see that day; but now I know that I shall never see it.'

He paused and looked at me, and added:

' Social evolution is exasperatingly slow, isn't it, sweet-heart?'

My arms were about him, and his head was on my breast.

---

[5] We cannot but marvel at Everhard's foresight. Before ever the thought of wonder cities like Ardis and Asgard entered the minds of the oligarchs, Everhard saw those cities and the inevitable necessity for their creation.

[6] And since that day of prophecy have passed away the three centuries of the Iron Heel and the four centuries of the Brother-hood of Man, and today we tread the roads and dwell in the cities that the oligarchs built. It is true, we are even now building still more wonderful wonder cities, but the wonder cities of the oligarchs endure, and I write these lines in Ardis, one of the most wonderful of them all.

'Sing me to sleep,' he murmured whimsically. 'I have had a visioning, and I wish to forget.'

CHAPTER 15

Last Days

I T W A S near the end of January, 1913, that the changed attitude of the Oligarchy towards the favoured unions was made public. The newspapers published information of an unprecedented rise in wages and shortening of hours for the railroad employees, the iron and steel workers, and the engineers and machinists. But the whole truth was not told. The oligarchs did not dare permit the telling of the whole truth. In reality the wages had been raised much higher, and the privileges were correspondingly greater. All this was secret, but secrets will out. Members of the favoured unions told their wives, and the wives gossiped, and soon all the labour world knew what had happened.

It was merely the logical development of what in the nineteenth century had been known as grab-sharing. In the industrial warfare of that time, profit-sharing had been tried. That is, the capitalists had striven to placate the workers by interesting them financially in their work. But profit-sharing, as a system, was ridiculous and impossible. Profit-sharing could be successful only in isolated cases in the midst of a system of industrial strife; for if all labour and all capital shared profits, the same conditions would obtain as did obtain when there was no profit-sharing.

So, out of the unpractical idea of profit-sharing, arose the practical idea of grab-sharing. ' Give us more pay and charge it to the public,' was the slogan of the strong unions. And here and there this selfish policy worked successfully. In charging it to the public, it was charged to the great mass of unorganised labour and of weakly organised labour. These workers actually paid the increased wages of their stronger brothers who were members of unions that were labour monopolies. This idea, as I say, was merely carried to its logical conclusion, on a large scale, by the combination of the oligarchs and the favoured unions.[1]

---

[1] All the railroad unions entered into this combination with the oligarchs, and it is of interest to note that the first definite applica-

As soon as the secret of the defection of the favoured unions leaked out, there were rumblings and mutterings in the labour world. Next the favoured unions withdrew from the international organisations and broke off all affiliations. Then came trouble and violence. The members of the favoured unions were branded as traitors, and in saloons and brothels, on the streets and at work, and, in fact, everywhere, they were assaulted by the comrades they had so treacherously deserted.

Countless heads were broken, and there were many killed. No member of the favoured unions was safe. They gathered together in bands in order to go to work or to return from work. They walked always in the middle of the street. On the sidewalk they were liable to have their skulls crushed by bricks and cobblestones thrown from windows and housetops. They were permitted to carry weapons, and the authorities aided them in every way. Their persecutors were sentenced to long terms in prison, where they were harshly treated; while no man, not a member of the favoured unions, was permitted to carry weapons. Violation of this law was made a high misdemeanour and punished accordingly.

Outraged labour continued to wreak vengeance on the traitors. Caste lines formed automatically. The children of the traitors were persecuted by the children of the workers who had been betrayed, until it was impossible for the former to play on the streets or to attend the public schools. Also, the wives and families of the traitors were ostracised, while the corner groceryman who sold provisions to them was boycotted.

As a result, driven back upon themselves from every side, the traitors and their families became clannish. Finding it impossible to dwell in safety in the midst of the betrayed

---

tion of the policy of profit-grabbing was made by a railroad union in the nineteenth century A.D., namely, the Brotherhood of Locomotive Engineers. P. M. Arthur was for twenty years Grand Chief of the Brotherhood. After the strike on the Pennsylvania Railroad in 1877, he broached a scheme to have the Locomotive Engineers make terms with the railroads and to 'go it alone' so far as the rest of the labour unions were concerned. This scheme was eminently successful. It was as successful as it was selfish, and out of it was coined the word 'arthurisation' to denote grab-sharing on the part of labour unions. This word 'arthurisation' has long puzzled the etymologists, but its derivation, I hope, is now made clear.

proletariat, they moved into new localities inhabited by themselves alone. In this they were favoured by the oligarchs. Good dwellings, modern and sanitary, were built for them, surrounded by spacious yards, and separated here and there by parks and playgrounds. Their children attended schools especially built for them, and in these schools manual training and applied science were specialised upon. Thus, and unavoidably, at the very beginning, out of this segregation arose caste. The members of the favoured unions became the aristocracy of labour. They were set apart from the rest of labour. They were better housed, better clothed, better fed, better treated. They were grab-sharing with a vengeance.

In the meantime, the rest of the working class was more harshly treated. Many little privileges were taken away from it, while its wages and its standard of living steadily sank down. Incidentally its public schools deteriorated, and education slowly ceased to be compulsory. The increase in the younger generation of children who could not read nor write was perilous.

The capture of the world-market by the United States had disrupted the rest of the world. Institutions and governments were everywhere crashing or transforming. Germany, Italy, France, Australia, and New Zealand were busy forming co-operative commonwealths. The British Empire was falling apart. England's hands were full. In India revolt was in full swing. The cry in all Asia was, ' Asia for the Asiatics!' And behind this cry was Japan, ever urging and aiding the yellow and brown races against the white. And while Japan dreamed of continental empire and strove to realise the dream, she suppressed her own proletarian revolution. It was a simple war of the castes, Coolie *versus* Samurai, and the coolie socialists were executed by tens of thousands. Forty thousand were killed in the street-fighting of Tokio, and in the futile assault on the Mikado's palace. Kobe was a shambles; the slaughter of the cotton operatives by machine-guns became classic as the most terrific execution ever achieved by modern war machines. Most savage of all was the Japanese Oligarchy that arose. Japan dominated the East, and took to herself the whole Asiatic portion of the world-market, with the exception of India.

England managed to crush her own proletarian revolution and to hold on to India, though she was brought to the verge of exhaustion. Also, she was compelled to let her great

colonies slip away from her. So it was that the socialists succeeded in making Australia and New Zealand into co-operative commonwealths. And it was for the same reason that
Canada was lost to the mother country. But Canada crushed
her own socialist revolution, being aided in this by the Iron
Heel. At the same time, the Iron Heel helped Mexico and
Cuba to put down revolt. The result was that the Iron Heel
was firmly established in the New World. It had welded into
one compact political mass the whole of North America from
the Panama Canal to the Arctic Ocean.

And England, at the sacrifice of her great colonies, had
succeeded only in retaining India. But this was no more than
temporary. The struggle with Japan and the rest of Asia for
India was merely delayed. England was destined shortly to
lose India, while behind that event loomed the struggle
between a united Asia and the world.

And while all the world was torn with conflict, we of the
United States were not placid and peaceful. The defection of
the great unions had prevented our proletarian revolt, but
violence was everywhere. In addition to the labour troubles,
and the discontent of the farmers and of the remnant of the
middle class, a religious revival had blazed up. An offshoot
of the Seventh Day Adventists sprang into sudden prominence, proclaiming the end of the world.

'Confusion thrice confounded!' Ernest cried. 'How can
we hope for solidarity with all these cross purposes and
conflicts?'

And truly the religious revival assumed formidable propor-
tions. The people, what of their wretchedness, and of their
disappointment in all things earthly, were ripe and eager for
a heaven where industrial tyrants entered no more than
camels passed through needle-eyes. Wild-eyed, itinerant
preachers swarmed over the land; and despite the prohibition
of the civil authorities, and the persecution for disobedience,
the flames of religious frenzy were fanned by countless camp-
meetings.

It was the last days, they claimed, the beginning of the end
of the world. The four winds had been loosed. God had
stirred the nations to strife. It was a time of visions and
miracles, while seers and prophetesses were legion. The
people ceased work by hundreds of thousands and fled to the
mountains, there to await the imminent coming of God and
the rising of the hundred and forty and four thousand to

heaven. But in the meantime God did not come, and they starved to death in great numbers. In their desperation they ravaged the farms for foods, and the consequent tumult and anarchy in the country districts but increased the woes of the poor expropriated farmers.

Also, the farms and warehouses were the property of the Iron Heel. Armies of troops were put into the field, and the fanatics were herded back at the bayonet point to their tasks in the cities. There they broke out in ever recurring mobs and riots. Their leaders were executed for sedition or confined in madhouses. Those who were executed went to their deaths with all the gladness of martyrs. It was a time of madness. The unrest spread. In the swamps and deserts and waste places, from Florida to Alaska, the small groups of Indians that survived were dancing ghost dances and waiting the coming of a Messiah of their own.

And through it all, with a serenity and certitude that was terrifying, continued to rise the form of that monster of the ages, the Oligarchy. With iron hand and iron heel it mastered the surging millions, out of confusion brought order, out of the very chaos wrought its own foundation and structure.

'Just wait till we get in,' the Grangers said—Calvin said it to us in our Pell Street quarters. 'Look at the states we've captured. With you socialists to back us, we'll make them sing another song when we take office.'

'The millions of the discontented and the impoverished are ours,' the socialists said. 'The Grangers have come over to us, the farmers, the middle class, and the labourers. The capitalist system will fall to pieces. In another month we send fifty men to Congress. Two years hence every office will be ours, from the President down to the local dog-catcher.'

To all of which Ernest would shake his head and say:

'How many rifles have you got? Do you know where you can get plenty of lead? When it comes to powder, chemical mixtures are better than mechanical mixtures, you take my word.'

CHAPTER 16

The End

WHEN IT came time for Ernest and me to go to Washington, father did not accompany us. He had become enamoured of proletarian life. He looked upon our slum neighbourhood as a great sociological laboratory, and he had embarked upon an apparently endless orgy of investigation. He chummed with the labourers, and was an intimate in scores of homes. Also, he worked at odd jobs, and the work was play as well as learned investigation, for he delighted in it and was always returning home with copious notes and bubbling over with new adventures. He was the perfect scientist.

There was no need for his working at all, because Ernest managed to earn enough from his translating to take care of the three of us. But father insisted on pursuing his favourite phantom, and a protean phantom it was, judging from the jobs he worked at. I shall never forget the evening he brought home his street pedlar's outfit of shoe-laces and suspenders, nor the time I went into the little corner grocery to make some purchase and had him wait on me. After that I was not surprised when he tended bar for a week in the saloon across the street. He worked as a night watchman, hawked potatoes on the street, pasted labels in a cannery warehouse, was utility man in a paper-box factory, and water-carrier for a street railway construction gang, and even joined the Dishwashers' Union just before it fell to pieces.

I think the Bishop's example, so far as wearing-apparel was concerned, must have fascinated father, for he wore the cheap cotton shirt of the labourer and the overalls with the narrow strap about the hips. Yet one habit remained to him from the old life; he always dressed for dinner, or supper, rather.

I could be happy anywhere with Ernest; and father's happiness in our changed circumstances rounded off my own happiness.

'When I was a boy,' father said, 'I was very curious. I wanted to know why things were and how they came to pass. That was why I became a physicist. The life in me today is just as curious as it was in my boyhood, and it's the being curious that makes life worth living.'

Sometimes he ventured north of Market Street into the shopping and theatre district, where he sold papers, ran errands, and opened cabs. There, one day, closing a cab, he encountered Mr Wickson. In high glee father described the incident to us that evening.

'Wickson looked at me sharply when I closed the door on him, and muttered, "Well, I'll be damned." Just like that he said it, "Well, I'll be damned." His face turned red, and he was so confused that he forgot to tip me. But he must have recovered himself quickly, for the cab hadn't gone fifty feet before it turned around and came back. He leaned out of the door.

'"Look here, professor," he said, "this is too much. What can I do for you?"

'"I closed the cab door for you," I answered. "According to common custom you might give me a dime."

'"Bother that!" he snorted. "I mean something substantial."

'He was certainly serious—a twinge of ossified conscience or something; and so I considered with grave deliberation for a moment.

'His face was quite expectant when I began my answer, but you should have seen it when I finished.

'"You might give me back my home," I said, "and my stock in the Sierra Mills."'

Father paused.

'What did he say?' I questioned eagerly.

'What could he say? He said nothing. But I said, "I hope you are happy." He looked at me curiously. "Tell me, are you happy?" I asked.

'He ordered the cabman to drive on, and went away swearing horribly. And he didn't give me the dime, much less the home and stock; so you see, my dear, your father's street-arab career is beset with disappointments.'

And so it was that father kept on at our Pell Street quarters, while Ernest and I went to Washington. Except for the final consummation, the old order had passed away, and the final consummation was nearer than I dreamed. Contrary to our expectation, no obstacles were raised to prevent the socialist Congressmen from taking their seats. Everything went smoothly, and I laughed at Ernest when he looked upon the very smoothness as something ominous.

We found our socialist comrades confident, optimistic of their strength and of the things they would accomplish. A few Grangers who had been elected to Congress increased our strength, and an elaborate programme of what was to be done was prepared by the united forces. In all of which Ernest joined loyally and energetically, though he could not forbear, now and again, from saying, apropos of nothing in particular, 'When it comes to powder, chemical mixtures are better than mechanical mixtures, you take my word.'

The trouble arose first with the Grangers in the various states they had captured at the last election. There were a dozen of these states, but the Grangers who had been elected were not permitted to take office. The incumbents refused to get out. It was very simple. They merely charged illegality in the elections and wrapped up the whole situation in the inter-minable red tape of the law. The Grangers were powerless. The courts were the last recourse, and the courts were in the hands of their enemies.

This was the moment of danger. If the cheated Grangers became violent, all was lost. How we socialists worked to hold them back! There were days and nights when Ernest never closed his eyes in sleep. The big leaders of the Grangers saw the peril, and were with us to a man. But it was all of no avail. The Oligarchy wanted violence, and it set its agents-provocateurs to work. Without discussion, it was the agents-provocateurs who caused the Peasant Revolt.

In a dozen states the revolt flared up. The expropriated farmers took forcible possession of the state governments. Of course this was unconstitutional, and of course the United States put its soldiers into the field. Everywhere the agents-provocateurs urged the people on. These emissaries of the Iron Heel disguised themselves as artisans, farmers, and farm labourers. In Sacramento, the capital of California, the Grangers had succeeded in maintaining order. Thousands of secret agents were rushed to the devoted city. In mobs composed wholly of themselves, they fired and looted buildings and factories. They worked the people up until they joined them in the pillage. Liquor in large quantities was distributed among the slum classes further to inflame their minds. And then, when all was ready, appeared upon the scene the soldiers of the United States, who were, in reality, the soldiers of the Iron Heel. Eleven thousand men, women, and children were shot down on the streets of Sacramento or murdered in their houses. The national government took possession of the state government, and all was over for California.

And as with California, so elsewhere. Every Granger state was ravaged with violence and washed in blood. First, disorder was precipitated by the secret agents and the Black Hundreds, then the troops were called out. Rioting and mob-rule reigned throughout the rural districts. Day and night the smoke of burning farms, warehouses, villages, and cities filled the sky. Dynamite appeared. Railroad bridges and tunnels were blown up and trains were wrecked. The poor farmers were shot and hanged in great numbers. Reprisals were bitter, and many plutocrats and army officers were murdered. Blood and vengeance were in men's hearts. The regular troops fought the farmers as savagely as had they been Indians. And the regular troops had cause. Twenty-eight hundred of them had been annihilated in a tremendous series of dynamite explosions in Oregon, and in a similar manner, a number of train loads, at different times and places, had been destroyed. So it was that the regular troops fought for their lives as well as did the farmers.

As for the militia, the militia law of 1903 was put into effect, and the workers of one state were compelled, under pain of death, to shoot down their comrade-workers in other states. Of course, the militia law did not work smoothly at first. Many militia officers were murdered, and many militia-men were executed by drumhead court martial. Ernest's prophecy was strikingly fulfilled in the cases of Mr Kowalt and Mr Asmunsen. Both were eligible for the militia, and both were drafted to serve in the punitive expedition that was dispatched from California against the farmers of Missouri. Mr Kowalt and Mr Asmunsen refused to serve. They were given short shift. Drumhead court martial was their portion, and military execution their end. They were shot with their backs to the firing squad.

Many young men fled into the mountains to escape serving in the militia. There they became outlaws, and it was not until more peaceful times that they received their punishment. It was drastic. The government issued a proclamation for all law-abiding citizens to come in from the mountains for a period of three months. When the proclaimed date arrived, half a million soldiers were sent into the mountainous districts everywhere. There was no investigation, no trial. Wherever a man was encountered, he was shot down on the spot. The troops operated on the basis that no man not an outlaw remained in the mountains. Some bands, in strong positions, fought gallantly, but in the end every deserter from the militia met death.

A more immediate lesson, however, was impressed on the minds of the people by the punishment meted out to the Kansas militia. The great Kansas Mutiny occurred at the very beginning of military operations against the Grangers. Six thousand of the militia mutinied. They had been for several weeks very turbulent and sullen, and for that reason had been kept in camp. Their open mutiny, however, was without doubt precipitated by the agents-provocateurs.

On the night of the 22nd of April they arose and murdered their officers, only a small remnant of the latter escaping. This was beyond the scheme of the Iron Heel, for the agents-provocateurs had done their work too well. But everything was grist to the Iron Heel. It had prepared for the outbreak, and the killing of so many officers gave it justification for what followed. As by magic, forty thousand soldiers of the regular army surrounded the malcontents. It was a trap. The wretched militiamen found that their machine-guns had been tampered with, and that the cartridges from the captured magazines did not fit their rifles. They hoisted the white flag of surrender, but it was ignored. There were no survivors. The entire six thousand were annihilated. Common shell and shrapnel were thrown in upon them from a distance, and when, in their desperation, they charged the encircling lines, they were mowed down by the machine-guns. I talked with an eye-witness, and he said that the nearest any militiaman approached the machine-guns was a hundred and fifty yards. The earth was carpeted with the slain, and a final charge of cavalry, with trampling of horse's hoofs, revolvers, and sabres, crushed the wounded into the ground.

Simultaneously with the destruction of the Grangers came the revolt of the coal miners. It was the expiring effort of organised labour. Three-quarters of a million of miners went out on strike. But they were too widely scattered over the country to advantage from their own strength. They were segregated in their own districts and beaten into submission. This was the first great slave-drive. Pocock[1] won his spurs as

---

[1] Albert Pocock, another of the notorious strike-breakers of earlier

a slave-driver and earned the undying hatred of the proletariat. Countless attempts were made upon his life, but he
seemed to bear a charmed existence. It was he who was
responsible for the introduction of the Russian passport system among the miners, and the denial of their right of removal
from one part of the country to another.

In the meantime, the socialists held firm. While the
Grangers expired in flame and blood, and organised labour
was disrupted, the socialists held their peace and perfected
their secret organisation. In vain the Grangers pleaded with
us. We rightly contended that any revolt on our part was
virtually suicide for the whole Revolution. The Iron Heel,
at first dubious about dealing with the entire proletariat at
one time, had found the work easier than it had expected,
and would have asked nothing better than an uprising on
our part. But we avoided the issue, in spite of the fact that
agents-provocateurs swarmed in our midst. In those early
days the agents of the Iron Heel were clumsy in their methods.
They had much to learn, and in the meantime our Fighting
Groups weeded them out. It was bitter, bloody work, but we
were fighting for life and for the Revolution, and we had to
fight the enemy with its own weapons. Yet we were fair. No
agent of the Iron Heel was executed without a trial. We may
have made mistakes, but if so, very rarely. The bravest and
the most combative and self-sacrificing of our comrades went
into the Fighting Groups. Once, after ten years had passed,
Ernest made a calculation from figures furnished by the
chiefs of the Fighting Groups, and his conclusion was that the
average life of a man or woman after becoming a member
was five years. The comrades of the Fighting Groups were

---

years, who, to the day of his death successfully held all the coal
miners of the country to their task. He was succeeded by his son,
Lewis Pocock, and for five generations this remarkable line of
slave-drivers handled the coal mines. The elder Pocock, known as
Pocock I, has been described as follows: ' A long, lean head, semi-
circled by a fringe of brown and grey hair, with big cheek-bones
and a heavy chin . . . a pale face, lustreless grey eyes, a metallic
voice, and a languid manner.' He was born of humble parents and
began his career as a bar-tender. He next became a private
detective for a street railway corporation, and by suppressive steps
developed into a professional strike-breaker. Pocock V, the last
of the line, was blown up in a pump house by a bomb during
a petty revolt of the miners in the Indian Territory. This occurred
in A.D. 2073.

heroes all, and the peculiar thing about it was that they were opposed to the taking of life. They violated their own natures, yet they loved liberty and knew of no sacrifice too great to make for the Cause. [2]

The task we set ourselves was threefold. First, the weeding out from our circles of the secret agents of the Oligarchy. Second, the organising of the Fighting Groups, and, outside of them, of the general secret organisation of the Revolution. And third, the introduction of our own secret agents into every branch of the Oligarchy—into the labour castes and especially among the telegraphers and secretaries and clerks, into the army, the agents-provocateurs, and the slave-drivers. It was slow work and perilous, and often were our efforts rewarded with costly failures.

The Iron Heel had triumphed in open warfare, but we held

---

[2] These Fighting Groups were modelled somewhat after the Fighting Organisation of the Russian Revolution, and, despite the unceasing efforts of the Iron Heel, these Groups persisted throughout the three centuries of its existence. Composed of men and women actuated by lofty purpose and unafraid to die, the Fighting Groups exercised tremendous influence and tempered the savage brutality of the rulers. Not alone was their work confined to unseen warfare with the secret agents of the Oligarchy. The oligarchs themselves were compelled to listen to the decrees of the Groups, and often, when they disobeyed, were punished by death —and likewise with the subordinates of the oligarchs, with the officers of the army and the leaders of the labour castes.

Stern justice was meted out by these organised avengers, but most remarkable was their passionless and judicial procedure. There were no snap judgments. When a man was captured he was given fair trial and opportunity for defence. Of necessity, many men were tried and condemned by proxy, as in the case of General Lampton. This occurred in A.D. 2138. Possibly the most bloodthirsty and malignant of all the mercenaries that ever served the Iron Heel, he was informed by the Fighting Groups that they had tried him, found him guilty, and condemned him to death—and this, after three warnings for him to cease from his ferocious treatment of the proletariat. After his condemnation he surrounded himself with a myriad protective devices. Years passed, and in vain the Fighting Groups strove to execute their decree. Comrade after comrade, men and women, failed in their attempts, and were cruelly executed by the Oligarchy. It was the case of General Lampton that revived crucifixion as a legal method of execution. But in the end the condemned man found his executioner in the form of a slender girl of seventeen, Madeline Provence, who, to accomplish her purpose, served two years in his palace as a seamstress to the household. She died in solitary confinement after horrible and prolonged torture; but today she stands in imperishour own in the new warfare, strange and awful and subterranean, that we instituted. All was unseen, much was unguessed; the blind fought the blind; and yet through it all was order, purpose, control. We permeated the entire organisation of the Iron Heel with our agents, while our own organisation was permeated with the agents of the Iron Heel. It was warfare dark and devious, replete with intrigue and conspiracy, plot and counterplot. And behind all, ever menacing, was death, violent and terrible. Men and women disappeared, our nearest and dearest comrades. We saw them today. Tomorrow they were gone; we never saw them again, and we knew that they had died.

There was no trust, no confidence anywhere. The man who plotted beside us, for all we knew, might be an agent of the Iron Heel. We mined the organisation of the Iron Heel with our secret agents, and the Iron Heel countermined with its secret agents inside its own organisation. And it was the same with our organisation. And despite the absence of confidence and trust we were compelled to base our every effort on confidence and trust. Often were we betrayed. Men were weak. The Iron Heel could offer money, leisure, the joys and pleasures that waited in the repose of the wonder cities. We could offer nothing but the satisfaction of being faithful to a noble ideal. As for the rest, the wages of those who were loyal were unceasing peril, torture, and death.

Men were weak, I say, and because of their weakness we were compelled to make the only other reward that was within our power. It was the reward of death. Out of necessity

---

able bronze in the Pantheon of Brotherhood in the wonder city of Serles.

We, who by personal experience know nothing of bloodshed, must not judge harshly the heroes of the Fighting Groups. They gave up their lives for humanity, no sacrifice was too great for them to accomplish, while inexorable necessity compelled them to bloody expression in an age of blood. The Fighting Groups constituted the one thorn in the side of the Iron Heel that the Iron Heel could never remove. Everhard was the father of this curious army, and its accomplishments and successful persistence for three hundred years bear witness to the wisdom with which he organised and the solid foundation he laid for the succeeding generations to build upon. In some respects, despite his great economic and sociological contributions, and his work as a general leader in the Revolution, his organisation of the Fighting Groups must be regarded as his greatest achievement.

we had to punish our traitors. For every man who betrayed us, from one to a dozen faithful avengers were loosed upon his heels. We might fail to carry out our decrees against our enemies, such as the Pococks, for instance; but the one thing we could not afford to fail in was the punishment of our own traitors. Comrades turned traitor by permission, in order to win to the wonder cities and there execute our sentences on the real traitors. In fact, so terrible did we make ourselves, that it became a greater peril to betray us than to remain loyal to us.

The Revolution took on largely the character of religion. We worshipped at the shrine of the Revolution, which was the shrine of liberty. It was the divine flashing through us. Men and women devoted their lives to the Cause, and new-born babes were sealed to it as of old they had been sealed to the service of God. We were lovers of Humanity.

CHAPTER 17

The Scarlet Livery

W I T H T H E destruction of the Granger states, the Grangers in Congress disappeared. They were being tried for high treason, and their places were taken by the creatures of the Iron Heel. The socialists were in a pitiful minority, and they knew that their end was near. Congress and the Senate were empty pretences, farces. Public questions were gravely debated and passed upon according to the old forms, while in reality all that was done was to give the stamp of constitutional procedure to the mandates of the Oligarchy.

Ernest was in the thick of the fight when the end came. It was in the debate on the bill to assist the unemployed. The hard times of the preceding year had thrust great masses of the proletariat beneath the starvation line, and the continued and wide-reaching disorder had but sunk them deeper. Millions of people were starving, while the oligarchs and their supporters were surfeiting on the surplus.[1] We called these wretched people the people of the abyss,[2] and it was to alleviate their awful suffering that the socialists had

---

[1] The same conditions obtained in the nineteenth century A.D., under British rule in India. The natives died of starvation by the million, while their rulers robbed them of the fruits of their toil and expended it on magnificent pageants and mumbo-jumbo fooleries. Perforce, in this enlightened age, we have much to blush for in the acts of our ancestors. Our only consolation is philosophic. We must accept the capitalistic stage in social evolution as about on a par with the earlier monkey age. The human had to pass through those stages in its rise from the mire and slime of low organic life. It was inevitable that much of the mire and slime should cling and be not easily shaken off.

[2] *The people of the abyss*—this phrase was struck out by the genius of H. G. Wells in the late nineteenth century A.D. Wells was a sociological seer, sane and normal as well as warm human. Many fragments of his work have come down to us, while two of his greatest achievements, *Anticipations* and *Mankind in the Making,* have come down intact. Before the oligarchs, and before Everhard, Wells speculated upon the building of the wonder cities, though in his writings they are referred to as 'pleasure cities.'

introduced the unemployed bill. But this was not to the fancy of the Iron Heel. In its own way it was preparing to set these millions to work, but the way was not our way, wherefore it had issued its orders that our bill should be voted down. Ernest and his fellows knew that their effort was futile, but they were tired of the suspense. They wanted something to happen. They were accomplishing nothing, and the best they hoped for was the putting of an end to the legislative farce in which they were unwilling players. They knew not what end would come, but they never anticipated a more disastrous end than the one that did come.

I sat in the gallery that day. We all knew that something terrible was imminent. It was in the air, and its presence was made visible by the armed soldiers drawn up in lines in the corridors, and by the officers grouped in the entrances to the House itself. The Oligarchy was about to strike. Ernest was speaking. He was describing the sufferings of the unemployed, as if with the wild idea of in some way touching their hearts and consciences; but the Republican and Democratic members sneered and jeered at him, and there was uproar and confusion. Ernest abruptly changed front.

' I know nothing that I may say can influence you,' he said. ' You have no souls to be influenced. You are spineless, flaccid things. You pompously call yourselves Republicans and Democrats. There is no Republican Party. There is no Democratic Party. There are no Republicans nor Democrats in this House. You are lick-spittlers and panderers, the creatures of the Plutocracy. You talk verbosely in antiquated terminology of your love of liberty, and all the while you wear the scarlet livery of the Iron Heel.'

Here the shouting and the cries of ' Order! order!' drowned his voice, and he stood disdainfully till the din had somewhat subsided. He waved his hand to include all of them, turned to his own comrades, and said:

' Listen to the bellowing of the well-fed beasts.'

Pandemonium broke out again. The Speaker rapped for order and glanced expectantly at the officers in the doorways. There were cries of ' Sedition!' and a great rotund New York member began shouting ' Anarchist!' at Ernest. And Ernest was not pleasant to look at. Every fighting fibre of him was quivering, and his face was the face of a fighting animal, withal he was cool and collected.

' Remember,' he said, in a voice that made itself heard

above the din, 'that as you show mercy now to the proletariat, some day will that same proletariat show mercy to
you.'

The cries of 'Sedition!' and 'Anarchist!' redoubled.

'I know that you will not vote for this bill,' Ernest went
on. 'You have received the command from your masters to
vote against it, and yet you call me anarchist. You who have
destroyed the government of the people, and who shamelessly
flaunt your scarlet shame in public places, call me anarchist.
I do not believe in hell-fire and brimstone; but in moments
like this I regret my unbelief. Nay, in moments like this I
almost do believe. Surely there must be a hell, for in no less
place could it be possible for you to receive punishment
adequate to your crimes. So long as you exist, there is a vital
need for hell-fire in the Cosmos.'

There was a movement in the doorways. Ernest, the
Speaker, all the members turned to see.

'Why do you not call your soldiers in, Mr Speaker, and
bid them do their work?' Ernest demanded. 'They should
carry out your plan with expedition.'

'There are other plans afoot,' was the retort. 'That is why
the soldiers are present.'

'Our plans, I suppose,' Ernest sneered. 'Assassination or
something kindred.'

But at the word 'assassination' the uproar broke out again.
Ernest could not make himself heard, but he remained on his
feet waiting for a lull. And then it happened. From my place
in the gallery I saw nothing except the flash of the explosion.
The roar of it filled my ears, and I saw Ernest reeling and
falling in a swirl of smoke, and the soldiers rushing up all
the aisles. His comrades were on their feet, wild with anger,
capable of any violence. But Ernest steadied himself for a
moment, and waved his arms for silence.

'It is a plot!' his voice rang out in warning to his comrades. 'Do nothing, or you will be destroyed.'

Then he slowly sank down, and the soldiers reached him.
The next moment soldiers were clearing the galleries and I
saw no more.

Though he was my husband, I was not permitted to get to
him. When I announced who I was, I was promptly placed
under arrest. And at the same time were arrested all socialist
Congressmen in Washington, including the unfortunate Simpson, who lay ill with typhoid fever in his hotel.

The trial was prompt and brief. The men were fore-
doomed. The wonder was that Ernest was not executed. This
was a blunder on the part of the Oligarchy, and a costly one.
But the Oligarchy was too confident in those days. It was
drunk with success, and little did it dream that that small
handful of heroes had within them the power to rock it to its
foundations. Tomorrow, when the Great Revolt breaks out
and all the world resounds with the tramp, tramp of the
millions, the Oligarchy will realise, and too late, how mightily
that band of heroes has grown.[3]

As a revolutionist myself, as one on the inside who knew
the hopes and fears and secret plans of the revolutionists, I
am fitted to answer, as very few are, the charge that they
were guilty of exploding the bomb in Congress. And I can
say flatly, without qualification or doubt of any sort, that the
socialists, in Congress and out, had no hand in the affair.
Who threw the bomb we do not know, but the one thing we
are absolutely sure of is that we did not throw it.

On the other hand, there is evidence to show that the Iron
Heel was responsible for the act. Of course, we cannot prove
this. Our conclusion is merely presumptive. But here are such
facts as we do know. It had been reported to the Speaker of
the House, by secret-service agents of the government, that
the socialist Congressmen were about to resort to terroristic
tactics, and that they had decided upon the day when their

[3] Avis Everhard took for granted that her narrative would be
read in her own day, and so omits to mention the outcome of the
trial for high treason. Many other similar disconcerting omissions
will be noticed in the Manuscript. Fifty-two socialist Congressmen
were tried, and all were found guilty. Strange to relate, not one
received the death sentence. Everhard and eleven others, among
whom were Theodore Donnelson and Matthew Kent, received life
imprisonment. The remaining forty received sentences varying
from thirty to forty-five years; while Arthur Simpson, referred to
in the Manuscript as being ill of typhoid fever at the time of the
explosion, received only fifteen years. It is the tradition that he
died of starvation in solitary confinement, and this harsh treatment is explained as having been caused by his uncompromising
stubbornness and his fiery and tactless hatred for all men that
served the despotism. He died in Cabanas in Cuba, where three of
his comrades were also confined. The fifty-two socialist Congressmen were confined in military fortresses scattered all over the
United States. Thus, Du Bois and Woods were held in Porto Rico,
while Everhard and Merryweather were placed in Alcatraz, an
island in San Francisco Bay that had already seen long service as
a military prison.

tactics would go into effect. This day was the very day of the explosion. Wherefore the Capitol had been packed with troops in anticipation. Since we knew nothing about the bomb, and since a bomb actually was exploded, and since the authorities had prepared in advance for the explosion, it is only fair to conclude that the Iron Heel did know. Furthermore, we charge that the Iron Heel was guilty of the outrage, and that the Iron Heel planned and perpetrated the outrage for the purpose of foisting the guilt on our shoulders and bringing about our destruction.

From the Speaker the warning leaked out to all the creatures in the House that wore the scarlet livery. They knew, while Ernest was speaking, that some violent act was to be committed. And to do them justice, they honestly believed that the act was to be committed by the socialists. At the trial, and still with honest belief, several testified to having seen Ernest prepare to throw the bomb, and that it exploded prematurely. Of course they saw nothing of the sort. In the fevered imagination of fear they thought they saw, that was all.

As Ernest said at the trial: ' Does it stand to reason, if I were going to throw a bomb, that I should elect to throw a feeble little squib like the one that was thrown? There wasn't enough powder in it. It made a lot of smoke, but hurt no one except me. It exploded right at my feet, and yet it did not kill me. Believe me, when I get to throwing bombs, I'll do damage. There'll be more than smoke in my petards.'

In return it was argued by the prosecution that the weakness of the bomb was a blunder on the part of the socialists, just as its premature explosion, caused by Ernest's losing his nerve and dropping it, was a blunder. And to clinch the argument, there were the several Congressmen who testified to having seen Ernest fumble and drop the bomb.

As for ourselves, not one of us knew how the bomb was thrown. Ernest told me that the fraction of an instant before it exploded he both heard and saw it strike at his feet. He testified to this at the trial, but no one believed him. Besides the whole thing, in popular slang, was ' cooked up '. The Iron Heel had made up its mind to destroy us, and there was no withstanding it.

There is a saying that truth will out. I have come to doubt the saying. Nineteen years have elapsed, and despite our untiring efforts, we have failed to find the man who really did throw the bomb. Undoubtedly he was some emissary of the Iron Heel, but he has escaped detection. We have never got the slightest clue to his identity. And now, at this late date, nothing remains but for the affair to take its place among the mysteries of history.[4]

[4] Avis Everhard would have had to live for many generations ere she could have seen the clearing up of this particular mystery. A little less than a hundred years ago, and a little more than six hundred years after her death, the confession of Pervaise was discovered in the secret archives of the Vatican. It is perhaps well to tell a little something about this obscure document, which, in the main, is of interest to the historian only.

Pervaise was an American, of French descent, who, in A.D. 1913, was lying in the Tombs Prison, New York City, awaiting trial for murder. From his confession we learn that he was not a criminal. He was warm-blooded, passionate, emotional. In an insane fit of jealousy he killed his wife—a very common act in those times. Pervaise was mastered by the fear of death, all of which is recounted at length in his confession. To escape death he would have done anything, and the police agents prepared him by assuring him that he could not possibly escape conviction of murder in the first degree when his trial came off. In those days, murder in the first degree was a capital offence. The guilty man or woman was placed in a specially constructed death-chair, and, under the supervision of competent physicians, was destroyed by a current of electricity. This was called electrocution, and it was very popular during that period. Anaesthesia, as a mode of compulsory death, was not introduced until later.

This man, good at heart but with a ferocious animalism close at the surface of his being, lying in jail and expectant of nothing less than death, was prevailed upon by the agents of the Iron Heel to throw the bomb in the House of Representatives. In his confession he states explicitly that he was informed that the bomb was to be a feeble thing and that no lives would be lost. This is directly in line with the fact that the bomb was lightly charged, and that its explosion at Everhard's feet was not deadly.

Pervaise was smuggled into one of the galleries ostensibly closed for repairs. He was to select the moment for the throwing of the bomb, and he naïvely confesses that in his interest in Everhard's tirade and the general commotion raised thereby, he nearly forgot his mission.

Not only was he released from prison in reward for his deed, but he was granted an income for life. This he did not long enjoy. In A.D. 1914, in September, he was stricken with rheumatism of the heart, and lived for three days. It was then that he sent for the Catholic priest, Father Peter Durban, and to him made confession. So important did it seem to the priest that he had the confession taken down in writing and sworn to. What happened after this we can only surmise. The document was certainly important enough to find its way to Rome. Powerful influences must have been brought to bear, hence its suppression. For centuries no hint of its existence reached the world. It was not until in the last century that Lorbia, the brilliant Italian scholar, stumbled upon it quite by chance during his researches in the Vatican.

There is today no doubt whatever that the Iron Heel was responsible for the bomb that exploded in the House of Representatives in A.D. 1913. Even though the Pervaise confession had never come to light, no reasonable doubt could obtain; for the act in question, that sent fifty-two Congressmen to prison, was on a par with countless other acts committed by the oligarchs, and, before them, by the capitalists.

There is the classic instance of the ferocious and wanton judicial murder of the innocent and so-called Haymarket Anarchists in Chicago in the penultimate decade of the nineteenth century A.D. In a category by itself is the deliberate burning and destruction of capitalist property by the capitalists themselves. For such destruction of property innocent men were frequently punished—' railroaded ' in the parlance of the times.

In the labour troubles of the first decade of the twentieth century A.D., between the capitalists and the Western Federation of Miners, similar but more bloody tactics were employed. The railroad station at Independence was blown up by the agents of the capitalists. Thirteen men were killed, and many more were wounded. And then the capitalists, controlling the legislative and judicial machinery of the state of Colorado, charged the miners with the crime and came very near to convicting them. Romaines, one of the tools in this affair, like Pervaise, was lying in jail in another state, Kansas, awaiting trial, when he was approached by the agents of the capitalists. But, unlike Pervaise, the confession of Romaines was made public in his own time.

Then, during this same period, there was the case of Moyer and Haywood, two strong, fearless leaders of labour. One was president and the other was secretary of the Western Federation of Miners. The ex-governor of Idaho had been mysteriously murdered. The crime, at the time, was openly charged to the mine owners by the socialists and miners. Nevertheless, in violation of the national and state constitutions, and by means of conspiracy on the parts of the governors of Idaho and Colorado, Moyer and Haywood were kidnapped, thrown into jail, and charged with the murder. It was this instance that provoked from Eugene V. Debs, national leader of the American socialists at the time, the following words: ' *The labour leaders that cannot be bribed nor bullied, must be ambushed and murdered. The only crime of Moyer and Haywood is that they have been unswervingly true to the working class. The capitalists have stolen our country, debauched our politics, defiled our judiciary, and ridden over us roughshod, and now they propose to murder those who will not abjectly surrender to their brutal dominion. The governors of Colorado and Idaho are but executing the mandates of their masters, the Plutocracy. The issue is the Workers versus the Plutocracy. If they strike the first violent blow, we will strike the last.*'

CHAPTER 18

In the Shadow of Sonoma

O F M Y S E L F, during this period, there is not much to say. For six months I was kept in prison, though charged with no crime. I was a *suspect*—a word of fear that all revolutionists were soon to come to know. But our own nascent secret service was beginning to work. By the end of my second month in prison, one of the jailers made himself known as a revolutionist in touch with the organisation. Several weeks later, Joseph Parkhurst, the prison doctor who had just been appointed, proved himself to be a member of one of the Fighting Groups.

Thus, throughout the organisation of the Oligarchy, our own organisation, web-like and spidery, was insinuating itself. And so I was kept in touch with all that was happening in the world without. And furthermore, every one of our imprisoned leaders was in contact with brave comrades who masqueraded in the livery of the Iron Heel. Though Ernest lay in prison three thousand miles away, on the Pacific Coast, I was in unbroken communication with him, and our letters passed regularly back and forth.

The leaders, in prison and out, were able to discuss and direct the campaign. It would have been possible, within a few months, to have effected the escape of some of them; but since imprisonment proved no bar to our activities, it was decided to avoid anything premature. Fifty-two Congressmen were in prison, and fully three hundred more of our leaders. It was planned that they should be delivered simultaneously. If part of them escaped, the vigilance of the oligarchs might be aroused so as to prevent the escape of the remainder. On the other hand, it was held that a simultaneous jail-delivery all over the land would have immense psychological influence on the proletariat. It would show our strength and give confidence.

So it was arranged, when I was released at the end of six months, that I was to disappear and prepare a secure hiding-place for Ernest. To disappear was in itself no easy thing. No sooner did I get my freedom than my footsteps began to be dogged by the spies of the Iron Heel. It was necessary that they should be thrown off the track, and that I should win to California. It is laughable, the way this was accomplished.

Already the passport system, modelled on the Russian, was developing. I dared not cross the continent in my own character. It was necessary that I should be completely lost if ever I was to see Ernest again, for by trailing me after he escaped, he would be caught once more. Again, I could not disguise myself as a proletarian and travel. There remained the disguise of a member of the Oligarchy. While the arch-oligarchs were no more than a handful, there were myriads of lesser ones of the type, say, of Mr Wickson—men, worth a few millions, who were adherents of the arch-oligarchs. The wives and daughters of these lesser oligarchs were legion, and it was decided that I should assume the disguise of such a one. A few years later this would have been impossible, because the passport system was to become so perfect that no man, woman, nor child in all the land was unregistered and unaccounted for in his or her movements.

When the time was ripe, the spies were thrown off my track. An hour later Avis Everhard was no more. At that time one Felice Van Verdighan, accompanied by two maids and a lap-dog, with another maid for the lap-dog,[1] entered a drawing-room on a Pullman,[2] and a few minutes later was speeding west.

The three maids who accompanied me were revolutionists. Two were members of the Fighting Groups, and the third, Grace Holbrook, entered a group the following year, and six months later was executed by the Iron Heel. She it was who waited upon the dog. Of the other two, Bertha Stole disappeared twelve years later, while Anna Roylston still lives and plays an increasingly important part in the Revolution.[3]

---

[1] This ridiculous picture well illustrates the heartless conduct of the masters. While people starved, lap-dogs were waited upon by maids. This was a serious masquerade on the part of Avis Everhard. Life and death and the Cause were in the issue; therefore the picture must be accepted as a true picture. It affords a striking commentary of the times.

[2] *Pullman*—the designation of the more luxurious railway cars of the period and so named from the inventor.

[3] Despite continual and almost inconceivable hazards, Anna Roylston lived to the royal age of ninety-one. As the Pococks defied the executioners of the Fighting Groups, so she defied the executioners of the Iron Heel. She bore a charmed life, and prospered

Without adventure we crossed the United States to California. When the train stopped at Sixteenth Street Station, in Oakland, we alighted, and there Felice Van Verdighan, with her two maids, her lap-dog, and her lap-dog's maid, disappeared for ever. The maids, guided by trusty comrades, were led away. Other comrades took charge of me. Within half an hour after leaving the train I was on board a small fishing boat and out on the waters of San Francisco Bay. The winds baffled, and we drifted aimlessly the greater part of the night. But I saw the lights of Alcatraz where Ernest lay, and found comfort in the thought of nearness to him. By dawn, what with the rowing of the fishermen, we made the Marin Islands. Here we lay in hiding all day, and on the following night, swept on by a flood tide and a fresh wind, we crossed San Pablo Bay in two hours and ran up Petaluma Creek.

Here horses were ready and another comrade, and without delay we were away through the starlight. To the north I could see the loom of Sonoma Mountain, towards which we rode. We left the old town of Sonoma to the right and rode up a canyon that lay between outlying buttresses of the mountain. The wagon-road became a wood-road, the wood-road became a cow-path, and the cow-path dwindled away and ceased among the upland pastures. Straight over Sonoma Mountain we rode. It was the safest route. There was no one to mark our passing.

Dawn caught us on the northern brow, and in the grey light we dropped down through chaparral into red-wood canyons deep and warm with the breath of passing summer. It was old country to me that I knew and loved, and soon I became the guide. The hiding place was mine. I had selected it. We let down the bars and crossed an upland meadow. Next, we went over a low, oak-covered ridge and descended into a smaller meadow. Again we climbed a ridge, this time riding under red-limed madroños and manzanitas of deeper red. The first rays of the sun streamed upon our backs as we

---

amid dangers and alarms. She herself was an executioner for the Fighting Groups, and, known as the Red Virgin, she became one of the inspired figures of the Revolution. When she was an old woman of sixty-nine she shot 'Bloody' Halcliffe down in the midst of his armed escort and got away unscathed. In the end she died peaceably of old age in a secret refuge of the revolutionists in the Ozark mountains.

climbed. A flight of quail thrummed off through the thickets. A big jack-rabbit crossed our path, leaping swiftly and silently like a deer. And then a deer, a many-pronged buck, the sun flashing red-gold from neck and shoulders, cleared the crest of the ridge before us and was gone.

We followed in his wake a space, then dropped down a zigzag trail that he disdained into a group of noble redwoods that stood about a pool of water murky with minerals from the mountain side. I knew every inch of the way. Once a writer friend of mine had owned the ranch; but he, too, had become a revolutionist, though more disastrously than I, for he was already dead and gone, and none knew where nor how. He alone, in the days he had lived, knew the secret of the hiding place for which I was bound. He had bought the ranch for beauty, and paid a round price for it, much to the disgust of the local farmers. He used to tell with great glee how they were wont to shake their heads mournfully at the price, to accomplish ponderously a bit of mental arithmetic, and then to say, ' But you can't make six per cent on it.'

But he was dead now, nor did the ranch descend to his children. Of all men, it was now the property of Mr Wickson, who owned the whole eastern and northern slopes of Sonoma Mountain, running from the Spreckels estate to the divide of Bennett Valley. Out of it he had made a magnificent deer-park, where, over thousands of acres of sweet slopes and glades and canyons, the deer ran almost in primitive wildness. The people who had owned the soil had been driven away. A state home for the feeble-minded had also been demolished to make room for the deer.

To cap it all, Wickson's hunting lodge was a quarter of a mile from my hiding-place. This, instead of being a danger, was an added security. We were sheltered under the very ægis of one of the minor oligarchs. Suspicion, by the nature of the situation, was turned aside. The last place in the world the spies of the Iron Heel would dream of looking for me, and for Ernest when he joined me, was Wickson's deer-park.

We tied our horses among the redwoods at the pool. From a cache behind a hollow rotting log my companion brought out a variety of things—a fifty-pound sack of flour, tinned foods of all sorts, cooking utensils, blankets, a canvas tarpaulin, books and writing material, a great bundle of letters, a five-gallon can of kerosene, and, last and most important, a large coil of stout rope. So large was the supply of things that a number of trips would be necessary to carry them to the refuge.

But the refuge was very near. Taking the rope and leading the way, I passed through a glade of tangled vines and bushes that ran between two wooded knolls. The glade ended abruptly at the steep bank of a stream. It was a little stream, rising from springs, and the hottest summer never dried it up. On every hand were tall wooded knolls, a group of them, with all the seeming of having been flung there from some careless Titan's hand. There was no bed-rock in them. They rose from their bases hundreds of feet, and they were composed of red volcanic earth, the famous wine-soil of Sonoma. Through these the tiny stream had cut its deep and precipitous channel.

It was quite a scramble down to the stream bed, and, once on the bed, we went down stream perhaps for a hundred feet. And then we came to the great hole. There was no warning of the existence of the hole, nor was it a hole in the common sense of the word. One crawled through tight-locked briars and branches, and found oneself on the very edge, peering out and down through a green screen. A couple of hundred feet in length and width, it was half of that in depth. Possibly because of some fault that had occurred when the knolls were flung together, and certainly helped by freakish erosion, the hole had been scooped out in the course of centuries by the wash of water. Nowhere did the raw earth appear. All was garmented by vegetation, from tiny maiden-hair and gold-back ferns to mighty redwoods and Douglas spruces. These great trees even sprang out from the walls of the hole. Some leaned over at angles as great as forty-five degrees, though the majority towered straight up from the soft and almost perpendicular earth walls.

It was a perfect hiding-place. No one ever came there, not even the village boys of Glen Ellen. Had this hole existed in the bed of a canyon a mile long, or several miles long, it would have been well known. But this was no canyon. From beginning to end the length of the stream was no more than five hundred yards. Three hundred yards above the hole the stream took its rise in a spring at the foot of a flat meadow. A hundred yards below the hole the stream ran out into open country, joining the main stream and flowing across rolling and grass-covered land.

My companion took a turn of the rope around a tree, and with me fast on the other end, lowered away. In no time I was on the bottom. And in but a short while he had carried all the articles from the cache and lowered them down to me. He hauled the rope up and hid it, and before he went away called down to me a cheerful parting.

Before I go on I want to say a word for this comrade, John Carlson, a humble figure of the Revolution, one of the countless faithful ones in the ranks. He worked for Wickson, in the stables near the hunting lodge. In fact it was on Wickson's horses that we had ridden over Sonoma Mountain. For nearly twenty years now John Carlson has been custodian of the refuge. No thought of disloyalty, I am sure, has ever entered his mind during all that time. To betray his trust would have been in his mind a thing undreamed. He was phlegmatic, stolid to such a degree that one could not but wonder how the Revolution had any meaning to him at all. And yet love of freedom glowed sombrely and steadily in his dim soul. In ways it was indeed good that he was not flighty and imaginative. He never lost his head. He could obey orders, and he was neither curious nor garrulous. Once I asked how it was that he was a Revolutionist.

'When I was a young man I was a soldier,' was his answer. 'It was in Germany. There all young men must be in the army. So I was in the army. There was another soldier there, a young man too. His father was what you call an agitator, and his father was in jail for lese-majesty—what you call speaking the truth about the Emperor. And the young man, the son, talked with me much about people, and work, and the robbery of the people by the capitalists. He made me see things in new ways, and I became a socialist. His talk was very true and good, and I have never forgotten. When I came to the United States I hunted up the socialists. I became a member of a section—that was in the day of the S.L.P. Then later, when the split came, I joined the local of the S.P. I was working in a livery stable in San Francisco then. That was before the Earthquake. I have paid my dues for twenty-two years. I am yet a member, and I yet pay my dues, though it is very secret now. I will always pay my dues, and when the co-operative commonwealth comes, I will be glad.'

Left to myself, I proceeded to cook breakfast on the oil stove and to prepare my home. Often, in the early morning, or in the evening after dark, Carlson would steal down to the refuge and work for a couple of hours. At first my home was the tarpaulin. Later, a small tent was put up. And still later, when we became assured of the perfect security of the place, a small house was erected. This house was completely hidden from any chance eye that might peer down from the edge of the hole. The lush vegetation of that sheltered spot made a natural shield. Also, the house was built against the perpendicular wall; and in the wall itself, shored by strong timbers, well drained and ventilated, we excavated two small rooms. Oh, believe me, we had many comforts. When Biedenbach, the German terrorist, hid with us some time later, he installed a smoke-consuming device that enabled us to sit by crackling wood fires on winter nights.

And here I must say a word for that gentle-souled terrorist than whom there is no comrade in the Revolution more fearfully misunderstood. Comrade Biedenbach did not betray the cause. Nor was he executed by the comrades, as is commonly supposed. This canard was circulated by the creatures of the Oligarchy. Comrade Biedenbach was absent-minded, forgetful. He was shot by one of our lookouts at the cave-refuge at Carmel, through failure on his part to remember the secret signals. It was all a sad mistake. And that he betrayed his Fighting Group is an absolute lie. No truer, more loyal man ever laboured for the Cause.[4]

For nineteen years now the refuge that I selected has been almost continuously occupied, and in all that time, with one exception, it has never been discovered by an outsider. And yet it was only a quarter of a mile from Wickson's hunting lodge, and a short mile from the village of Glen Ellen. I was able, always, to hear the morning and evening trains arrive and depart, and I used to set my watch by the whistle at the brickyards.[5]

---

[4] Search as we may through all the material of those times that has come down to us, we can find no clue to the Biedenbach here referred to. No mention is made of him anywhere save in the Everhard Manuscript.

[5] If the curious traveller will turn south from Glen Ellen, he will find himself on a boulevard that is identical with the old country road of seven centuries ago. A quarter of a mile from Glen Ellen, after the second bridge is passed, to the right will be noticed a barranca that runs like a scar across the rolling land towards a group of wooded knolls. The barranca is the site of the ancient right of way that in the time of private property in land ran across

the holding of one Chauvet, a French pioneer of California who came from his native country in the fabled days of gold. The wooded knolls are the same knolls referred to by Avis Everhard.

The great Earthquake of A.D. 2368 broke off the side of one of these knolls and toppled it into the hole where the Everhards made their refuge. Since the finding of the Manuscript excavations have been made, and the house, the two cave rooms, and all the accumulated rubbish of long occupancy have been brought to light. Many valuable relics have been found, among which, curious to relate, is the smoke-consuming device of Biedenbach's mentioned in the narrative. Students interested in such matters should read the brochure of Arnold Bentham soon to be published.

A mile north-west from the wooded knolls, brings one to the site of Wake Robin Lodge at the junction of Wild-Water and Sonoma Creeks. It may be noticed, in passing, that Wild-Water was originally called Graham Creek, and was so named on the early local maps. But the later name sticks. It was at Wake Robin Lodge that Avis Everhard later lived for short periods, when, disguised as an agent-provocateur of the Iron Heel, she was enabled to play with impunity her part among men and events. The official permission to occupy Wake Robin Lodge is still on the records, signed by no less a man than Wickson, the minor oligarch of the Manuscript.

CHAPTER 19

Transformation

'YOU MUST make yourself over again,' Ernest wrote to me. 'You must cease to be. You must become another woman —and not merely in the clothes you wear, but inside your skin under the clothes. You must make yourself over again so that even I would not know you—your voice, your gestures, your mannerisms, your carriage, your walk, everything.'

This command I obeyed. Every day I practised for hours in burying for ever the old Avis Everhard beneath the skin of another woman whom I may call my other self. It was only by long practice that such results could be obtained. In the mere detail of voice intonation I practised almost perpetually till the voice of my new self became fixed, automatic. It was this automatic assumption of a rôle that was considered imperative. One must become so adept as to deceive oneself. It was like learning a new language, say the French. At first, speech in French is self-conscious, a matter of the will. The student thinks in English and then transmutes into French, or reads in French but transmutes into English before he can understand. Then later, becoming firmly grounded, automatic, the student reads, writes, and *thinks* in French, without any recourse to English at all.

And so with our disguises. It was necessary for us to practise until our assumed rôles became real; until to be our original selves would require a watchful and strong exercise of will. Of course, at first, much was mere blundering experiment. We were creating a new art, and we had much to discover. But the work was going on everywhere; masters in the art were developing, and a fund of tricks and expedients was being accumulated. This fund became a sort of textbook that was passed on, a part of the curriculum, as it were, of the school of Revolution.[1]

[1] Disguise did become a veritable art during that period. The revolutionists maintained schools of acting in all their refuges. They scorned accessories, such as wigs and beards, false eyebrows, and such aids of the theatrical actors. The game of revolution was a game of life and death, and mere accessories were

It was at this time that my father disappeared. His letters, which had come to me regularly, ceased. He no longer appeared at our Pell Street quarters. Our comrades sought him everywhere. Through our secret service we ransacked every prison in the land. But he was lost as completely as if the earth had swallowed him up, and to this day no clue to his end has ever been discovered.[2]

Six lonely months I spent in the refuge, but they were not idle months. Our organisation went on apace, and there were mountains of work always waiting to be done. Ernest and his fellow-leaders, from their prisons, decided what should be done; and it remained for us on the outside to do it. There was the organisation of the mouth-to-mouth propaganda; the organisation, with all its ramifications, of our spy system; the establishment of our secret printing-presses; and the establishment of our underground railways, which meant the knitting together of all our myriads of places of refuge, and the formation of new refuges where links were missing in the chains we ran over all the land.

So I say, the work was never done. At the end of six months my loneliness was broken by the arrival of two comrades. They were young girls, brave souls and passionate lovers of liberty: Lora Peterson, who disappeared in 1922, and Kate Bierce, who later married du Bois,[3] and who is still with us with eyes lifted to tomorrow's sun that heralds in the new age.

The two girls arrived in a flurry of excitement, danger, and sudden death. In the crew of the fishing boat that conveyed them across San Pablo Bay was a spy. A creature of the Iron Heel, he had successfully masqueraded as a revolutionist and penetrated deep into the secrets of our organisation. Without

---

traps. Disguise had to be fundamental, intrinsic, part and parcel of one's being, second nature. The Red Virgin is reported to have been one of the most adept in the art, to which must be ascribed her long and successful career.

[2] Disappearance was one of the horrors of the time. As a *motif*, in song and story, it constantly crops up. It was an inevitable concomitant of the subterranean warfare that raged through those three centuries. This phenomenon was almost as common in the oligarch class and the labour castes as it was in the ranks of the revolutionists. Without warning, without trace, men and women, and even children, disappeared and were seen no more, their ends shrouded in mystery.

[3] Du Bois, the present librarian of Ardis, is a lineal descendant of this revolutionary pair.

doubt he was on my trail, for we had long since learned that my disappearance had been cause of deep concern to the secret service of the Oligarchy. Luckily, as the outcome proved, he had not divulged his discoveries to anyone. He had evidently delayed reporting, preferring to wait until he had brought things to a successful conclusion by discovering my hiding-place and capturing me. His information died with him. Under some pretext, after the girls had landed at Petaluma Creek and taken to the horses, he managed to get away from the boat.

Part way up Sonoma Mountain, John Carlson let the girls go on, leading his horse, while he went back on foot. His suspicions had been aroused. He captured the spy, and as to what then happened Carlson gave us a fair idea.

' I fixed him,' was Carlson's unimaginative way of describing the affair. ' I fixed him,' he repeated, while a sombre light burnt in his eyes, and his huge, toil-distorted hands opened and closed eloquently. ' He made no noise. I hid him, and tonight I will go back and bury him deep.'

During that period I used to marvel at my own metamorphosis. At times it seemed impossible either that I had ever lived a placid, peaceful life in a college town, or else that I had become a revolutionist inured to scenes of violence and death. One or the other could not be. One was real, the other was a dream, but which was which? Was this present life of a revolutionist, hiding in a hole, a nightmare? or was I a revolutionist who had somewhere, somehow, dreamed that in some former existence, I had lived in Berkeley and never known of life more violent than teas and dances, debating societies, and lecture rooms? But then I suppose this was a common experience of all of us who had rallied under the red banner of the brotherhood of man.

I often remembered figures from that other life, and, curiously enough, they appeared and disappeared now and again, in my new life. There was Bishop Morehouse. In vain we searched for him after our organisation had developed. He had been transferred from asylum to asylum. We traced him from the state hospital for the insane at Napa to the one in Stockton, and from there to the one in the Santa Clara Valley called Agnews, and there the trail ceased. There was no record of his death. In some way he must have escaped. Little did I dream of the awful manner in which I was to see him once again—the fleeting glimpse of him in the whirlwind carnage of the Chicago Commune.

Jackson who had lost his arm in the Sierra Mills and who had been the cause of my own conversion into a revolutionist, I never saw again; but we all knew what he did before he died. He never joined the revolutionists. Embittered by his fate, brooding over his wrongs, he became an anarchist—not a philosophic anarchist, but a mere animal, mad with hate and lust for revenge. And well he revenged himself. Evading the guards, in the night time while all were asleep he blew the Pertonwaithe palace into atoms. Not a soul escaped, not even the guards. And in prison, while awaiting trial, he suffocated himself under his blankets.

Dr Hammerfield and Dr Ballingford achieved quite different fates from that of Jackson. They have been faithful to their salt, and they have been correspondingly rewarded with ecclesiastical palaces wherein they dwell at peace with the world. Both are apologists for the Oligarchy. Both have grown very fat. 'Doctor Hammerfield,' as Ernest once said, 'has succeeded in modifying his metaphysics so as to give God's sanction to the Iron Heel, and also to include much worship of beauty and to reduce to an invisible wraith the gaseous vertebrate described by Haeckel—the difference between Dr Hammerfield and Dr Ballingford being that the latter has made the God of the oligarchs a little more gaseous and a little less vertebrate.'

Peter Donnelly, the scab foreman at the Sierra Mills whom I encountered while investigating the case of Jackson was a surprise to all of us. In 1918 I was present at a meeting of the 'Frisco Reds. Of all our Fighting Groups this one was the most formidable, ferocious, and merciless. It was really not a part of our organisation. Its members were fanatics, madmen. We dared not encourage such a spirit. On the other hand, though they did not belong to us, we remained on friendly terms with them. It was a matter of vital importance that brought me there that night. I, alone in the midst of a score of men, was the only person unmasked. After the business that brought me there was transacted, I was led away by one of them. In a dark passage this guide struck a match, and holding it close to his face, slipped back his mask. For a moment I gazed upon the passion-wrought features of Peter Donnelly. Then the match went out.

'I just wanted you to know it was me,' he said in the darkness. 'D'you remember Dallas, the superintendent?'

I nodded at recollection of the vulpine-faced superintendent of the Sierra Mills.

' Well, I got him first,' Donnelly said with pride. ' 'Twas after that I joined the Reds.'

' But how comes it that you are here?' I queried. ' Your wife and children?'

' Dead,' he answered. ' That's why. No,' he went on hastily, ' 'tis not revenge for them. They died easily in their beds—sickness, you see, one time and another. They tied my arms while they lived. And now that they're gone, 'tis revenge for my blasted manhood I'm after. I was once Peter Donnelly, the scab foreman. But tonight I'm Number 27, of the 'Frisco Reds. Come on now, and I'll get you out of this.'

More I heard of him afterward. In his own way he had told the truth when he said all were dead. But one lived, Timothy, and him his father considered dead because he had taken service with the Iron Heel in the Mercenaries.[4] A member of the 'Frisco Reds pledged himself to twelve annual executions. The penalty for failure was death. A member who failed to complete his number committed suicide. These executions were not haphazard. This group of madmen met frequently and passed wholesale judgements upon offending members and servitors of the Oligarchy. The executions were afterward apportioned by lot.

In fact the business that brought me there the night of my visit was such a trial. One of our own comrades, who for years had successfully maintained himself in a clerical position in the local bureau of the secret service of the Iron Heel, had fallen under the ban of the 'Frisco Reds and was being tried. Of course he was not present, and of course his judges did not know that he was one of our men. My mission had been to testify to his identity and loyalty. It may be wondered how we came to know of the affair at all. The explanation is simple. One of our secret agents was a member of the 'Frisco Reds. It was necessary for us to keep an eye on friend as well as foe, and this group of madmen was not too unim-

[4] In addition to the labour castes, there arose another caste, the military. A standing army of professional soldiers was created, officered by members of the Oligarchy and known as the Mercenaries. This institution took the place of the militia, which had proved impracticable under the new régime. Outside the regular secret service of the Iron Heel there was further established a secret service of the Mercenaries, this latter forming a connecting link between the police and the military.

portant to escape our surveillance.

But to return to Peter Donnelly and his son. All went well with Donnelly until, in the following year, he found among the sheaf of executions that fell to him the name of Timothy Donnelly. Then it was that that family clannishness, which was his to so extraordinary a degree, asserted itself. To save his son he betrayed his comrades. In this he was partially blocked, but a dozen of the 'Frisco Reds were executed, and the group was well-nigh destroyed. In retaliation the survivors meted out to Donnelly the death he had earned by his treason.

Nor did Timothy Donnelly long survive. The 'Frisco Reds pledged themselves to his execution. Every effort was made by the Oligarchy to save him. He was transferred from one part of the country to another. Three of the Reds lost their lives in vain efforts to get him. The Group was composed only of men. In the end they fell back on a woman, one of our comrades, and none other than Anna Roylston. Our Inner Circle forbade her, but she had ever a will of her own and disdained discipline. Furthermore, she was a genius and lovable, and we could never discipline her anyway. She is in a class by herself and not amenable to the ordinary standards of the revolutionists.

Despite our refusal to grant permission to do the deed, she went on with it. Now Anna Roylston was a fascinating woman. All she had to do was to beckon a man to her. She broke the hearts of scores of our young comrades, and scores of others she captured, and by their heart-strings led into our organisation. Yet she steadfastly refused to marry. She dearly loved children, but she held that a child of her own would claim her from the Cause, and that it was the Cause to which her life was devoted.

It was an easy task for Anna Roylston to win Timothy Donnelly. Her conscience did not trouble her, for at that very time occurred the *Nashville Massacre*, when the Mercenaries, Donnelly in command, literally murdered eight hundred weavers of that city. But she did not kill Donnelly. She turned him over, a prisoner, to the 'Frisco Reds. This happened only last year, and now she has been renamed. The revolutionists everywhere are calling her the ' Red Virgin '.[5]

---

[5] It was not until the Second Revolt was crushed that the 'Frisco Reds flourished again. And for two generations the Group flour-

Colonel Ingram and Colonel Van Gilbert are two more familiar figures that I was later to encounter. Colonel Ingram rose high in the Oligarchy and became Minister to Germany. He was cordially detested by the proletariat of both countries. It was in Berlin that I met him, where, as an accredited international spy of the Iron Heel, I was received by him and afforded much assistance. Incidentally, I may state that in my dual rôle I managed a few important things for the Revolution.

Colonel Van Gilbert became known as ' Snarling ' Van Gilbert. His important part was played in drafting the new code after the Chicago Commune. But before that, as trial judge, he had earned sentence of death by his fiendish malignancy. I was one of those that tried him and passed sentence upon him. Anna Roylston carried out the execution.

Still another figure arises out of the old life—Jackson's lawyer. Least of all would I have expected again to meet this man, Joseph Hurd. It was a strange meeting. Late at night, two years after the Chicago Commune, Ernest and I arrived together at the Benton Harbour refuge. This was in Michigan, across the lake from Chicago. We arrived just at the conclusion of the trial of a spy. Sentence of death had been passed, and he was being led away. Such was the scene as we came upon it. The next moment the wretched man had wrenched free from his captors and flung himself at my feet, his arms clutching me about the knees in a vice-like grip as he prayed in a frenzy for mercy. As he turned his agonised face up to me, I recognised him as Joseph Hurd. Of all the terrible things I have witnessed, never have I been so unnerved as by this frantic creature's pleading for life. He was mad for life. It was pitiable. He refused to let go of me, despite the hands of a dozen comrades. And when at last he was dragged shrieking away, I sank down fainting upon the floor. It is far easier to see brave men die than to hear a coward beg for life.[6]

---

ished. Then an agent of the Iron Heel managed to become a member, penetrated all its secrets, and brought about its total annihilation. This occurred in A.D. 2002. The members were executed one at a time, at intervals of three weeks, and their bodies exposed in the labour Ghetto of San Francisco.

[6] The Benton Harbour refuge was a catacomb, the entrance of which was cunningly contrived by way of a well. It has been maintained in a fair state of preservation, and the curious visitor

may today tread its labyrinths to the assembly hall, where, without doubt, occurred the scene described by Avis Everhard. Farther on are the cells where the prisoners were confined, and the death chamber where the executions took place. Beyond is the cemetery —long, winding galleries hewn out of the solid rock, with recesses on either hand, wherein, tier above tier, lie the revolutionists just as they were laid away by their comrades long years agone.

CHAPTER 20

A Lost Oligarch

B u t i n remembering the old life I have run ahead of my story into the new life. The wholesale jail delivery did not occur until well along into 1915. Complicated as it was, it was carried through without a hitch, and as a very creditable achievement it cheered us on in our work. From Cuba to California, out of scores of jails, military prisons, and fortresses, in a single night, we delivered fifty-one of our fifty-two Congressmen, and in addition over three hundred other leaders. There was not a single instance of miscarriage. Not only did they escape, but every one of them won to the refuges planned. The one comrade Congressman we did not get was Arthur Simpson, and he had already died in Cubañas after cruel tortures.

The eighteen months that followed was perhaps the happiest period of my life with Ernest. During that time we were never apart. Later, when we went back into the world, we were separated much. Not more impatiently do I await the flame of tomorrow's revolt than did I that night await the coming of Ernest. I had not seen him for so long, and the thought of a possible hitch or error in our plans that would keep him still in his island prison almost drove me mad. The hours passed like ages. I was all alone. Biedenbach, and three young men who had been staying in the refuge, were out and over the mountain, heavily armed and prepared for anything. The refuges all over the land were quite empty, I imagine, of comrades that night.

Just as the sky paled with the first warning of dawn I heard the signal from above and gave the answer. In the darkness I almost embraced Biedenbach, who came down first; but the next moment I was in Ernest's arms. And in that moment, so complete had been my transformation, I discovered it was only by an effort of will that I could be the old Avis Everhard, with the old mannerisms and smiles, phrases and intonations of voice. It was by strong effort only that I was able to maintain my old identity; I could not allow myself to forget for an instant, so automatically imperative had become the new personality I had created.

Once inside the little cabin, I saw Ernest's face in the light. With the exception of the prison pallor, there was no change in him—at least, not much. He was my same lover-husband and hero. And yet there was a certain ascetic lengthening of the lines of his face. But he could well stand it, for it seemed to add a certain nobility of refinement to the riotous excess of life that had always marked his features. He might have been a trifle graver than yore, but the glint of laughter still was in his eyes. He was twenty pounds lighter, but in splendid physical condition. He had kept up exercise during the whole period of confinement, and his muscles were like iron. In truth, he was in better condition than when he had entered prison. Hours passed before his head touched pillow and I had soothed him off to sleep. But there was no sleep for me. I was too happy, and the fatigue of jail-breaking and riding horseback had not been mine.

While Ernest slept, I changed my dress, arranged my hair differently, and came back to my new automatic self. Then, when Biedenbach and the other comrades awoke, with their aid I concocted a little conspiracy. All was ready and we were in the cave-room that served for kitchen and dining-room when Ernest opened the door and entered. At that moment Biedenbach addressed me as Mary, and I turned and answered him. Then I glanced at Ernest with curious interest, such as any young comrade might betray on seeing for the first time so noted a hero of the Revolution. But Ernest's glance took me in and quested impatiently past and around the room. The next moment I was being introduced to him as Mary Holmes.

To complete the deception, an extra plate was laid, and when we sat down to table one chair was not occupied. I could have cried out with joy as I noted Ernest's increasing uneasiness and impatience. Finally he could stand it no longer.

'Where's my wife?' he demanded bluntly.

'She is still asleep,' I answered.

It was the crucial moment. But my voice was a strange voice, and in it he recognised nothing familiar. The meal went on. I talked a great deal, and enthusiastically, as a hero-worshipper might talk, and it was obvious that he was my hero. I rose to a climax of enthusiasm and worship, and, before he could guess my intention, threw my arms around his neck and kissed him on the lips. He held me from him at arm's length and stared about in annoyance and perplexity. The four men greeted him with roars of laughter, and explanations were made. At first he was sceptical. He scrutinised me keenly and was half convinced, then shook his head and would not believe. It was not until I became the old Avis Everhard and whispered secrets in his ear that none knew but he and Avis Everhard, that he accepted me as his really, truly wife.

It was later in the day that he took me in his arms, manifesting great embarrassment and claiming polygamous emotions.

'You are my Avis,' he said, 'and you are also someone else. You are two women, and therefore you are my harem. At any rate, we are safe now. If the United States becomes too hot for us, why, I have qualified for citizenship in Turkey.'[1]

Life became for me very happy in the refuge. It is true, we worked hard and for long hours; but we worked together. We had each other for eighteen precious months, and we were not lonely, for there was always a coming and going of leaders and comrades—strange voices from the under-world of intrigue and revolution, bringing stranger tales of strife and war from all our battle-line. And there was much fun and delight. We were not mere gloomy conspirators. We toiled hard and suffered greatly, filled the gaps in our ranks and went on, and through all the labour and the play and interplay of life and death we found time to laugh and love. There were artists, scientists, scholars, musicians, and poets among us; and in that hole in the ground culture was higher and finer than in the palaces or wonder-cities of the oligarchs. In truth, many of our comrades toiled at making beautiful those same palaces and wonder-cities.[2]

Nor were we confined to the refuge itself. Often at night we rode over the mountains for exercise, and we rode on Wickson's horses. If only he knew how many revolutionists his horses have carried! We even went on picnics to isolated spots we knew, where we remained all day, going before day-

---

[1] At that time polygamy was still practised in Turkey.
[2] This is not braggadocio on the part of Avis Everhard. The flower of the artistic and intellectual world were revolutionists. With the exception of a few of the musicians and singers, and of a few of the oligarchs, all the great creators of the period whose names have come down to us were revolutionists.

light and returning after dark. Also, we used Wickson's cream and butter;[3] and Ernest was not above shooting Wickson's quail and rabbits, and, on occasion, his young bucks.

Indeed, it was a safe refuge. I have said that it was discovered only once, and this brings me to the clearing up of the mystery of the disappearance of young Wickson. Now that he is dead, I am free to speak. There was a nook on the bottom of the great hole where the sun shone for several hours and which was hidden from above. Here we had carried many loads of gravel from the creek-bed, so that it was dry and warm, a pleasant basking place; and here, one afternoon, I was drowsing, half asleep, over a volume of Mendenhall.[4] I was so comfortable and secure that even his flaming lyrics failed to stir me.

I was aroused by a clod of earth striking at my feet. Then, from above, I heard a sound of scrambling. The next moment a young man, with a final slide down the crumbling wall, alighted at my feet. It was Philip Wickson, though I did not know him at the time. He looked at me coolly and uttered a low whistle of surprise.

'Well,' he said; and the next moment, cap in hand, he was saying, 'I beg your pardon. I did not expect to find anyone here.'

I was not so cool. I was still a tyro so far as concerned knowing how to behave in desperate circumstances. Later on, when I was an international spy, I should have been less clumsy, I am sure. As it was, I scrambled to my feet and cried out the danger call.

'Why did you do that?' he asked, looking at me searchingly.

It was evident that he had no suspicion of our presence when making the descent. I recognised this with relief.

'For what purpose do you think I did it?' I countered. I was indeed clumsy in those days.

'I don't know,' he answered, shaking his head. 'Unless

[3] Even as late as that period, cream and butter were still crudely extracted from cow's milk. The laboratory preparation of foods had not yet begun.

[4] In all the extant literature and documents of that period, continual reference is made to the poems of Rudolph Mendenhall. By his comrades he was called 'The Flame.' He was undoubtedly a great genius; yet beyond weird and haunting fragments of his verse, quoted in the writings of others, nothing of his has come down to us. He was executed by the Iron Heel in A.D. 1928.

you've got friends about. Anyway, you've got some explanations to make. I don't like the look of it. You are trespassing. This is my father's land, and—'

But at that moment, Biedenbach, ever polite and gentle, said from behind him in a low voice, 'Hands up, my young sir.'

Young Wickson put his hands up first, then turned to confront Biedenbach, who held a thirty-thirty automatic rifle on him. Wickson was imperturbable.

'Oh, ho,' he said, 'a nest of revolutionists—and quite a hornet's nest, it would seem. Well you won't abide here long, I can tell you.'

'Maybe you'll abide here long enough to reconsider that statement,' Biedenbach said quietly. 'And in the meanwhile I must ask you to come inside with me.'

'Inside?' The young man was genuinely astonished. 'Have you a catacomb here? I have heard of such things.'

'Come on and see,' Biedenbach answered, with his adorable accent.

'But it is unlawful,' was the protest.

'Yes, by your law,' the terrorist replied significantly. 'But by our law, believe me, it is quite lawful. You must accustom yourself to the fact that you are in another world than the one of oppression and brutality in which you have lived.'

'There is room for argument there,' Wickson muttered.

'Then stay with us and discuss it.'

The young fellow laughed and followed his captor into the house. He was led into the inner cave room, and one of the young comrades left to guard him, while we discussed the situation in the kitchen.

Biedenbach, with tears in his eyes, held that Wickson must die, and was quite relieved when we outvoted him and his horrible proposition. On the other hand, we could not dream of allowing the young oligarch to depart.

'I'll tell you what to do,' Ernest said. 'We'll keep him and give him an education.'

'I bespeak the privilege, then, of enlightening him in jurisprudence,' Biedenbach cried.

And so a decision was laughingly reached. We would keep Philip Wickson a prisoner and educate him in our ethics and sociology. But in the meantime there was work to be done. All trace of the young oligarch must be obliterated. There were the marks he had left when descending the crumbling wall of the hole. This task fell to Biedenbach, and, slung on a rope from above, he toiled cunningly for the rest of the day till no sign remained. Back up the canyon from the lip of the hole all marks were likewise removed. Then at twilight came John Carlson, who demanded Wickson's shoes.

The young man did not want to give up his shoes, and even offered to fight for them, till he felt the horseshoer's strength in Ernest's hands. Carlson afterward reported several blisters and much grievous loss of skin due to the smallness of the shoes, but he succeeded in doing gallant work with them. Back from the lip of the hole, where ended the young man's obliterated trail, Carlson put on the shoes and walked away to the left. He walked for miles around knolls, over ridges and through canyons, and finally covered the trail in the running water of a creek-bed. Here he removed the shoes, and, still hiding the trail for a distance, at last put on his own shoes. A week later Wickson got back his shoes.

That night the hounds were out, and there was little sleep in the refuge. Next day, time and again, the baying hounds came down the canyon, plunged off to the left on the trail Carlson had made for them, and were lost to ear in the farther canyons high up the mountain. And all the time our men waited in the refuge, weapons in hand—automatic revolvers and rifles, to say nothing of half a dozen infernal machines of Biedenbach's manufacture. A more surprised party of rescuers could not be imagined, had they ventured down into our hiding-place.

I have now given the true disappearance of Philip Wickson, one-time oligarch, and, later, comrade in the Revolution. For we converted him in the end. His mind was fresh and plastic, and by nature he was very ethical. Several months later we rode him, on one of his father's horses, over Sonoma Mountain to Petaluma Creek and embarked him in a small fishing-launch. By easy stages we smuggled him along our underground railway to the Carmel refuge.

There he remained eight months, at the end of which time, for two reasons, he was loath to leave us. One reason was that he had fallen in love with Anna Roylston, and the other was that he had become one of us. It was not until he became convinced of the hopelessness of his love affair that he acceded to our wishes and went back to his father. Ostensibly an oligarch until his death, he was in reality one of the most valuable of our agents. Often and often had the Iron

Heel been dumbfounded by the miscarriage of its plans and operations against us. If it but knew the number of its own members who are our agents, it would understand. Young Wickson never wavered in his loyalty to the Cause. In truth, his very death was incurred by his devotion to duty. In the great storm of 1927, while attending a meeting of our leaders, he contracted the pneumonia of which he died.[5]

[5] The case of this young man was not unusual. Many young men of the Oligarchy, impelled by sense of right conduct, or their imaginations captured by the glory of the Revolution, ethically or romantically devoted their lives to it. In similar way, many sons of the Russian nobility played their parts in the earlier and protracted revolution in that country.

CHAPTER 21

The Roaring Abysmal Beast

DURING THE long period of our stay in the refuge, we were kept closely in touch with what was happening in the world without, and we were learning thoroughly the strength of the Oligarchy with which we were at war. Out of the flux of transition the new institutions were forming more definitely and taking on the appearance and attributes of permanence. The oligarchs had succeeded in devising a governmental machine, as intricate as it was vast, that worked—and this despite all our efforts to clog and hamper.

This was a surprise to many of the revolutionists. They had not conceived it possible. Nevertheless the work of the country went on. The men toiled in the mines and fields—perforce they were no more than slaves. As for the vital industries, everything prospered. The members of the great labour castes were contented and worked on merrily. For the first time in their lives they knew industrial peace. No more were they worried by slack times, strike and lock out, and the union label. They lived in more comfortable homes and in delightful cities of their own—delightful compared with the slums and ghettos in which they had formerly dwelt. They had better food to eat, less hours of labour, more holidays, and a greater amount and variety of interests and pleasures. And for their less fortunate brothers and sisters, the unfavoured labourers, the driven people of the abyss, they cared nothing. An age of selfishness was dawning upon mankind. And yet this is not altogether true. The labour castes were honeycombed by our agents—men whose eyes saw, beyond the belly-need, the radiant figure of liberty and brotherhood.

Another great institution that had taken form and was working smoothly was the Mercenaries. This body of soldiers had been evolved out of the old regular army and was now a million strong, to say nothing of the colonial forces. The mercenaries constituted a race apart. They dwelt in cities of their own which were practically self-governed, and they were granted many privileges. By them a large portion of the perplexing surplus was consumed. They were losing all touch and sympathy with the rest of the people, and, in fact, were developing their own class morality and consciousness. And yet we had thousands of our agents among them.[1]

The oligarchs themselves were going through a remarkable and, it must be confessed, unexpected development. As a class, they disciplined themselves. Every member had his work to do in the world, and this work he was compelled to do. There were no more idle-rich young men. Their strength was used to give united strength to the Oligarchy. They served as leaders of troops and as lieutenants and captains of industry. They found careers in applied science, and many of them became great engineers. They went into the multitudinous divisions of the government, took service in the colonial possessions, and by tens of thousands went into the various secret services. They were, I may say, apprenticed to education, to art, to the church, to science, to literature; and in those fields they served the important function of moulding the thought-processes of the nation in the direction of the perpetuity of the Oligarchy.

They were taught, and later they in turn taught, that what they were doing was right. They assimilated the aristocratic idea from the moment they began, as children, to receive impressions of the world. The aristocratic idea was woven into the making of them until it became bone of them and flesh of them. They looked upon themselves as wild-animal trainers, rulers of beasts. From beneath their feet rose always the subterranean rumbles of revolt. Violent death ever stalked in their midst; bomb and knife and bullet were looked upon as so many fangs of the roaring abysmal beast they must dominate if humanity were to persist. They were the saviours of humanity, and they regarded themselves as heroic and sacrificing labourers for the highest good.

They, as a class, believed that they alone maintained civilisation. It was their belief that if ever they weakened, the great beast would engulf them and everything of beauty and wonder and joy and good in its cavernous and slime-dripping maw. Without them, anarchy would reign and humanity would drop backward into the primitive night out

[1] The Mercenaries, in the last days of the Iron Heel, played an important rôle. They constituted the balance of power in the struggles between the labour castes and the oligarchs, and now to one side and now to the other threw their strength according to the play of intrigue and conspiracy.

of which it had so painfully emerged. The horrid picture of anarchy was held always before their children's eyes until they in turn, obsessed by this cultivated fear, held the picture of anarchy before the eyes of the children that followed them. This was the beast to be stamped upon, and the highest duty of the aristocrat was to stamp upon it. In short, they alone, by their unremitting toil and sacrifice, stood between weak humanity and the all-devouring beast; and they believed it, firmly believed it.

I cannot lay too great stress upon this high ethical righteousness of the whole oligarch class. This has been the strength of the Iron Heel, and too many of the comrades have been slow or loath to realise it. Many of them have ascribed the strength of the Iron Heel to its system of reward and punishment. This is a mistake. Heaven and hell may be the prime factors of zeal in the religion of a fanatic; but for the great majority of the religious, heaven and hell are incidental to right and wrong. Love of the right, desire for the right, unhappiness with anything less than the right—in short, right conduct, is the prime factor of religion. And so with the Oligarchy. Prisons, banishment and degradation, honours and palaces and wonder-cities, are all incidental. The great driving force of the oligarchs is the belief that they are doing right. Never mind the exceptions, and never mind the oppression and injustice in which the Iron Heel was conceived. All is granted. The point is that the strength of the Oligarchy today lies in its satisfied conception of its own righteousness.[2]

For that matter, the strength of the Revolution, during these frightful twenty years, has resided in nothing else than the sense of righteousness. In no other way can be explained our sacrifices and martyrdoms. For no other reason did Rudolph Mendenhall flame out his soul for the Cause and

---

[2] Out of the ethical incoherency and inconsistency of capitalism, the oligarchs emerged with a new ethic, coherent and definite, sharp and severe as steel, the most absurd and unscientific and at the same time the most potent ever possessed by any tyrant class. The oligarchs believed their ethics, in spite of the fact that biology and evolution gave them the lie; and, because of their faith, for three centuries they were able to hold back the mighty tide of human progress—a spectacle, profound, tremendous, puzzling to the metaphysical moralist, and one that to the materialist is the cause of many doubts and reconsiderations.

sing his wild swan-song that last night of life. For no other
reason did Hulbert die under torture, refusing to the last
to betray his comrades. For no other reason has Anna Roylston refused blessed motherhood. For no other reason has
John Carlson been the faithful and unrewarded custodian of
the Glen Ellen Refuge. It does not matter, young or old,
man or woman, high or low, genius or clod, go where one
will among the comrades of the Revolution, the motor-force
will be found to be a great and abiding desire for the right.

But I have run away from my narrative. Ernest and I
well understood, before we left the refuge, how the strength
of the Iron Heel was developing. The labour castes, the Mercenaries, and the great hordes of secret agents and police of
various sorts were all pledged to the Oligarchy. In the main
and ignoring the loss of liberty, they were better off than they
had been. On the other hand, the great helpless mass of the
population, the people of the abyss, was sinking into a brutish
apathy of content with misery. Whenever strong proletarians
asserted their strength in the midst of the mass, they were
drawn away from the mass by the oligarchs and given better
conditions by being made members of the labour castes or of
the Mercenaries. Thus discontent was lulled and the proletariat robbed of its natural leaders.

The condition of the people of the abyss was pitiable.
Common school education, so far as they were concerned, had
ceased. They lived like beasts in great squalid labour-ghettos,
festering in misery and degradation. All their old liberties were
gone. They were labour-slaves. Choice of work was denied
them. Likewise was denied them the right to move from place
to place, or the right to bear or possess arms. They were not
land-serfs like the farmers. They were machine-serfs and
labour-serfs. When unusual needs arose for them, such as the
building of the great highways and air-lines, of canals,
tunnels, subways, and fortifications, levies were made on the
labour-ghettos, and tens of thousands of serfs, willy-nilly,
were transported to the scene of operations. Great armies of
them are toiling now at the building of Ardis, housed in
wretched barracks where family life cannot exist, and where
decency is displaced by dull bestiality. In all truth, there in
the labour-ghettos is the roaring abysmal beast the oligarchs
fear so dreadfully—but it is the beast of their own making.
In it they will not let the ape and tiger die.

And just now the word has gone forth that new levies are

being imposed for the building of Asgard, the projected wonder-city that will far exceed Ardis when the latter is completed.[3] We of the revolution will go on with that great work, but it will not be done by the miserable serfs. The walls and towers and shafts of that fair city will arise to the sound of singing, and into its beauty and wonder will be woven, not sighs and groans, but music and laughter.

Ernest was madly impatient to be out in the world and doing, for our ill-fated First Revolt, that miscarried in the Chicago Commune, was ripening fast. Yet he possessed his soul with patience, and during the time of his torment, when Hadly, who had been brought for the purpose from Illinois, made him over into another man,[4] he revolved great plans in his head for the organisation of the learned proletariat, and for the maintenance of at least the rudiments of education amongst the people of the abyss—all this, of course, in the event of the First Revolt being a failure.

It was not until January, 1917, that we left the refuge. All had been arranged. We took our place at once as agents-provocateurs in the scheme of the Iron Heel. I was supposed to be Ernest's sister. By oligarchs and comrades on the inside who were high in authority, place had been made for us, we were in possession of all necessary documents, and our pasts were accounted for. With help on the inside, this was not

---

[3] Ardis was completed in A.D. 1942, while Asgard was not completed until A.D. 1984. It was fifty-two years in the building, during which time a permanent army of half a million serfs was employed. At times these numbers swelled to over a million—without any account being taken of the hundreds of thousands of the labour castes and the artists.

[4] Among the revolutionists were many surgeons, and in vivisection they attained marvellous proficiency. In Avis Everhard's words, they could literally make a man over. To them the elimination of scars and disfigurements was a trivial detail. They changed the features with such microscopic care that no traces were left of their handiwork. The nose was a favourite organ to work upon. Skin-grafting and hair-transplanting were among their commonest devices. The changes in expression they accomplished were wizard-like. Eyes and eyebrows, lips, mouths, and ears were radically altered. By cunning operations on tongue, throat, larynx, and nasal cavities a man's whole enunciation and manner of speech could be changed. Desperate times give need for desperate remedies, and the surgeons of the Revolution rose to the need. Among other things, they could increase an adult's stature by as much as four or five inches and decrease it by one or two inches. What they did is today a lost art. We have no need for it.

difficult, for in that shadow-world of secret service identity was nebulous. Like ghosts, the agents came and went, obeying commands, fulfilling duties, following clues, making their reports often to officers they never saw or co-operating with other agents they had never seen before and would never see again.

CHAPTER 22

The Chicago Commune

A S agents-provocateurs, not alone were we able to travel a great deal, but our very work threw us in contact with the proletariat and with our comrades, the revolutionists. Thus we were in both camps at the same time, ostensibly serving the Iron Heel and secretly working with all our might for the Cause. There were many of us in the various secret services of the Oligarchy, and despite the shakings-up and reorganisations the secret services have undergone, they have never been able to weed all of us out.

Ernest had largely planned the First Revolt, and the date set had been somewhere early in the spring of 1918. In the fall of 1917 we were not ready; much remained to be done, and when the Revolt was precipitated, of course it was doomed to failure. The plot of necessity was frightfully intricate, and anything premature was sure to destroy it. This the Iron Heel foresaw and laid its schemes accordingly.

We had planned to strike our first blow at the nervous system of the Oligarchy. The latter had remembered the general strike, and had guarded against the defection of the telegraphers by installing wireless stations, in the control of the Mercenaries. We, in turn, had countered this move. When the signal was given, from every refuge, all over the land, and from the cities, and towns, and barracks, devoted comrades were to go forth and blow up the wireless stations. Thus at the first shock would the Iron Heel be brought to earth and lie practically dismembered.

At the same moment, other comrades were to blow up the bridges and tunnels and disrupt the whole network of railroads. Still further, other groups of comrades, at the signal, were to seize the officers of the Mercenaries and the police, as well as all oligarchs of unusual ability or who held executive positions. Thus would the leaders of the enemy be removed from the field of the local battles that would inevitably be fought all over the land.

Many things were to occur simultaneously when the signal went forth. The Canadian and Mexican patriots, who were

far stronger than the Iron Heel dreamed, were to duplicate
our tactics. Then there were comrades (these were the
women, for the men would be busy elsewhere) who were to
post the proclamations from our secret presses. Those of us
in the higher employ of the Iron Heel were to proceed immediately to make confusion and anarchy in all our departments. Inside the Mercenaries were thousands of our comrades. Their work was to blow up the magazines and to
destroy the delicate mechanism of all the war machinery. In
the cities of the Mercenaries and of the labour castes similar
programmes of disruption were to be carried out.

In short, a sudden colossal, stunning blow was to be struck.
Before the paralysed Oligarchy could recover itself, its end
would have come. It would have meant terrible times and
great loss of life, but no revolutionist hesitates at such things.
Why, we even depended much, in our plan, on the unorganised people of the abyss. They were to be loosed on
the palaces and cities of the masters. Never mind the destruction of life and property. Let the abysmal brute roar and the
police and Mercenaries slay. The abysmal brute would roar
anyway, and the police and Mercenaries would slay anyway. It would merely mean that various dangers to us were
harmlessly destroying one another. In the meantime we
would be doing our own work, largely unhampered, and
gaining control of all the machinery of society.

Such was our plan, every detail of which had to be worked
out in secret, and, as the day drew near, communicated to
more and more comrades. This was the danger point, the
stretching of the conspiracy. But that danger-point was never
reached. Through its spy-system the Iron Heel got wind of
the Revolt and prepared to teach us another of its bloody
lessons. Chicago was the devoted city selected for the instruc-
tion, and well were we instructed.

Chicago[1] was the ripest of all—Chicago which of old

---

[1] Chicago was the industrial inferno of the nineteenth century A.D.
A curious anecdote has come down to us of John Burns, a great
English labour leader and one time member of the British Cabinet.
In Chicago, while on a visit to the United States, he was asked by
a newspaper reporter for his opinion of that city. 'Chicago,' he
answered, 'is a pocket edition of hell.' Some time later as he was
going aboard his steamer to sail to England, he was approached
by another reporter, who wanted to know if he had changed his
opinion of Chicago. 'Yes, I have,' was his reply. 'My present
opinion is that hell is a pocket edition of Chicago.'

time was the city of blood and which was to earn anew its name. There the revolutionary spirit was strong. Too many bitter strikes had been curbed there in the days of capitalism for the workers to forget and forgive. Even the labour castes of the city were alive with revolt. Too many heads had been broken in the early strike. Despite their changed and favourable conditions, their hatred for the master class had not died. This spirit had infected the Mercenaries, of which three regiments in particular were ready to come over to us *en masse*.

Chicago had always been the storm-centre of the conflict between labour and capital, a city of street-battles and violent death, with a class-conscious capitalist organisation and a class-conscious workman organisation, where, in the old days, the very school-teachers were formed into labour unions and affiliated with the hod-carriers and bricklayers in the American Federation of Labour. And Chicago became the storm-centre of the premature First Revolt.

The trouble was precipitated by the Iron Heel. It was cleverly done. The whole population, including the favoured labour castes, was given a course of outrageous treatment. Promises and agreements were broken, and most drastic punishments visited upon even petty offenders. The people of the abyss were tormented out of their apathy. In fact, the Iron Heel was preparing to make the abysmal beast roar. And hand in hand with this in all precautionary measures in Chicago, the Iron Heel was inconceivably careless. Discipline was relaxed among the Mercenaries that remained, while many regiments had been withdrawn and sent to various parts of the country.

It did not take long to carry out this programme—only several weeks. We of the Revolution caught vague rumours of the state of affairs, but had nothing definite enough for an understanding. In fact, we thought it was a spontaneous spirit of revolt that would require careful curbing on our part, and never dreamed that it was deliberately manufactured—and it had been manufactured so secretly, from the very innermost circle of the Iron Heel, that we had got no inkling. The counter-plot was an able achievement, and ably carried out.

I was in New York when I received the order to proceed immediately to Chicago. The man who gave me the order was one of the oligarchs, I could tell that by his speech, though I did not know his name nor see his face. His instructions were too clear for me to make a mistake. Plainly I read between the lines that our plot had been discovered, that we had been countermined. The explosion was ready for the flash of powder, and countless agents of the Iron Heel, including me, either on the ground or being sent there, were to supply that flash. I flatter myself that I maintained my composure under the keen eye of the oligarch, but my heart was beating madly. I could almost have shrieked and flown at his throat with my naked hands before his final cold-blooded instructions were given.

Once out of his presence, I calculated the time, I had just the moments to spare, if I were lucky, to get in touch with some local leader before catching my train. Guarding against being trailed, I made a rush of it for the Emergency Hospital. Luck was with me, and I gained access at once to comrade Galvin, the surgeon-in-chief. I started to gasp out my information, but he stopped me.

'I already know,' he said quietly, though his Irish eyes were flashing. 'I knew what you had come for. I got the word fifteen minutes ago, and I have already passed it along. Everything shall be done here to keep the comrades quiet. Chicago is to be sacrificed, but it shall be Chicago alone.'

'Have you tried to get word to Chicago?' I asked.

He shook his head. 'No telegraphic communication. Chicago is shut off. It's going to be hell there.'

He paused a moment, and I saw his white hand clinch. Then he burst out:

'By God! I wish I were going to be there!'

'There is yet a chance to stop it,' I said, 'if nothing happens to the train and I can get there in time. Or if some of the other secret-service comrades who have learned the truth can get there in time.'

'You on the inside were caught napping this time,' he said.

I nodded my head humbly.

'It was very secret,' I answered. 'Only the inner chiefs could have known up to today. We haven't yet penetrated that far, so we couldn't escape being kept in the dark. If only Ernest were here. Maybe he is in Chicago now, and all is well.'

Dr Galvin shook his head. 'The last news I heard of him was that he had been sent to Boston or New Haven. This secret service for the enemy must hamper him a lot, but it's better than lying in a refuge.'

I started to go, and Galvin wrung my hand.

'Keep a stout heart,' were his parting words. 'What if the First Revolt is lost? There will be a second, and we will be wiser then. Good-bye and good luck. I don't know whether I'll ever see you again. It's going to be hell there, but I'd give ten years of my life for your chance to be in it.'

The Twentieth Century[2] left New York at six in the evening, and was supposed to arrive at Chicago at seven next morning. But it lost time that night. We were running behind another train. Among the travellers in my Pullman was comrade Hartman, like myself in the secret service of the Iron Heel. He it was who told me of the train that immediately preceded us. It was an exact duplicate of our train, though it contained no passengers. The idea was that the empty train should receive the disaster were an attempt made to blow up the Twentieth Century. For that matter there were very few people on the train—only a baker's dozen in our car.

'There must be some big men on board,' Hartman concluded. 'I noticed a private car on the rear.'

Night had fallen when we made our first change of engine, and I walked down the platform for a breath of fresh air and to see what I could see. Through the windows of the private car I caught a glimpse of three men whom I recognised. Hartman was right. One of the men was General Altendorff; and the other two were Mason and Vanderbold, the brains of the inner circle of the Oligarchy's secret service.

It was a quiet moonlight night, but I tossed restlessly and could not sleep. At five in the morning I dressed and abandoned my bed.

I asked the maid in the dressing-room how late the train was, and she told me two hours. She was a mulatto woman, and I noticed that her face was haggard, with great circles under the eyes, while the eyes themselves were wide with some haunting fear.

'What is the matter?' I asked.

'Nothing, miss; I didn't sleep well, I guess,' was her reply.

I looked at her closely, and tried her with one of our signals. She responded, and I made sure of her.

'Something terrible is going to happen in Chicago,' she

[2] This was reputed to be the fastest train in the world then. It was quite a famous train.

said. ' There's that fake[3] train in front of us. That and the troop-trains have made us late.'

' Troop-trains?' I queried.

She nodded her head. ' The line is thick with them. We've been passing them all night. And they're all heading for Chicago. And bringing them over the air-line—that means business.

' I've a lover in Chicago,' she added apologetically. ' He's one of us, and he's in the Mercenaries, and I'm afraid for him.'

Poor girl. Her lover was in one of the three disloyal regiments.

Hartman and I had breakfast together in the dining-car, and I forced myself to eat. The sky had clouded, and the train rushed on like a sullen thunderbolt through the grey pall of advancing day. The very negroes that waited on us knew that something terrible was impending. Oppression sat heavily upon them; the lightness of their natures had ebbed out of them; they were slack and absent-minded in their service, and they whispered gloomily to one another in the far end of the car next to the kitchen. Hartman was hopeless over the situation.

' What can we do?' he demanded for the twentieth time, with a helpless shrug of the shoulders.

He pointed out of the window. ' See, all is ready. You can depend upon it that they're holding them like this, thirty or forty miles outside the city, on every road.'

He had reference to troop-trains on the side-track. The soldiers were cooking their breakfasts over fires built on the ground beside the track, and they looked up curiously at us as we thundered past without slackening our terrific speed.

All was quiet as we entered Chicago. It was evident nothing had happened yet. In the suburbs the morning papers came on board the train. There was nothing in them, and yet there was much in them for those skilled in reading between the lines that it was intended the ordinary reader should not read into the text. The fine hand of the Iron Heel was apparent in every column. Glimmerings of weakness in the armour of the Oligarchy were given. Of course, there was nothing definite. It was intended that the reader should feel

[3] False.

his way to these glimmerings. It was cleverly done. As fiction, those morning papers of October 27 were masterpieces.

The local news was missing. This in itself was a masterstroke. It shrouded Chicago in mystery, and it suggested to the average Chicago reader that the Oligarchy did not dare to give the local news. Hints that were untrue, of course, were given of insubordination all over the land, crudely disguised with complacent references to punitive measures to be taken. There were reports of numerous wireless stations that had been blown up, with heavy rewards offered for the detection of the perpetrators. Of course no wireless stations had been blown up. Many similar outrages, that dovetailed with the plot of the revolutionists, were given. The impression to be made on the minds of the Chicago comrades was that the general revolt was beginning, albeit with a confusing miscarriage in many details. It was impossible for one uninformed to escape the vague yet certain feeling that all the land was ripe for the revolt that had already begun to break out.

It was reported that the defection of the Mercenaries in California had become so serious that half a dozen regiments had been disbanded and broken, and that their members with their families had been driven from their own city and on into the labour-ghettos. And the California Mercenaries were in reality the most faithful of all to their salt! But how was Chicago, shut off from the rest of the world, to know? Then there was a ragged telegram describing an outbreak of the populace in New York City, in which the labour castes were joining, concluding with the statement (intended to be accepted as a bluff)[4] that the troops had the situation in hand.

And as the oligarchs had done with the morning papers, so had they done in a thousand other ways. These we learned afterward, as for example, the secret messages of the oligarchs, sent with the express purpose of leaking to the ears of the revolutionists, that had come over the wires, now and again, during the first part of the night.

' I guess the Iron Heel won't need our services,' Hartman remarked, putting down the paper he had been reading, when the train pulled into the central depôt. ' They wasted their time sending us here. Their plans have evidently prospered

[4] A lie.

better than they expected. Hell will break loose any second now.'

He turned and looked down the train as we alighted. 'I thought so,' he muttered. 'They dropped that private car when the papers came aboard.'

Hartman was hopelessly depressed. I tried to cheer him up, but he ignored my effort and suddenly began talking very hurriedly, in a low voice, as we passed through the station. At first I could not understand.

'I have not been sure,' he was saying, 'and I have told no one. I have been working on it for weeks, and I cannot make sure. Watch out for Knowlton. I suspect him. He knows the secrets of a score of our refuges. He carries the lives of hundreds of us in his hands, and I think he is a traitor. It's more a feeling on my part than anything else. But I thought I marked a change in him a short while back. There is the danger that he has sold us out, or is going to sell us out. I am almost sure of it. I wouldn't whisper my suspicions to a soul, but, somehow, I don't think I'll leave Chicago alive. Keep your eye on Knowlton. Trap him. Find out. I don't know anything more. It is only an intuition, and so far I have failed to find the slightest clue.' We were just stepping out upon the sidewalk. 'Remember,' Hartman concluded earnestly. 'Keep your eyes upon Knowlton.'

And Hartman was right. Before a month went by Knowlton paid for his treason with his life. He was formally executed by the comrades in Milwaukee.

All was quiet on the streets—too quiet. Chicago lay dead. There was no roar and rumble of traffic. There were not even cabs on the streets. The surface cars and the elevated were not running. Only occasionally, on the sidewalks, were there stray pedestrians, and these pedestrians did not loiter. They went their ways with great haste and definiteness, withal there was a curious indecision in their movements, as though they expected the buildings to topple over on them or the sidewalks to sink under their feet or fly up in the air. A few gamins, however, were around, in their eyes a suppressed eagerness in anticipation of wonderful and exciting things to happen.

From somewhere, far to the south, the dull sound of an explosion came to our ears. That was all. Then quiet again, though the gamins had startled and listened, like young deer, at the sound. The doorways to all the buildings were closed; the shutters to the shops were up. But there were many police and watchmen in evidence, and now and again automobile patrols of the Mercenaries slipped swiftly past.

Hartman and I agreed that it was useless to report ourselves to the local chiefs of the secret service. Our failure so to report would be excused, we knew, in the light of subsequent events. So we headed for the great labour-ghetto on the South Side in the hope of getting in contact with some of the comrades. Too late! We knew it. But we could not stand still and do nothing in those ghastly, silent streets. Where was Ernest? I was wondering. What was happening in the cities of the labour castes and Mercenaries? In the fortresses?

As if in answer, a great screaming roar went up, dim with distance, punctuated with detonation after detonation.

'It's the fortresses,' Hartman said. 'God pity those three regiments!'

At a crossing we noticed, in the direction of the stockyards, a gigantic pillar of smoke. At the next crossing several similar smoke pillars were rising skyward in the direction of the West Side. Over the city of the Mercenaries we saw a great captive war-balloon that burst even as we looked at it, and fell in flaming wreckage towards the earth. There was no clue to that tragedy of the air. We could not determine whether the balloon had been manned by comrades or enemies. A vague sound came to our ears, like the bubbling of a gigantic cauldron a long way off, and Hartman said it was machine-guns and automatic rifles.

And still we walked in immediate quietude. Nothing was happening where we were. The police and the automobile patrols went by, and once half a dozen fire-engines, returning evidently from some conflagration. A question was called to the firemen by an officer in an automobile, and we heard one shout in reply: 'No water! They've blown up the mains!'

'We've smashed the water supply,' Hartman cried excitedly to me. 'If we can do all this in a premature, isolated, abortive attempt, what can't we do in a concerted, ripened effort all over the land?'

The automobile containing the officer who had asked the question darted on. Suddenly there was a deafening roar. The machine, with its human freight, lifted in an upburst of smoke, and sank down a mass of wreckage and death.

Hartman was jubilant. 'Well done! well done!' he was repeating, over and over, in a whisper. 'The proletariat gets its lesson today, but it gives one too.'

Police were running for the spot. Also, another patrol machine had halted. As for myself, I was in a daze. The suddenness of it was stunning. How had it happened? I knew not how, and yet I had been looking directly at it. So dazed was I for the moment that I was scarcely aware of the fact that we were being held up by the police. I abruptly saw that a policeman was in the act of shooting Hartman. But Hartman was cool and was giving the proper passwords. I saw the levelled revolver hesitate, then sink down, and heard the disgusted grunt of the policeman. He was very angry, and was cursing the whole secret service. It was always in the way, he was averring, while Hartman was talking back to him and with fitting secret-service pride explaining to him the clumsiness of the police.

The next moment I knew how it happened. There was quite a group about the wreck, and two men were just lifting up the wounded officer to carry him to the other machine. A panic seized all of them, and they scattered in every direction, running in blind terror, the wounded officer, roughly dropped, being left behind. The cursing policeman alongside of me also ran, and Hartman and I ran too, we knew not why, obsessed with the same blind terror to get away from that particular spot.

Nothing really happened then, but everything was explained. The flying men were sheepishly coming back, but all the while their eyes were raised apprehensively to the many-windowed, lofty buildings that towered like the sheer walls of a canyon on each side of the street. From one of those countless windows the bomb had been thrown, but which window? There had been no second bomb, only a fear of one.

Thereafter we looked with speculative comprehension at the windows. Any of them contained possible death. Each building was a possible ambuscade. This was warfare in that modern jungle, a great city. Every street was a canyon, every building a mountain. We had not changed much from primitive man, despite the war automobiles that were sliding by.

Turning a corner, we came upon a woman. She was lying on the pavement in a pool of blood. Hartman bent over and examined her. As for myself, I turned deathly sick. I was to see many dead that day, but the total carnage was not to affect me as did this first forlorn body lying there at my feet abandoned on the pavement. ' Shot in the breast,' was Hartman's report. Clasped in the hollow of her arm, as a child might be clasped, was a bundle of printed matter. Even in death she seemed loath to part with that which had caused her death; for when Hartman had succeeded in withdrawing the bundle, we found that it consisted of large printed sheets, the proclamations of the revolutionists.

' A comrade,' I said.

But Hartman only cursed the Iron Heel, and we passed on. Often we were halted by the police and patrols, but our passwords enabled us to proceed. No more bombs fell from the windows, the last pedestrians seemed to have vanished from the streets, and our immediate quietude grew more profound; though the gigantic cauldron continued to bubble in the distance, dull roars of explosions came to us from all directions, and the smoke-pillars were towering more ominously in the heavens.

CHAPTER 23

The People of the Abyss

SUDDENLY A change came over the face of things. A tingle of excitement ran along the air. Automobiles fled past, two, three, a dozen, and from them warnings were shouted to us. One of the machines swerved wildly at high speed half a block down, and the next moment, already left well behind it, the pavement was torn into a great hole by a bursting bomb. We saw the police disappearing down the cross-streets on the run, and knew that something terrible was coming. We could hear the rising roar of it.

'Our brave comrades are coming,' Hartman said.

We could see the front of their column filling the street from gutter to gutter, as the last war-automobile fled past. The machine stopped for a moment just abreast of us. A soldier leaped from it, carrying something carefully in his hands. This, with the same care, he deposited in the gutter. Then he leaped back to his seat and the machine dashed on, took the turn at the corner, and was gone from sight. Hartman ran to the gutter and stooped over the object.

'Keep back,' he warned me.

I could see he was working rapidly with his hands. When he returned to me the sweat was heavy on his forehead.

'I disconnected it,' he said, 'and just in the nick of time. The soldier was clumsy. He intended it for our comrades, but he didn't give it enough time. It would have exploded prematurely. Now it won't explode at all.'

Everything was happening rapidly now. Across the street and half a block down, high up in a building, I could see heads peering out. I had just pointed them out to Hartman, when a sheet of flame and smoke ran along that portion of the face of the building where the heads had appeared, and the air was shaken by the explosion. In places the stone facing of the building was torn away, exposing the iron construction beneath. The next moment similar sheets of flame and smoke smote the front of the building across the street opposite it. Between the explosions we could hear the rattle of the automatic pistols and rifles. For several minutes this mid-air battle continued, then died out. It was patent that our comrades were in one building, that Mercenaries were in the other, and that they were fighting across the street. But we could not tell which was which—which building contained our comrades and which the Mercenaries.

By this time the column on the street was almost on us. As the front of it passed under the warring buildings, both went into action again—one building dropping bombs into the street, being attacked from across the street, and in return replying to that attack. Thus we learned which building was held by our comrades, and they did good work, saving those in the street from the bombs of the enemy.

Hartman gripped my arm and dragged me into a wide entrance.

' They're not our comrades,' he shouted in my ear.

The inner doors to the entrance were locked and bolted. We could not escape. The next moment the front of the column went by. It was not a column, but a mob, an awful river that filled the street, the people of the abyss mad with drink and wrong, up at last and roaring for the blood of their masters. I had seen the people of the abyss before, gone through its ghettos, and thought I knew it; but I found that I was now looking on it for the first time. Dumb apathy had vanished. It was now dynamic—a fascinating spectacle of dread. It surged past my vision in concrete waves of wrath, snarling and growing carnivorous, drunk with whisky from pillaged warehouses, drunk with hatred, drunk with lust for blood—men, women, and children, in rags and tatters, dim ferocious intelligences with all the godlike blotted from their features and all the fiendlike stamped in, apes, and tigers, anæmic consumptives and great hairy beasts of burden, wan faces from which vampire society had sucked the juice of life, bloated forms swollen with physical grossness and corruption, withered hags and death's heads bearded like patriarchs, festering youth and festering age, faces of fiends, crooked, twisted, misshapen monsters blasted with the ravages of disease and all the horrors of chronic innutrition—the refuse and the scum of life, a raging, screaming, screeching, demoniacal horde.

And why not? The people of the abyss had nothing to lose but the misery and pain of living. And to gain?—nothing, save one final, awful glut of vengeance. And as I looked the thought came to me that in that rushing stream of human lava were men, comrades and heroes, whose mission had been to rouse the abysmal beast and to keep the enemy occupied in coping with it.

And now a strange thing happened to me. A transformation came over me. The fear of death, for myself and for others, left me. I was strangely exalted, another being in another life. Nothing mattered. The Cause for this one time was lost, but the Cause would be here tomorrow, the same Cause, ever fresh and ever burning. And thereafter, in the orgy of horror that raged through the succeeding hours, I was able to take a calm interest. Death meant nothing, life meant nothing. I was an interested spectator of events, and, sometimes swept on by the rush, was myself a curious participant. For my mind had leaped to a star-cool altitude and grasped a passionless transvaluation of values. Had it not done this, I know that I should have died.

Half a mile of the mob had swept by when we were discovered. A woman in fantastic rags, with cheeks cavernously hollow and with narrow black eyes like burning gimlets, caught a glimpse of Hartman and me. She let out a shrill shriek and bore in upon us. A section of the mob tore itself loose and surged in after her. I can see her now, as I write these lines, a leap in advance, her grey hair flying in thin tangled strings, the blood dripping down her forehead from some wound in the scalp, in her right hand a hatchet, her left hand, lean and wrinkled, a yellow talon, gripping the air convulsively. Hartman sprang in front of me. This was no time for explanations. We were well dressed, and that was enough. His fist shot out, striking the woman between her burning eyes. The impact of the blow drove her backward, but she struck the wall of her on-coming fellows and bounced forward again, dazed and helpless, the brandished hatchet falling feebly on Hartman's shoulder.

The next moment I knew not what was happening. I was overborne by the crowd. The confined space was filled with shrieks and yells and curses. Blows were falling on me. Hands were ripping and tearing at my flesh and garments. I felt that I was being torn to pieces. I was being borne down, suffocated. Some strong hand gripped my shoulder in the thick of the press and was dragging fiercely at me. Between pain and pressure I fainted. Hartman never came out of that entrance. He had shielded me and received the first brunt of the attack. This had saved me, for the jam had quickly become too dense for anything more than the mad gripping and tearing of hands.

I came to in the midst of wild movement. All about me was the same movement. I had been caught up in a monstrous flood that was sweeping me I knew not whither. Fresh air was on my cheek and biting sweetly in my lungs. Faint and dizzy, I was vaguely aware of a strong arm around my body under the arms, and half-lifting me and dragging me along. Feebly my own limbs were helping me. In front of me I could see the moving back of a man's coat. It had been slit from top to bottom along the centre seam, and it pulsed rhythmically, the slit opening and closing regularly with every leap of the wearer. This phenomenon fascinated me for a time, while my senses were coming back to me. Next I became aware of stinging cheeks and nose, and could feel blood dripping on my face. My hat was gone. My hair was down and flying, and from the stinging of the scalp I managed to recollect a hand in the press of the entrance that had torn at my hair. My chest and arms were bruised and aching in a score of places.

My brain grew clearer, and I turned as I ran and looked at the man who was holding me up. He it was who had dragged me out and saved me. He noticed my movement.

' It's all right!' he shouted hoarsely. ' I knew you on the instant.'

I failed to recognise him, but before I could speak I trod upon something that was alive and that squirmed under my foot. I was swept on by those behind, and could not look down and see, and yet I knew that it was a woman who had fallen, and who was being trampled into the pavement by thousands of successive feet.

' It's all right,' he repeated. ' I'm Garthwaite.'

He was bearded and gaunt and dirty, but I succeeded in remembering him as the stalwart youth that had spent several months in our Glen Ellen refuge three years before. He passed me the signals of the Iron Heel's secret service, in token that he, too, was in its employ.

' I'll get you out of this as soon as I can get a chance,' he assured me. ' But watch your footing. On your life don't stumble and go down.'

All things happened abruptly on that day, and with an abruptness that was sickening the mob checked itself. I came in violent collision with a large woman in front of me (the

man with the split coat had vanished), while those behind
collided against me. A devilish pandemonium reigned—
shrieks, curses, and cries of death, while above all rose the
churning rattle of machine-guns and the put-a-put, put-a-put
of rifles. At first I could make out nothing. People were
falling about me right and left. The woman in front doubled
up and went down, her hands on her abdomen in a frenzied
clutch. A man was quivering against my legs in a death-
struggle.

It came to me that we were at the head of the column.
Half a mile of it had disappeared—where or how I never
learned. To this day I do not know what became of that
half-mile of humanity—whether it was blotted out by some
frightful bolt of war, whether it was scattered and destroyed
piece-meal, or whether it escaped. But there we were, at the
head of the column instead of in its middle, and we were
being swept out of life by a torrent of shrieking lead.

As soon as death had thinned the jam, Garthwaite, still
grasping my arm, led a rush of survivors into the wide
entrance of an office building. Here, at the rear, against the
doors, we were pressed by a panting, gasping mass of
creatures. For some time we remained in this position without
a change in the situation.

'I did it beautifully,' Garthwaite was lamenting to me.
'Ran you right into a trap. We had a gambler's chance in the
street, but in here there is no chance at all. It's all over but
the shouting. Vive la Revolution!'

Then, what he expected began. The Mercenaries were
killing without quarter. At first, the surge back upon us was
crushed, but as the killing continued the pressure was eased.
The dead and dying went down and made room. Garthwaite
put his mouth to my ear and shouted, but in the frightful din
I could not catch what he said. He did not wait. He seized me
and threw me down. Next he dragged a dying woman over on
top of me, and, with much squeezing and shoving, crawled in
beside me and partly over me. A mound of dead and dying
began to pile up over us, and over this mound, pawing and
moaning, crept those that still survived. But these too, soon
ceased, and a semi-silence settled down, broken by groans and
sobs and sounds of strangulation.

I should have been crushed had it not been for Garthwaite.
As it was, it seemed inconceivable that I could bear the
weight I did and live. And yet, outside of pain, the only

feeling I possessed was one of curiosity. How was it going to end? What would death be like? Thus did I receive my red baptism in that Chicago shambles. Prior to that, death to me had been a theory; but ever afterward death has been a simple fact that does not matter, it is so easy.

But the Mercenaries were not content with what they had done. They invaded the entrance, killing the wounded and searching out the unhurt that, like ourselves, were playing dead. I remember one man they dragged out of a heap who pleaded abjectly until a revolver shot cut him short. Then there was a woman who charged from a heap, snarling and shooting. She fired six shots before they got her, though what damage she did we could not know. We could follow these tragedies only by the sound. Every little while flurries like this occurred, each flurry culminating in the revolver shot that put an end to it. In the intervals we could hear the soldiers talking and swearing as they rummaged among the carcasses, urged on by their officers to hurry up.

At last they went to work on our heap, and we could feel the pressure diminish as they dragged away the dead and wounded. Garthwaite began uttering aloud the signals. At first he was not heard. Then he raised his voice.

'Listen to that,' we heard a soldier say. And next the sharp voice of an officer. 'Hold on there! Careful as you go!'

Oh, that first breath of air as we were dragged out! Garthwaite did the talking at first, but I was compelled to undergo a brief examination to prove service with the Iron Heel.

'Agents-provocateurs all right,' was the officer's conclusion. He was a beardless young fellow, a cadet, evidently of some great oligarch family.

'It's a hell of a job,' Garthwaite grumbled. 'I'm going to try and resign and get into the army. You fellows have a snap.'

'You've earned it,' was the young officer's answer. 'I've got some pull, and I'll see if it can be managed. I can tell them how I found you.'

He took Garthwaite's name and number, then turned to me.

'And you?'

'Oh, I'm going to be married,' I answered lightly, 'and then I'll be out of it all.'

And so we talked, while the killing of the wounded went on. It is all a dream now, as I look back on it; but at the time it was the most natural thing in the world. Garthwaite and the young officer fell into an animated conversation over the difference between so-called modern warfare and the present street fighting and skyscraper fighting that was taking place all over the city. I followed them intently, fixing up my hair at the same time and pinning together my torn skirts. And all the time the killing of the wounded went on. Sometimes the revolver shots drowned the voices of Garthwaite and the officer, and they were compelled to repeat what they had been saying.

I lived through three days of the Chicago Commune, and the vastness of it and of the slaughter may be imagined when I say that in all that time I saw practically nothing outside the killing of the people of the abyss and the mid-air fighting between skyscrapers. I really saw nothing of the heroic work done by the comrades. I could hear the explosions of their mines and bombs, and see the smoke of their conflagrations, and that was all. The mid-air part of one great deed I saw, however, and that was the balloon attacks made by our comrades on the fortresses. That was on the second day. The three disloyal regiments had been destroyed in the fortresses to the last man. The fortresses were crowded with Mercenaries, the wind blew in the right direction, and up went our balloons from one of the office buildings in the city.

Now Biedenbach, after he left Glen Ellen, had invented a most powerful explosive—'expedite' he called it. This was the weapon the balloons used. They were only hot-air balloons, clumsily and hastily made, but they did the work. I saw it all from the top of an office building. The first balloon missed the fortresses completely and disappeared into the country; but we learned about it afterward. Burton and O'Sullivan were in it. As they were descending they swept across a railroad directly over a troop-train that was heading at full speed for Chicago. They dropped their whole supply of expedite upon the locomotive. The resulting wreck tied the line up for days. And the best of it was that, released from the weight of expedite, the balloon shot up into the air and did not come down for half a dozen miles, both heroes escaping unharmed.

The second balloon was a failure. Its flight was lame. It floated too low and was shot full of holes before it could reach the fortresses. Hertford and Guinness were in it, and they were blown to pieces along with the field into which they fell. Biedenbach was in despair—we heard all about it afterward—and he went up alone in the third balloon. He, too, made a low flight, but he was in luck, for they failed seriously to puncture his balloon. I can see it now as I did then, from the lofty top of the building—that inflated bag drifting along the air and that tiny speck of a man clinging on beneath. I could not see the fortress, but those on the roof with me said he was directly over it. I did not see the expedite fall when he cut it loose. But I did see the balloon suddenly leap up into the sky. An appreciable time after that the great column of the explosion towered in the air, and after that, in turn, I heard the roar of it. Biedenbach the gentle had destroyed a fortress. Two other balloons followed at the same time. One was blown to pieces in the air, the expedite exploding, and the shock of it disrupting the second balloon, which fell prettily into the remaining fortress. It couldn't have been better planned, though the two comrades in it sacrificed their lives.

But to return to the people of the abyss. My experiences were confined to them. They raged and slaughtered and destroyed all over the city proper, and were in turn destroyed; but never once did they succeed in reaching the city of the oligarchs over on the west side. The oligarchs had protected themselves well. No matter what destruction was wreaked in the heart of the city, they, and their womenkind and children, were to escape, unhurt. I am told that their children played in the parks during those terrible days, and that their favourite game was an imitation of their elders stamping upon the proletariat.

But the Mercenaries found it no easy task to cope with the people of the abyss and at the same time fight with the comrades. Chicago was true to her traditions, and though a generation of revolutionists was wiped out, it took along with it pretty close to a generation of its enemies. Of course, the Iron Heel kept the figures secret, but, at a very conservative estimate, at least one hundred and thirty thousand Mercenaries were slain. But the comrades had no chance. Instead of the whole country being hand in hand in revolt, they were all alone, and the total strength of the Oligarchy could have been directed against them if necessary. As it was, hour after hour, day after day, in endless train loads, by hundreds of thousands, the Mercenaries were hurled into Chicago.

And there were so many of the people of the abyss! Tiring of the slaughter, a great herding movement was begun by the soldiers, the intent of which was to drive the street mobs like cattle, into Lake Michigan. It was at the beginning of this movement that Garthwaite and I had encountered the young officer. This herding movement was practically a failure, thanks to the splendid work of the comrades. Instead of the great host the Mercenaries had hoped to gather together, they succeeded in driving no more than forty thousand of the wretches into the lake. Time and again, when a mob of them was well in hand and being driven along the streets to the water, the comrades would create a diversion and the mob would escape through the consequent hole torn in the encircling net.

Garthwaite and I saw an example of this shortly after meeting with the young officer. The mob of which we had been a part, and which had been put in retreat, was prevented from escaping to the south and east by strong bodies of troops. The troops we had fallen in with had held it back on the west. The only outlet was north, and north it went toward the lake, driven on from east and west and south by machine-gun fire and automatics. Whether it divined that it was being driven toward the lake, or whether it was merely a blind squirm of the monster, I do not know; but at any rate the mob took a cross street to the west, turned down the next street, and came back upon its track, heading south toward the great ghetto.

Garthwaite and I at that time were trying to make our way westward to get out of the territory of street fighting, and we were caught right in the thick of it again. As we came to the corner we saw the howling mob bearing down upon us. Garthwaite seized my arm and we were just starting to run, when he dragged me back from in front of the wheels of half a dozen war automobiles, equipped with machine-guns, that were rushing for the spot. Behind them came the soldiers with their automatic rifles. By the time they took position, the mob was upon them, and it looked as though they would be overwhelmed before they could get into action.

Here and there a soldier was discharging his rifle, but this scattered fire had no effect in checking the mob. On it came, bellowing with brute rage. It seemed the machine-guns could not get started. The automobiles on which they were mounted blocked the street, compelling the soldiers to find positions in, between, and on the sidewalks. More and more soldiers were arriving, and in the jam we were unable to get away. Garthwaite held me by the arm, and we pressed close against the front of a building.

The mob was no more than twenty-five feet away when the machine-guns opened up; but before that flaming sheet of death nothing could live. The mob came on, but it could not advance. It piled up in a heap, a mound, a huge and growing wave of dead and dying. Those behind urged on, and the column, from gutter to gutter, telescoped upon itself. Wounded creatures, men and women, were vomited over the top of that awful wave and fell squirming down the face of it till they thrashed about under the automobiles and against the legs of the soldiers. The latter bayoneted the struggling wretches, though one I saw who gained his feet and flew at a soldier's throat with his teeth. Together they went down, soldier and slave, into the welter.

The firing ceased. The work was done. The mob had been stopped in its wild attempt to break through. Orders were being given to clear the wheels of the war-machines. They could not advance over that wave of dead, and the idea was to run them down the cross street. The soldiers were dragging the bodies away from the wheels when it happened. We learned afterwards how it happened. A block distant a hundred of our comrades had been holding a building. Across roofs and through buildings they made their way, till they found themselves looking down upon the close-packed soldiers. Then it was counter-massacre.

Without warning a shower of bombs fell from the top of the building. The automobiles were blown to fragments, along with many soldiers. We, with the survivors, swept back in mad retreat. Half a block down another building opened fire on us. As the soldiers had carpeted the street with dead slaves, so, in turn, did they themselves become carpet. Garthwaite and I bore charmed lives. As we had done before, so again we sought shelter in an entrance. But he was not to be caught napping this time. As the roar of the bombs died away, he began peering out.

'The mob's coming back!' he called to me. 'We've got to get out of this!'

We fled, hand in hand, down the bloody pavement, slipping and sliding, and making for the corner. Down the cross street we could see a few soldiers still running. Nothing was happening to them. The way was clear. So we paused a moment and looked back. The mob came on slowly. It was busy arming itself with the rifles of the slain and killing the wounded. We saw the end of the young officer who had rescued us. He painfully lifted himself on his elbow and turned loose with his automatic pistol.

' There goes my chance of promotion,' Garthwaite laughed, as a woman bore down on the wounded man, brandishing a butcher's cleaver. ' Come on. It's the wrong direction, but we'll get out somehow.'

And we fled eastward through the quiet streets, prepared at every cross street for anything to happen. To the south a monster conflagration was filling the sky, and we knew that the great ghetto was burning. At last I sank down on the sidewalk. I was exhausted and could go no further. I was bruised and sore and aching in every limb; yet I could not escape smiling at Garthwaite, who was rolling a cigarette and saying:

' I know I'm making a mess of rescuing you, but I can't get head nor tail of the situation. It's all a mess. Every time we try to break out, something happens and we're turned back. We're only a couple of blocks now from where I got you out of that entrance. Friend and foe are all mixed up. It's chaos. You can't tell who is in those darned buildings. Try to find out, and you get a bomb on your head. Try to go peaceably on your way, and you run into a mob and are killed by machine-guns, or you run into the Mercenaries and are killed by your own comrades from a roof. And on top of it all the mob comes along and kills you too.'

He shook his head dolefully, lighted his cigarette, and sat down beside me.

' And I'm that hungry,' he added, ' I could eat cobblestones.'

The next moment he was on his feet again and out in the street prying up a cobblestone. He came back with it and assaulted the window of a store behind us.

' It's ground floor and no good,' he explained as he helped me through the hole he had made; ' but it's the best we can do. You get a nap and I'll reconnoitre. I'll finish this rescue all right, but I want time, time, lots of it—and something to eat.'

It was a harness store we found ourselves in, and he fixed

me up a couch of horse blankets in the private office well to the rear. To add to my wretchedness a splitting headache was coming on, and I was only too glad to close my eyes and try to sleep.

' I'll be back,' were his parting words. ' I don't hope to get an auto, but I'll surely bring some grub,[1] anyway.'

And that was the last I saw of Garthwaite for three years. Instead of coming back, he was carried away to a hospital with a bullet through his lungs and another through the fleshy part of his neck.

[1] Food.

CHAPTER 24

Nightmare

I HAD not closed my eyes the night before on the Twentieth Century, and what of that and of my exhaustion I slept soundly. When I first awoke, it was night. Garthwaite had not returned. I had lost my watch and had no idea of the time. As I lay with my eyes closed, I heard the same dull sound of distant explosions. The inferno was still raging. I crept through the store to the front. The reflection from the sky of vast conflagrations made the street almost as light as day. One could have read the finest print with ease. From several blocks away came the crackle of small hand-bombs and the churning of machine-guns, and from a long way off came a long series of heavy explosions. I crept back to my horse blankets and slept again.

When next I awoke a sickly yellow light was filtering in on me. It was dawn of the second day. I crept to the front of the store. A smoke pall, shot through with lurid gleams, filled the sky. Down the opposite side of the street tottered a wretched slave. One hand he held tightly against his side and behind him he left a bloody trail. His eyes roved everywhere, and they were filled with apprehension and dread. Once he looked straight across at me, and in his face was all the dumb pathos of the wounded and hunted animal. He saw me, but there was no kinship between us, and with him, at least, no sympathy of understanding; for he cowered perceptibly and dragged himself on. He could expect no aid in all God's world. He was a helot in the great hunt of helots that the masters were making. All he could hope for, all he sought, was some hole to crawl away in and hide like any animal. The sharp clang of a passing ambulance at the corner gave him a start. Ambulances were not for such as he. With a groan of pain he threw himself into a doorway. A minute later he was out again and desperately hobbling on.

I went back to my horse blankets and waited an hour for Garthwaite. My headache had not gone away. On the contrary, it was increasing. It was by an effort of will only that I was able to open my eyes and look at objects. And with the opening of my eyes and the looking came intolerable torment. Also, a great pulse was beating in my brain. Weak and reeling, I went out through the broken window and down the street, seeking to escape, instinctively and gropingly from the awful shambles. And thereafter I lived nightmare. My memory of what happened in the succeeding hours is the memory one would have of nightmare. Many events are focused sharply on my brain, but between these indelible pictures I retain are intervals of unconsciousness. What occurred in those intervals I know not, and never shall know.

I remember stumbling at the corner over the legs of a man. It was the poor hunted wretch that had dragged himself past my hiding-place. How distinctly do I remember his poor, pitiful, gnarled hands as he lay there on the pavement—hands that were more hoof and claw than hands, all twisted and distorted by the toil of all his days, with on the palms a horny growth of callous half an inch thick. And as I picked myself up and started on, I looked into the face of the thing and saw that it still lived; for the eyes, dimly intelligent, were looking at me and seeing me.

After that came a kindly blank. I knew nothing, saw nothing, merely tottered on in my quest for safety. My next nightmare vision was a quiet street of the dead. I came upon it abruptly, as a wanderer in the country would come upon a flowing stream. Only this stream I gazed upon did not flow. It was congealed in death. From pavement to pavement, and covering the sidewalks, it lay there, spread out quite evenly, with only here and there a lump or mound of bodies to break the surface. Poor driven people of the abyss, hunted helots— they lay there as the rabbits in California after a drive.[1] Up the street and down I looked. There was no movement, no sound. The quiet buildings looked down upon the scene from their many windows. And once, and once only, I saw an arm that moved in that dead stream. I swear I saw it move, with a strange writhing gesture of agony, and with it lifted a head, gory with nameless horror, that gibbered at me and then lay down again and moved no more.

[1] In those days, so sparsely populated was the land that wild animals often became pests. In California the custom of rabbit-driving obtained. On a given day all the farmers in a locality would assemble and sweep across the country in converging lines, driving the rabbits by scores of thousands into a prepared enclosure, where they were clubbed to death by men and boys.

I remember another street, with quiet buildings on either side, and the panic that smote me into consciousness as again I saw the people of the abyss, but this time in a stream that flowed and came on. And then I saw there was nothing to fear. The stream moved slowly, while from it arose groans and lamentations, cursings, babblings of senility, hysteria, and insanity; for these were the very young and the very old, the feeble and the sick, the helpless and the hopeless, all the wreckage of the ghetto. The burning of the great ghetto on the South Side had driven them forth into the inferno of the street fighting, and whither they wended and whatever became of them I did not know and never learned.[2]

I have faint memories of breaking a window and hiding in some shop to escape a street mob that was pursued by soldiers. Also, a bomb burst near me, once, in some still street, where, look as I would up and down, I could see no human being. But my next sharp recollection begins with the crack of a rifle and an abrupt becoming aware that I am being fired at by a soldier in an automobile. The shot missed, and the next moment I was screaming and motioning the signals. My memory of riding in the automobile is very hazy, though this ride, in turn, is broken by one vivid picture. The crack of the rifle of the soldier sitting beside me made me open my eyes, and I saw George Milford, whom I had known in the Pell Street days, sinking slowly down to the sidewalk. Even as he sank the soldier fired again, and Milford doubled in, then flung his body out, and fell sprawling. The soldier chuckled, and the automobile sped on.

The next I knew after that I was awakened out of a sound sleep by a man who walked up and down close beside me. His face was drawn and strained, and the sweat rolled down his nose from his forehead. One hand was clutched tightly against his chest by the other hand, and blood dripped down upon the floor as he walked. He wore the uniform of the Mercenaries. From without, as through thick walls, came the muffled roar of bursting bombs. I was in some building that was locked in combat with some other building.

A surgeon came in to dress the wounded soldier, and I learned that it was two in the afternoon. My headache was no

[2] It was a long question of debate, whether the burning of the South Side ghetto was accidental, or whether it was done by the Mercenaries; but it is definitely settled now that the ghetto was fired by the Mercenaries under orders from their chiefs.

better, and the surgeon paused from his work long enough
to give me a powerful drug that would depress the heart and
bring relief. I slept again, and the next I knew I was on top
of the building. The immediate fighting had ceased, and I
was watching the balloon attack on the fortresses. Someone
had an arm around me and I was leaning close against him.
It came to me quite as a matter of course that this was Ernest,
and I found myself wondering how he had got his hair and
eyebrows so badly singed.

It was by the merest chance that we had found each other
in that terrible city. He had had no idea that I had left New
York, and, coming through the room where I lay asleep, could
not at first believe that it was I. Little more I saw of the
Chicago Commune. After watching the balloon attack, Ernest
took me down into the heart of the building, where I slept the
afternoon out and the night. The third day we spent in the
building, and on the fourth, Ernest having got permission and
an automobile from the authorities, we left Chicago.

My headache was gone, but, body and soul, I was very
tired. I lay back against Ernest in the automobile, and with
apathetic eyes watched the soldiers trying to get the machine
out of the city. Fighting was still going on, but only in isolated localities. Here and there whole districts were still in
possession of the comrades, but such districts were surrounded
and guarded by heavy bodies of troops. In a hundred segregated traps were the comrades thus held while the work of
subjugating them went on. Subjugation meant death, for no
quarter was given, and they fought heroically to the last
man.[3]

Whenever we approached such localities, the guards turned
us back and sent us around. Once, the only way past two
strong positions of the comrades was through a burnt section
that lay between. From either side we could hear the rattle
and roar of war while the automobile picked its way through
smoking ruins and tottering walls. Often the streets were

[3] Numbers of the buildings held out over a week, while one held
out eleven days. Each building had to be stormed like a fort,
and the Mercenaries fought their way upward floor by floor. It
was deadly fighting. Quarter was neither given nor taken, and in
the fighting the revolutionists had the advantage of being above.
While the revolutionists were wiped out, the loss was not one-
sided. The proud Chicago proletariat lived up to its ancient
boast. For as many of itself as were killed, it killed that many of
the enemy.

blocked by mountains of debris that compelled us to go around. We were in a labyrinth of ruin, and our progress was slow.

The stockyards (ghetto, plant, and everything) were smouldering ruins. Far off to the right a wide smoke haze dimmed the sky. The town of Pullman, the soldier chauffeur told us, or what had been the town of Pullman, for it was utterly destroyed. He had driven the machine out there, with dispatches, on the afternoon of the third day. Some of the heaviest fighting had occurred there, he said, many of the streets being rendered impassable by the heaps of the dead.

Swinging around the shattered walls of a building, in the stockyards district, the automobile was stopped by a wave of dead. It was for all the world like a wave tossed up by the sea. It was patent to us what had happened. As the mob charged past the corner, it had been swept, at right angles and point-blank range, by the machine-guns drawn up on the cross street. But disaster had come to the soldiers. A chance bomb must have exploded among them, for the mob, checked until its dead and dying formed the wave, had white-capped and flung forward its foam of living, fighting slaves. Soldiers and slaves lay together, torn and mangled, around and over the wreckage of the automobiles and guns.

Ernest sprang out. A familiar pair of shoulders in a cotton shirt and a familiar fringe of white hair had caught his eye. I did not watch him, and it was not until he was back beside me and we were speeding on that he said:

' It was Bishop Morehouse.'

Soon we were in the green country, and I took one last glance back at the smoke-filled sky. Faint and far came the low thud of an explosion. Then I turned my face against Ernest's breast and wept softly for the Cause that was lost. Ernest's arm about me was eloquent with love.

' For this time lost, dear heart,' he said, ' but not for ever. We have learned. Tomorrow the Cause will rise again, strong with wisdom and discipline.'

The automobile drew up at a railroad station. Here we would catch a train to New York. As we waited on the platform, three trains thundered past, bound west to Chicago. They were crowded with ragged, unskilled labourers, people of the abyss.

' Slave-levies for the rebuilding of Chicago,' Ernest said. ' You see, the Chicago slaves are all killed.'

CHAPTER 25

The Terrorists

I T W A S not until Ernest and I were back in New York, and after weeks had elapsed, that we were able to comprehend thoroughly the full sweep of the disaster that had befallen the Cause. The situation was bitter and bloody. In many places, scattered over the country, slave revolts and massacres had occurred. The roll of the martyrs increased mightily. Countless executions took place everywhere. The mountains and waste regions were filled with outlaws and refugees who were being hunted down mercilessly. Our own refuges were packed with comrades who had prices on their heads. Through information furnished by its spies, scores of our refuges were raided by the soldiers of the Iron Heel.

Many of the comrades were disheartened, and they retaliated with terroristic tactics. The set-back to their hopes made them despairing and desperate. Many terrorist organisations unaffiliated with us sprang into existence and caused us much trouble.[1] These misguided people sacrificed their own lives

[1] The annals of this short-lived era of despair make bloody reading. Revenge was the ruling motive, and the members of the terroristic organisations were careless of their own lives and hopeless about the future. The Danites, taking their name from the avenging angels of the Mormon mythology, sprang up in the mountains of the Great West and spread over the Pacific Coast from Panama to Alaska. The Valkyries were women. They were the most terrible of all. No woman was eligible for membership who had not lost near relatives at the hands of the Oligarchy. They were guilty of torturing their prisoners to death. Another famous organisation of women was the Widows of War. A companion organisation to the Valkyries was the Berserkers. These men placed no value whatever upon their own lives, and it was they who totally destroyed the great Mercenary city of Bellona along with its population of over a hundred thousand souls. The Bedlamites and the Helldamites were twin slave organisations, while a new religious sect that did not flourish long was called the Wrath of God. Among others, to show the whimsicality of their deadly seriousness, may be mentioned the following: The Bleeding Hearts, Sons of the Morning, the Morning Stars, the Flamingoes, The Triple Triangles, The Three Bars, the Rubonics, the Vindicators, The Comanches, and The Erebusites.

wantonly, very often made our own plans go astray, and retarded our organisation.

And through it all moved the Iron Heel, impassive and deliberate, shaking up the whole fabric of the social structure in its search for the comrades, combing out the Mercenaries, the labour castes, and all its secret services, punishing without mercy and without malice, suffering in silence all retaliations that were made upon it and filling the gaps in its fighting line as fast as they appeared. And hand in hand with this, Ernest and the other leaders were hard at work reorganising the forces of the Revolution. The magnitude of the task may be understood when it is taken into[2]

---

[2] This is the end of the Everhard Manuscript. It breaks off abruptly in the middle of a sentence. She must have received warning of the coming of the Mercenaries, for she had time safely to hide the manuscript before she fled or was captured. It is to be regretted that she did not live to complete her narrative, for then, undoubtedly, would have been cleared away the mystery that has shrouded for seven centuries the execution of Ernest Everhard.